ABYSSAL

RIPLEY SHAINE

Modern Guard Publishing LLC
5900 Balcones Drive STE 100
Austin, TX 78731
rights@modernguardpublishing.com

Obsidian Quill is an imprint of Modern Guard Publishing LLC.
Visit our website at www.modernguardpublishing.com

Edited by Ripley Shaine
Cover art and design by Grace M.

Paperback ISBN **979-8-9990095-5-5**
Hardback ISBN **979-8-9990095-3-1**
Ebook ISBN **979-8-9990095-1-7**

First Edition 2026

For the team who made Alien: Isolation—
Thank you for proving that anxiety can, in fact, be a full-body
gaming experience…
and that I will never trust a locker, a vent, or my own
heartbeat ever again.

PREFACE

Abyssal didn't start as just a thesis—it started as a daydream. Something deep and strange and a little sparkly that I couldn't shake loose. After reading S.A. Barnes (Stacey Kade)'s sci-fi gems, I wondered: *what if I tried to write something like that? For women? About emotions, fear, connection... but also aliens and weird oceans?*

Then I played *Subnautica*, and honestly? That sealed the deal. I needed more. More alien oceans, more mysteries, more of that creeping-quiet terror of the deep. So I built my own.

This is a story for those who love the dark unknown, who find beauty in eerie things, and who sometimes wish they could breathe underwater just to explore what's hiding beneath. It's about fear, yes—but also about wonder. It's for the anxious girls, the curious ones, the ones who feel too much and still keep swimming.

I wrote parts of this book at 2 a.m., hunched over my laptop with a mug of tea that went cold hours ago. Some chapters came easily, like a current pulling me along; others, I wrestled with word by word, scene by scene. I rewrote. I doubted. I kept going. This story wouldn't leave me alone until it was finished—and honestly, I'm glad it didn't.

Of course, I'm not a scientist. I tried to get things *kinda* right, but science here is more of a helpful friend than a strict parent. This is fiction. It's meant to feel real in your heart, even if it bends the rules of gravity, biology, or, you know, thermodynamics.

So go ahead—let the real world slip away. Sink into the water. Don't worry about the rules. Just breathe in the story and let yourself drift.

"Hope" is the thing with feathers -
That perches in the soul -
And sings the tune without the words -
And never stops - at all -

And sweetest - in the Gale - is heard -
And sore must be the storm -
That could abash the little Bird
That kept so many warm -

I've heard it in the chillest land -
And on the strangest Sea -
Yet - never - in Extremity,
It asked a crumb - of me.

-Emily Dickinson-

Chapter 1: Arrival

The first thing I noticed about Thalassa IX was the water—endless, dark, and stretching to every horizon like some colossal mirror reflecting a stormy, gray sky. The second thing was how fucking cold it was.

The kind of cold that burrows under your layers, snakes up your spine, seeps into your bones. The kind that leaves your breath hanging in the air like smoke and freezes the ends of your eyelashes together. My gloves were thermal-regulation grade, my jacket insulated to the standards of the Outer Colonies, but none of that seemed to matter here.

The grav-wing behind me gave a thunderous roar, drowning out the low howl of the wind as it powered up again. Its engines hissed as it rose, angling sharply toward the Inception, our research vessel hanging in low orbit like a distant silver speck. Watching it climb away made my pulse hitch—a visceral reminder that, for now, escape was no longer an option.

Eighteen months. That was the length of my assignment. Longer than a standard scientific rotation, sure, but the pay had been more than worth it—especially considering I'd practically begged for the most remote outpost available. Far away from Earth. Far away from the questions, the cameras, the headlines.

The cold was just a bonus.

I flexed my gloved fingers, adjusted the weight of my pack across my shoulders, and tried to steady my breathing. In the distance, jagged peaks speared the low clouds — white-capped mountains rising like silent sentinels from Thalassa's twin continents. Both landmasses were leagues away, separated by the vast, unbroken ocean that covered ninety-six percent of this planet's surface. The only things breaking the monotony of the dark, heaving sea were a few scattered research platforms, like metallic islands lost in the abyss.

Up ahead, a narrow metal gangway stretched across the waves, leading to the habitation unit perched precariously on spindly supports above the churning water. It looked...temporary. Like a prefabricated shelter you'd pop open during a storm on Mars, not a long-term research station balanced over an alien ocean.

I steeled myself, hitching my pack higher, and started walking. Each step made the gangway creak and shudder beneath me, the sound barely audible over the crash of waves. My boots clanged against the grated floor, sending hollow echoes into the wind.

The ocean was alive all around me. Towering swells rolled beneath the metal walkway, their deep blue surfaces glinting with oily reflections of the heavy clouds above. The rhythmic crash of water against the supports echoed through my bones. It was beautiful, in a wild, unforgiving sort of way—but it also made my skin crawl. I couldn't shake the image of something massive lurking beneath the waves. Something old.

Something watching.

Get it together, Arizona, I scolded myself, shaking the thought away.

The isolation, the cold, the eerie beauty of Thalassa IX—it was exactly what I needed. No reporters, no public statements, no damn cameras shoved in my face. Just eighteen months of oceanic data collection, environmental surveys, and the kind of solitude that might finally clear my head. There was no use giving into paranoia, not when I'd asked for the isolation.

The gangway swayed as a gust of wind slammed into me, stealing the breath from my lungs. My heart stuttered in my chest. I glanced at the water—black and endless. If one of those monstrous waves rose high enough…

A shudder snaked down my spine.

The habitation unit's door loomed ahead—rounded, metallic, reinforced. Before I could reach for the console, the door hissed open. A figure stepped out, blocking the entrance.

Tall, broad-shouldered, clad in insulated gear with the collar popped high against the cold. His soft brown hair curled slightly at the edges, wind-tousled, and his eyes crinkled warmly beneath the brim of his hood.

"Dr. Birch?" His voice carried easily over the wind, warm with an accent that tugged faintly at my memory—Old Scotland, maybe?

I nodded, squinting against the ocean spray. Who else would I be? This rock wasn't exactly bustling with tourists.

"Come on, get in. We need to run you through decon before you freeze your arse off," he added, grin widening. "Colder than a yeti's balls out here."

I almost snorted despite myself. That accent—thicker now, unmistakably New Scotland. The colony had been one of the first to splinter off after the Exodus from Earth. Something about the endless green hills reminded the displaced Scots of home, or so I'd read. I'd never been.

He stepped aside, motioning for me to enter. Grateful to be out of the wind, I ducked through the doorway into the habitation unit.

The space was utilitarian—rounded walls lined with exposed piping, bundled cables, and control panels blinking with muted amber and green. The air smelled faintly metallic, tinged with salt carried in from the waves outside. Metal crates were stacked in tidy rows, papers and instruments scattered across them in an organized chaos that suggested use rather than neglect.

Behind me, the man sealed the hatch with a heavy clang, spinning the locking wheel into place. A green indicator lit above the frame as he pressed the button beside it.

"Warning: Decontamination sequence initiated," announced a soft, feminine voice—synthetic, but laced with human-like inflections. *"Please close your eyes."*

I barely had time to comply before a sudden burst of fine, stinging mist sprayed from concealed nozzles above, coating me from head to toe in an icy, chemical laced spray. The shock of cold stole my breath; droplets clung to my lashes and the seams of my jacket. I shivered, fighting the urge to recoil.

The man chuckled with his eyes open, unfazed.

"First time's always the worst. You'll get used to it," he said, peeling off his gloves with practiced ease. His hands were calloused but steady—not just a cook's hands, I realized.

Medic's hands, too.

My own hands shook incessantly. It made dealing with glass slides a pain in the ass.

I swiped at the droplets clinging to my jacket, glancing sideways at him. "You're… Leo Kilmartin, right? Chef and in-house doctor?"

"Guilty as charged." He extended his hand, grin easy. "And occasional tour guide, depending on how seasick you're feeling."

I shook his hand. His grip was firm, warm despite the chill clinging to me, and for a moment the tension coiling in my chest eased.

Outside, the waves battered the station's supports, in an endless rhythm. I would never get used to the creaking as the station swayed with rhythm of the sea.

I took a deep breath, trying (and failing) to calm the nerves curling low in my stomach, taking root in my veins.

There was something about Leo's easy smile and the hum of machinery that made me think— maybe, just maybe, I could survive eighteen months here.

The moment broke when the floor seemed to tilt beneath me—not violently, but enough to send a slow spin through my skull. My stomach lurched.

Gravity here was heavier than orbital drift; my body hadn't caught up. Leo caught the hesitation in my stance, brow furrowing slightly. "Pressure chamber will help," he said, taking the duffel from my shoulder before I could protest. "Med-bay's two corridors down—I'll stash your gear in your room, then meet you in the mess hall when you're done. Deal?"

I managed a nod, already feeling the edges of dizziness closing in.

"Deal."

He observed me for a moment, concern lacing his gaze.

"You'll make it alright?"

I waved him off as another wave of dizziness hit me. "Yeah, I'm fine."

We split at the junction—him vanishing with my things, me staggering toward the med-bay, guided by the hum of machinery and the hiss of the waves beyond the steel walls.

The air felt heavier here, as if the sea itself was pressing in.

And though Leo's easy smile lingered in my mind, so did the crawling sensation at the base of my skull—a whisper of unseen things waiting in the deep.

Chapter 2: Introductions

The mess hall was warmer than I expected—warmer than the decon chamber, warmer than the brittle corridors that led me in, warmer than the cold dread still clinging to my ribs.

And filled with voices. Actual voices.

For all my bravado, I hadn't realized how much I'd braced for silence. For an outpost stripped down to bone.

Four people sat around a brushed steel table, eating from mismatched ceramic bowls. The scent of simmering broth and fresh bread hung thick in the air. It was almost… cozy. A large pot steamed at the center, herbs and something tangy rising from it like a quiet promise.

"Birch, you made it," Leo called, grinning as he set a bowl down and waved me over—like we weren't stranded on a frozen water world on the edge of nowhere.

I straightened, tugged my sleeves, and crossed the room. The others glanced up—evaluating. Not unfriendly, but not exactly at ease.

"This is Dr. Arizona Birch," Leo said, leaning against the bulkhead. "Our new marine bio genius—and apparently brave enough to survive the gangway."

I gave a weak smile. "Genius might be overselling it. But I didn't die, so… progress."

The woman nearest laughed, her hair a mess of blonde braids pulled up and flecked with grease like war paint.

"Well, that already puts you ahead of our last arrival. Slipped, screamed, nearly took the whole gangway down. RIP, Derek's dignity. He lasted a whole four months."

She offered a grease-smudged hand. "Kaela Vrin. I fix things. And if I break them? I deny everything."

Her accent was Lunar-colonial—clipped, fast. Her eyes sparkled under the overhead lights.

"You break things often?" I asked, shaking her hand.

Kaela's grin sharpened. "Only the boring stuff."

Next to her sat a man built like a bulkhead—broad, composed, posture so rigid I knew he'd seen military training. Olen, I guessed, if I remembered the debrief correctly. He didn't offer a hand, just gave me a slow, silent nod. Cold read. Like he was scanning for weak points.

"Don't take it personally," Kaela stage whispered. "Olen's emotionally bonded to a pulse rifle."

The corner of Olen's mouth twitched. Barely. His gaze lingered on me too long. I didn't look away. Eventually, he nodded and turned back to his bowl.

Then the last one stood—lean, sharp-featured, dark hair swept back neatly. Gray eyes studied me like I was some new species, but there was warmth beneath the analysis. It pulled at me, dragging me into his orbit.

"Dr. Rhys Calum," he said, extending a hand. "Exo-linguistics, archaeology, and occasional offender of mealtime schedules."

I blinked, caught off guard by the dry humor. His handshake was firm, his skin cool. If he noticed how clammy mine was, he didn't comment on it.

"Welcome to Thalassa IX," he added, studying me again like I was an artifact still wrapped in sediment. The curiosity in his gaze held my attention for long after he looked away from me.

The introductions eased. I took the empty seat, and the bowl Leo passed me. The broth was hot, salty, rich with something vaguely kelpy—local, probably. I took a sip. A small, unbidden sound escaped me. Warmth spread through my chest, unclenching something I hadn't realized was clenched. For a moment, it felt like the heat might reach the edges of me—like I could thaw all the way through.

"Good, eh?" Leo said, grinning. It was the type of grin that told me he enjoyed cooking for others, and he enjoyed it when they enjoyed what he made.

I nodded into the bowl, the warmth settling deep. For the first time since arrival, the cold didn't feel permanent.

"Why is this outpost so small?" I asked between bites, when there was a lull in the inside jokes and mechanical musings.

Silence descended, though I didn't think my question was particularly scintillating. Kaela and Leo both looked at Olen, as if for direction but that didn't make sense. He was just hired security— he wasn't in charge of anything other than ensuring we didn't accidentally pick up an alien plague and bring it to one of the developed planets.

Olen cleared his throat and set his spoon down with slow deliberate movements. He picked up a napkin, dabbed it at the corners of his mouth.

"The sea gets to people. Most don't stay long enough for their beds to get warm." His eyes traveled the length of me. Not in a lecherous way, more assessing. As if he was looking for something and had found me lacking. I pressed my lips together.

"We'll see how long you last."

He returned to his soup. Kaela rolled her eyes at him then circled her spoon in the air. "Drama king," she said as droplets of soup sprayed through the air.

Leo and Dr. Calum laughed, some of the tension easing as conversation once again hummed around the table—blending with the mechanical murmur of the station: the click of filtration, the faint rattle of pipes, the groan of steel bracing against water. Half the Hab sat above the waves. The other half… below.

I suppressed a shiver and focused on the soup.

The power suddenly flicked off. No generators, no oxygen scrubbers, not a single sound rang through the air aside from the ocean roaring outside and the breaths of five humans.

I gasped at the power outage, but no one else seemed surprised.

Kaela looked at me, sympathy filling her wide brown eyes. "It happens sometimes. Because of the cold. Don't worry, it never lasts long."

She had barely finished speaking before the lights clicked back on.

The AI chimed overhead: *power restored.*

I stared around the lights above us, uncertain if I believed her. "And if it does?"

"Well, then," she shrugged, "the back up generators kick in ten minutes after the outage, or sooner if we turn them on manually."

Kaela then launched into a story about nearly frying the atmospheric regulators last week, spoon flashing as she gestured.

"I told Olen the system's ten years past warranty. You'd think the Directorate could afford to replace *something* critical."

Olen raised an eyebrow. "You wired the bypass backward."

"Semantics," Kaela said, unbothered.

Leo chuckled. "This place runs on caffeine and spite. Equal parts."

I smiled faintly. The teasing, the banter—it softened the edges of my nerves. Rhys didn't join in, but watched quietly, tracking the rhythm of the group like a scientist logging field data.

Still… under the warmth, something else stirred.

Kaela's laugh faltered a beat when our eyes met. Olen's spoon clinked too hard against the bowl. Even Leo, for all his warmth, held his body at a slight angle—like a ship trimming sails against uncertain wind. And Rhys… his gaze lingered, then flicked away.

They'd been briefed. Maybe not the full dossier, but enough. Enough to know the name *Birch* came with caveats.

Their questions skirted around it. The way people were careful *after.*

The memory surfaced without asking—the Directorate rep in a tailored suit, sitting in my mother's—*my*—living room, lips pressed into a line.

We regret to inform you that Professor Birch died in an accident related to unauthorized genetic experimentation.

Flat. Practiced. Followed quickly by:

The Directorate had no knowledge of these activities and cannot provide further detail for legal reasons.

I'd waited. For what, I didn't know—truth? A crack in the story?

Nothing.

My father vanished into a black hole of redacted files and unanswered messages. I was left with grief that calcified into suspicion, suspicion that rotted into rage. His research had been scrubbed, colleagues gone dark. And now, here I was— back in the Directorate's orbit, my last name a shadow I couldn't shake.

Maybe the crew didn't know the details. Most of it was scrubbed from the archives, but bits and pieces always slipped through. Either way, they were wary.

I couldn't decide which was worse—that they judged me for what my father *did*... or pitied me for believing he hadn't.

"Must be strange, coming all the way out here," Rhys said, voice low and calm. "Most people volunteer for Thalassa either to avoid something... or chase it."

I stirred my broth. "Maybe a little of both."

Kaela snorted. "Can't be here for the cuisine."

"Give it a week," Leo said. "Either the food grows on you, or you just give up."

"Mostly the second," Rhys muttered.

"You'll either love us," Kaela added, winking, "or want to throw us out the airlock by month three. No in-between."

That made me pause. The way she said *us*—like the place had already grafted them together. I wasn't part of that. Not yet. Maybe not ever. Would I last longer than the famed Derek?

The conversation drifted to marine samples and climate data I hadn't seen. I sat quietly at the table, letting the quiet exhaustion wash over me while I adjusted to being there. It wasn't home, but it wasn't hostile.

Not yet.

TO: Dr. Alan Birch <a.birch@aquaeris.com>
FROM: Arizona Birch <ari.birch@aquaeris.com>
SUBJECT: When are you coming home?

Hey Dad,

I know your rotation just started, but I'm already worried about you. I keep having nightmares about Mom. I know, I know—you'd say I'm being paranoid again. But when you won't even tell me what planet you're on…

I get it. Scientific ethics, NDAs, classified work, blah blah. But it still sucks. I miss you.

The Bill Nye shower is passing through tonight. I was hoping we could watch it together—make one of our ridiculous wishes. Instead, I'll be out there alone, staring up at the sky and pretending you're looking at the same streaks of light from wherever the hell you are.

Write back if you can. Even just a dumb riddle or a weather report. A new poem maybe.

Love,
Your Cal-Zona

Chapter 3: The Lab

The hab groaned around me as I lingered by the corridor—metal flexing as it rode the waves. Distant machinery pulsed steady and low, like a heartbeat.

"You want to see your lab?" Calum's voice cut the quiet.

He leaned by the bulkhead, hands in his jacket pockets, posture casual.

I hesitated. "Yeah… sure."

"It's below. Come on."

The words *down below* made my stomach turn, but I followed. The level we were on sat on top of the water, but the majority of the research station was underwater by necessity.

The corridor narrowed—walls curving inward, ceiling bristling with cables. We reached a circular hatch in the floor. Brushed steel. Damp with condensation.

Dr. Calum cracked it open with a practiced twist, revealing a ladder descending into shadow.

"She's all yours," he said, and started down.

I followed. The rungs were cold beneath my hands, the metal humming faintly. The deeper we went, the louder the sea became—pressing close.

Twenty feet down, another hatch. Calum opened it. Cool, filtered air swept past us.

I stepped through—and the warmth I'd carried from the mess hall died instantly. The air was sterile, colder by degrees. It slipped under my jacket-like fingers. The cold here didn't just touch skin—it *settled in*. Like it was trying to claim something deeper.

The lab unfurled around me, built like a ring at the base of the hab. Light glinted off sealed containers and sleek consoles. But I didn't see any of it.

I saw the walls.

Or rather—the *glass*.

Floor to ceiling, seamless panes curved around the lab, offering a panoramic view of the ocean outside. The abyss loomed, rippling with currents and shadows.

Life moved out there. Pale fish drifted through fronds of alien flora, their bodies pulsing in slow rhythm—too synchronized, too still. A dozen narrow eyes tracked the lab as they passed, unblinking. One brushed against the glass. The impact was soft, almost soundless. But the vibration lingered under my feet.

On one counter, a sealed sample container blinked red in a slow, steady rhythm. Inside, something coral-like pulsed faintly in response—as if the two were speaking a language I wasn't invited to hear. I turned to ask Rhys, but he was watching the reef instead, face unreadable.

My knees went soft before I realized I was swaying. I blinked hard. The ocean beyond the glass wasn't just vast—it was *alive*. It pulsed with its own slow hunger. My throat closed. I'd been underwater before. But this was different. This was like standing on the edge of something that had been waiting.

"You okay?" Calum asked, voice quiet.

I nodded too quickly. "Yeah. Just... wasn't expecting this."

"Takes getting used to." He stepped beside me, reflected faintly in the glass. "But you'll find your rhythm. Most do."

That confused me considering there was a grand total of five of us on this planet.

"I'm not great with tight spaces," I admitted. "Or water this deep."

"Thalassophobia?"

"Among other things." I shoved my hands in my jacket pockets. "Distraction helps."

"Good," he said. "You'll have your first dive simulation tomorrow."

I blinked. "Simulation?"

"The Directorate requires it. The Maw's... a lot."

"The Maw?"

"One of the deepest parts of the shelf," he said, eyes distant. "Water so black the sub's lights can't cut through. Honestly... it's creepy."

A beat passed.

"The simulation's terrifying," he added, "but necessary."

I swallowed. "Thanks for the warning."

"Anytime." His mouth twitched—not quite a smile. "I'll give you the full tour after. Kaela's probably going to show you the fun stuff, but scientist to scientist... mine's better."

I nodded, rubbing my arms. Goosebumps bloomed

beneath my sleeves. I barely registered his words. My mind was already sinking down into the dark.

Ω

A little while later, as I calibrated computers and digipads, a sharp *rap* against the glass made me flinch. I jolted hard enough to clip my elbow against the lab bench, pain sparking bright and sudden.

The filtration system hummed steadily overhead. Beyond the massive panes, the ocean shifted—slow, endless, blue-black. Nothing else moved.

Another knock. Louder this time.

Kaela's face appeared in the small circular window of the lab door, breath fogging the glass as she grinned and knocked again, deliberately obnoxious.

I let out a breath I hadn't realized I was holding and crossed the lab, thumbed the door control. It slid open with a hydraulic sigh.

"You settling in," Kaela said, stepping inside, arms crossed over grease-smeared coveralls, "or teaching Calum how to summon sea demons?"

"Just getting acquainted with the scenery," I said, jerking my chin toward the glass wall and the kaleidoscope of alien life beyond it.

Kaela glanced at the ocean. For a heartbeat, the grin slipped—replaced by something like awe, or maybe calculation. Then she shook it off.

"Yeah, well. You can commune with the fish later. C'mon. I'm supposed to show you your room before you collapse face-first into a workstation."

I hesitated, glancing back at the lab. At the glass. At the

faint pulse of light far beyond it.

Calum caught my eye and gave a small nod. "Go. We'll dig into samples tomorrow—once you've adjusted to being planetside."

"Appreciate it," I muttered.

The hatch sealed behind us with a dull clang. Without the lab's open space, the station felt tighter—pipes rattling faintly behind the walls, metal creaking as the habitat shifted against the currents.

Kaela walked ahead, bouncing lightly on her heels. "Alright. Grand tour, Birch edition. You've seen Sub-Lab One. Main lab's topside. Hydro-analysis is aft."

"Aft?" I asked.

She grinned. "Gotta keep ship terms alive. Even if this glorified tin can doesn't float."

We passed a junction where the corridor split—stairs spiraling upward on one side, sealed doors on the other, marked with faded hazard stripes.

"Engineering bay," Kaela said. "My kingdom. If something makes a weird noise, assume I caused it."

"Comforting."

"I keep us alive," she said lightly. "Mostly."

The corridor curved, reinforced with pressure seals. Condensation slicked the floor grates. Our footsteps echoed, swallowed quickly by the station's low, constant hum.

She stopped at a modest hall lined with doors. "Living quarters. Closet-sized, but private. Yours is seven."

The door slid open.

The room was small—bunk, locker, narrow desk—but the porthole dominated the far wall. Thick glass framed the ocean beyond, shadows drifting through blue and green light cast by bioluminescent growths clinging to the structure outside.

Cramped. Nowhere to pace. Nowhere to escape if the walls closed in.

But also… quiet. Like being tucked into something vast.

"Not bad," I said, setting my pack down. I'd let Leo take my other two bags, but this one almost never left my sight. I guessed I'd have to leave it behind when we were in the water.

"It grows on you," Kaela replied. "Like mold."

I snorted.

"You ready for your dive sim tomorrow?" she asked.

The word landed wrong—heavy, sudden.

"Dive feels generous," I said. "More like… controlled observation."

She rolled her eyes. "You won't be in a real sub, thousands of meters down, until a few days or maybe a week from now."

A flash of deep water pressed behind my eyes—black, endless, closing in. I forced a smirk.

"Can't wait to test the life expectancy of experimental submarines."

Kaela laughed, but something flickered in her eyes. Not fear, more like a flash of memory.

"I've only done a few jobs like this," she said after a beat. "Couldn't resist this one though. Ocean planet. Weird life. Big paycheck."

Her fingers worried a silver ring, spinning it again and again. I wondered who she'd left behind. Or what.

"You're from the Lunar colonies, right?" I asked.

"Sector Twelve," she said. "Big family. Loud. Crowded."

Her smile faltered, just slightly.

"I took this job for the quiet," she admitted. "Didn't expect to miss them so much."

I leaned against the bulkhead, feeling the vibration of the station through my spine. "Funny how distance works."

She gave a soft huff. "Yeah."

After a pause, she looked at me. "What about you? Your family okay with you being out here?"

The question dropped straight through me.

"I wouldn't know," I said lightly. "They're dead."

Silence.

"Oh," Kaela said, then winced. "I—sorry."

"It's fine." It wasn't. "You get used to it."

You don't.

She studied me for a long moment, something unreadable behind her eyes. Then her expression reset—too fast.

"You'll like it here," she said, patting my arm. "Even if this place…" She trailed off.

"Even if it what?"

She smiled, wide and artificial. "Has terrible coffee."

I almost laughed. Almost. I wasn't trying to be mean, I really wasn't. There was simply nothing in me left to give that day.

"Get some rest, Dr. Birch. Big day tomorrow."

She turned and left before I could reply. The quiet returned, heavier than before. I found myself wishing Dr. Calum would stop by, or maybe even Leo. Just someone to talk to.

I unpacked on autopilot. Clothes. Data pads. Tools. At the bottom of my pack, my fingers brushed a holo-frame.

My father's face—mid-laugh, eyes crinkled, alive. The ache in my chest sharpened, familiar and cruel. I shoved the frame into the drawer and shut it harder than necessary.

The bunk creaked as I lay down—the mattress pad far more comfortable than I expected. The station swayed gently, rocked by the ocean like a careful cradle. The hum of machines blended with the distant groan of metal and the whisper of water pressing in.

Sleep crept up on me, soft but quick.

And just as I slipped beneath it—

"Arizona."

My eyes flew open.

My heart hammered. The room was dark. Quiet. Empty.

Just the station breathing around me.

Just the ocean beyond the glass.

I told myself it was exhaustion. Memory. Guilt, finally catching up.

Still, I lay awake far longer than I should have, listening—waiting—for something I couldn't name.

Chapter 4: A New Dawn

The mess hall felt different in the morning.

It wasn't warmer—the temperature control was constant—but the light was gentler up here, nearer to the surface. A soft, simulated sunlight filtered through the ceiling panels, casting a pale gold wash across the brushed metal walls. Somewhere above, the reinforced dome of the topside habitat swayed faintly with the ocean's motion. The creaking frame didn't sound ominous anymore. The creaking simply filled the silent spaces in the Hab.

Kaela was already at the table when I stepped in, perched sideways on her chair like she might launch out of it. Leo stood behind the stovetop—hair an unruly brown mess, undershirt stained with coffee—scooping something vaguely porridge-like into bowls. Rhys sat at the far end with a datapad, scrolling silently. Olen leaned against the wall, arms crossed, watching them all like a man stationed on a different frequency.

"Morning, Birch!" Kaela called, waving a spoon at me. "Hope you're hungry. Today's special is protein sludge. Hand-whisked with despair."

Leo snorted. "It's oatmeal."

"It's lying," Kaela replied, letting said sludge drip off the spoon for effect.

I slid into the empty chair furthest from Olen, posture straight. The room smelled like overbrewed caffeine, warm grains, and faint ozone from the night-cycle machinery reboot.

Leo set a bowl in front of me with a half-bow. "Welcome to luxury dining on the Directorate's dime."

"Thanks," I muttered.

"It's not bad if you drown it in salt," Kaela offered.

"Or regret," Rhys added without looking up.

Kaela grinned. "See? He gets it."

I stirred my bowl, watching the others move in their quiet morning ritual. It was ordinary, easy. They didn't speak in full sentences half the time, but the way they passed bowls, leaned without thinking, exchanged dry jabs—this was their rhythm. A small crew, shrinking smaller. A world carved out of metal and routine.

I glanced up and caught Olen watching me. Not studying. Just *watching*. I met his gaze. It didn't soften.

"Morning, Olen," I said.

He didn't answer.

Kaela made a face. "Don't mind him. That's just his default programming."

Leo laughed around a mouthful of food. Rhys only blinked.

"I heard your training scores were below spec," Olen said flatly.

The conversation paused, just enough for the temperature to shift.

"I met the Directorate minimum," I said, keeping my tone even. A flush crept across my skin.

"Minimum gets people killed."

Kaela groaned. "Gods, Olen. Dial it back. She's been here a *day*."

"No such thing as a soft landing out here."

"I'll be fine," I said, sharper than I meant.

"Hope so," he said, and turned back to his bowl.

Kaela leaned toward me, voice conspiratorial. "It's not personal. He just thinks everyone's an idiot until proven otherwise. Took me three weeks to earn a full sentence."

"He talked to you?" Leo said. "Jealous."

I huffed a laugh, despite myself.

Rhys finally set his data pad down. His gray eyes flicked toward me—direct, thoughtful.

"Tea or coffee?"

I blinked. "Tea."

He stood, walked to the beverage unit, and retrieved a small stash tin from the upper cabinet.

Leo whistled low. "Ohhh, breaking out the good stuff."

"Don't be dramatic," Rhys said.

"He never offered *me* tea," Kaela muttered.

Rhys returned and set the mug in front of me. It smelled faintly floral—dried citrus, and something herbal underneath. Not standard ration supply.

"Where did this come from?" I stared up at him, awe leaking into my voice.

"Contraband," he said with a wink. "Don't tell Olen."

Unsure if he was joking, I looked up and smiled. He didn't smile back, but his gaze lingered—analytical, almost soft.

"Thanks," I said.

"You're welcome."

Kaela propped her chin in her palm. "So, how's our new crew-member doing?"

"We'll find out after today," Rhys said.

"What's today?" I asked, already bracing.

"Simulation," Olen reminded me, standing.

I exhaled through my nose. "Great. Nothing like a fake drowning before your real one."

"You won't drown," Olen said. "Unless you panic. Then it'll feel real."

Kaela kicked his boot under the table. "Such *bedside* charm."

"You'll be fine," Leo said. "Probably."

I raised my mug in mock-toast. "To near-death training exercises."

Leo clinked his against mine. "And to passing out in your wetsuit."

It wasn't warmth, but it was *something*. A rhythm. A strange kind of gravity, pulling me slowly into their orbit.

Ω

Later that morning, I found myself in Sub-Lab One again— smaller, quieter, a little less sterile than the others. I'd found a few ways to personalize it, soften it.

After several hours of cataloging samples and reading data cores, the silence between Rhys and me grew too loud.

Kaela and Leo had vanished into the engineering bay, somewhere behind the dull thrum of distant power tools. Olen was off doing Olen things—training, drills, scowling at static readouts. The upper level above us creaked now and then with movement, but here, below the surface, it felt like another world entirely.

"Did you ever work with my father?" I asked, not looking up.

It came out fast. Too fast.

Rhys paused. Just briefly. He didn't look up from the storage capsule he was sealing.

"What was his name?"

"Dr. Alan Birch. Geneticist and biologist."

"Ah," he said quietly.

That was it. Just *ah*.

My eyes narrowed. "You *don't* know him?"

Rhys set the container aside and leaned slightly on the edge of the workstation. His expression stayed neutral, but his voice was carefully even.

"I remember the name. But we never worked together."

My chest tightened—not with grief, exactly, but with something hollower. I'd expected… not fanfare, maybe, but something. Recognition. Weight. *Legacy.*

"I just assumed…" I trailed off. "He was a lead in the genetic survey initiative. I figured people would at least *remember* him."

Rhys's gray eyes met mine. Calm. Measured. Unreadable.

"He was a scientist," he said. "One of many. We don't all leave legacies out here. Most don't."

His tone was neutral, but there was a tension behind it. A thin wire stretched too tight. His words however… they became a sludge in my throat, sinking and settling in my stomach.

"Right," I said, and looked back down at the data pads. "Guess I built him up in my head. Gotta fill in the blanks with something."

The silence that followed was heavy.

"I didn't mean it as a dismissal," Rhys added quietly, after a moment.

I shrugged. "You're fine, Dr. Calum."

He crossed the lab slowly, stopping beside my station. The air between us felt close, but not claustrophobic.

"Arizona," he said.

I glanced up. "Yeah?"

"Call me Rhys. Not Dr. Calum."

That caught me off-guard. Not because he said it—but because of the way he said it. Soft. Unpressured. Like an offering.

"Okay," I said. "Rhys."

Something small inside me bloomed. It didn't discourage me from wondering about Rhys' connection to my father.

He nodded once, then pointed toward my screen. "That sample log's off. Chemistry doesn't match the previous readouts. Could be contamination."

"Or a variant strain," I said, leaning in. "Let me cross-check it."

His hand hovered near mine for a moment on the console's edge. Just enough to feel the static buzz of proximity. I could still smell the faint citrus of the tea he'd made. We worked in silence for a while—quiet clicks, soft hum of processors, distant sound of water flexing against the lab walls.

Part of me wasn't reading data. Part of me was stuck on the look Rhys had given me when I said my father's name.

He remembered Alan Birch. I was sure of it now. He just wasn't telling me why. Was it because of what my father supposedly did, or was it for a darker reason?

Chapter 5: The Simulation

The dive chamber was colder than I expected.

Maybe it was the lighting—dim, clinical, flickering slightly above us. Maybe it was the fact that we were below again, two decks down from the warmth of the mess hall, surrounded by ocean. Below my lab even. No more simulated sunlight. Just metal, machines, and pressure.

The walls of the simulation room were lined with thick cables and fiber conduits. A submersible pod—sleek, narrow, too small for comfort—sat mounted in the center. Open cockpit. Interior stripped to the bare essentials: screen array, throttle, pressure regulator, emergency feed. Space enough for one.

I stood at the edge, suited up. The synthetic dive fabric clung like a second skin, the rebreather unit tight across my chest.

Olen checked the seal around my wrist with a practiced yank. "Too loose," he muttered, adjusting it. "You're dead if this leaks at five thousand meters."

"Noted," I said flatly.

He didn't acknowledge it. Just moved to the next strap.

His presence was all angles—stern, economical, efficient. Like he resented every second this was taking.

"You'll run the simulation once. Three minutes of descent, three minutes of maneuvering, three minutes of ascent. Standard depth profile. No AI assist."

"Got it."

His eyes flicked to mine. "Don't try to prove anything. This isn't about guts. It's about control. Stick to procedure."

I nodded, jaw tight.

He stepped back. "Get in."

The sub's cockpit was even smaller than it looked from the outside. I eased in, knees brushing the side panels, screen arrays blinking to life as the system initialized. The hatch slid closed above me with a hiss.

Enclosure sealed.

Simulation loading.

Depth target: 4,800 meters.

Begin descent.

The chair vibrated beneath me as the world outside fell away. I knew it wasn't real—just projection, sensors, gravity adjustments, and screen trickery—but the illusion was flawless.

The water outside the simulated viewport grew darker. The filtered light from the shallows faded quickly, replaced by greenish murk, then shadows, then black. Weightless black.

I gripped the side controls tighter. Reminded myself to breathe.

In the observation room above, I could just make out silhouettes: Leo leaning forward, Kaela with her feet propped on a console, Rhys standing with his arms folded. Watching.

Olen's voice came through my headset. "Begin orientation maneuvers."

I adjusted the yaw, toggled the internal gyroscope, shifted the sub laterally. Smooth. Fluid. The training modules hadn't prepared me for how real the dark would feel. How much like that day it would feel.

My breath came shorter as I descended. The depth meter ticked past 3,000 meters.

3,800.

4,200.

The viewport offered only void now. Darkness that seemed to press back. No light. No motion. No boundary. I was alone. Alone in a capsule that felt more like a coffin than a vehicle.

The comm hissed faintly in my ear. "You're lagging. Adjust your pitch."

I swallowed and reached for the control—but my hand shook. Barely. Just enough to notice. Olen said nothing. His silence was worse. My heart started to pick up pace.

You're fine. It's just a sim.

Another voice echoed, unbidden.

"Arizona..."

Not Olen. Not the sim.

Familiar. Soft. Dad.

My breath caught.

I blinked hard. Nothing in the cockpit had changed, but suddenly it felt wrong. Off-kilter. Like the walls were closer, the lights too dim. I could feel the pressure around me—not just simulated water, but something watching. Something vast and unseen.

"Control's slipping," Olen said, calm but sharp. "You need to breathe and refocus."

I couldn't. The slight shaking of my hands became a tremor.

I was back in my mother's living room. The Directorate's voice on the vidcall, sterile and final. There was an accident. Genetic breach. Unauthorized. I was back in the archival servers, watching files vanish before I could open them. I was back in the dream—water pressing in on all sides, light vanishing, something vast below me, moving without shape.

I was… I was… I was…

My hands slipped off the console. Tears dripped from my cheeks.

Alarms pinged—low-level, warning me of a simulated pressure breach.

"You're losing the pod," Olen said. Still calm. Still cold.

"Pull her out," Leo's voice snapped in the background, his brogue intensified in his ire.

"No," Olen said. "Let her ride it out."

The screen flickered.

Outside—if there was an outside—something passed the viewport. Just a shimmer. A flicker of color, wrong and red, too close.

My chest convulsed. I gasped for breath, trying to claw my mind back from the spiral.

It's not real. It's not real. It's not real.

"Arizona."

This time, my mother's voice. Soft. Lilting. In the walls.

I pressed my hands to the sides of the cockpit and screamed. Not loud. Not long. Just enough to release something sharp and buried.

And then—

Stillness.

The screen blinked once. The simulation halted.

Descent complete.
Simulation terminated.
Vitals abnormal.
Recommend repeat.

The hatch hissed open.

I blinked against the sterile lights of the chamber. My skin was slick with sweat inside the suit. A persistent ringing sounded in my ears. My breath came out in rasps.

Olen stood above me, unreadable.

I pulled myself out, legs shaking.

"You froze," he said. Not an accusation. Just a statement in that flat voice of his.

"I came back," I rasped.

He gave a small nod. "Just enough. Barely."

Rhys appeared in the corridor, concern etched into the lines of his face. Kaela was close behind, wringing her hands. Leo lingered further back, visibly uneasy.

"You passed," Olen said. "Technically."

I didn't reply.

"You'll do it again tomorrow. And the day after. Until I'm satisfied you're qualified to go out there without endangering this team."

I stared at him. Rage and shame knotted under my ribs. "You let me spiral."

"I'm not your nanny, sweetheart. Same time tomorrow."

Olen didn't wait for a response. He turned and walked away, boots echoing down the corridor.

Kaela reached out to steady me. "You okay?"

I nodded. A lie. "Fine."

Leo cleared his throat. He looked like he was searching for the right words that might put me at ease. "If it helps, you'll never have to pilot alone unless it's an emergency. All you have to do is get through the simulation."

Rhys didn't speak, but he held my gaze as I moved past him. Quiet. Present. There was something wild and unsettled in his storm-grey eyes. If I wasn't careful, it might drag me down with him.

Ω

Evening in the mess hall felt different than morning.

The lights overhead dimmed to a warmer amber tone, mimicking sunset. The sway of the surface platform was gentler now, more rhythmic, like the station had finally exhaled.

Leo had made something resembling stew—thick, fragrant, full of things that didn't quite match but somehow worked. I had absolutely no cooking skills other than ordering delivery, so I was grateful for it despite the strongly fishy smell wafting off the stew.

Kaela leaned into him as they moved around the tiny galley, arms brushing, quiet touches exchanged without thought. It wasn't performative. It was lived-in. Comfortable.

They'd been together a long time, I realized. Longing spiked in my chest. Grief dominated most of my life; science the rest. Would I ever have that sort of quiet intimacy?

Olen sat at the far end of the table, boots planted wide,

posture rigid even at rest. He didn't speak unless addressed. When I asked for salt, he passed it down without a word. But, when it reached me, I caught it—a nod.

Barely a tilt of the chin. Nothing more. It was something. His version of a handshake, perhaps.

Kaela flopped into her usual seat and pointed her spoon at me. "Congrats on not dying in the sim."

"Thanks," I said dryly.

"You know he let me drown my first time?" she said, nodding toward Olen. "Full red-out. Nearly puked in the helmet."

"I was assessing response time," Olen said without looking up.

"Sure you were."

Leo handed me a steaming bowl and winked. "Don't take it personally. He calls me useless at least once a week. It's his love language."

Olen grunted, and I wasn't sure if that was confirmation or the beginnings of a threat.

I sat. The bench was cold, but the steam from the stew warmed my face. I realized I hadn't truly eaten since the protein sludge at breakfast. My body was catching up with my fear.

Kaela leaned toward me. "You really okay?"

"I will be."

She nodded, accepting that. "You did good, you know. He wouldn't have let you spiral if he didn't think you could pull yourself out."

"Nice of him to almost drown me out of respect."

She grinned. "It's practically a hug."

I smiled, the tension in my spine softening slightly.

Across the table, Rhys sat quiet, but not absent. He watched the conversation unfold like he was cataloguing behavior—small expressions, deflections, unspoken jokes. But when I glanced at him, his eyes met mine immediately.

Not wild now. Still unsettled.

Like he was waiting for me to ask more questions, to call him out on his obvious lies.

I didn't.

Not yet.

Instead, I focused on the meal. The sound of Kaela's spoon clinking against Leo's bowl. Olen's sharp inhale when Kaela tried to steal a bite from his plate. Rhys's tea cooling in front of him, untouched.

It was still new. Still tight in my chest. But for the first time since arriving, I didn't feel like a passenger orbiting someone else's system.

I was in the gravity of it now. I was starting to settle in.

Chapter 6: Small Wonders

It was late when Rhys found me.

I was back in Sub-Lab One, alone now, doodling absentmindedly in one of Dad's old journals. The others had drifted off—Kaela and Leo to their shared bunk, Olen to whatever rigid meditation passed for his downtime. I'd told myself I was just finishing a scan cycle, but really, I couldn't sleep. My skin still prickled from the dive. My lungs hadn't quite forgotten the way they'd locked tight inside the sim.

"You're still awake," Rhys said from the doorway.

I looked up. He leaned there casually, hands in his jacket pockets, a faint shadow under his eyes like he hadn't slept either.

"I was promised a tour," I said, more brightly than I felt.

He nodded once. "Walk with me?"

I hesitated, then peeled off my gloves and followed him into the corridor.

The station was quieter now. The hum of systems pulsed like a heartbeat, steady and far away. Pipes ticked faintly overhead. Our footsteps echoed in the curved hall as we moved past sealed bulkheads and flickering indicator panels.

"We haven't had many like you," he said as we walked. "Biologists who make it this far."

"It hasn't been that long. I assumed there'd be more of us," I said. "Given the nature of the mission."

"There were. Early on. Budget cuts," he said with a shrug.

We passed through a reinforced door into a secondary research bay—smaller, colder. On one of the tables, a sealed sample container glowed faintly from within. Inside: a small, branching structure of coral, threads of green and violet weaving through its crystalline arms. The colors pulsed back and forth like twinkling stars.

Rhys stepped up beside it, motioned me closer.

"This is what we're here for," he said. "The Nylaris Coral."

Bitterness filled his voice, but I barely registered it as I studied the coral. "It's stunning."

"It's more than that. It has regenerative properties—unlike anything we've seen. Reacts to electrical fields, even neural signals in some cases. There's a theory it can interface with the human nervous system. Potential applications in neurodegenerative diseases, trauma repair..."

"Stem-pathway scaffolding," I murmured. "Or artificial memory anchoring."

Rhys looked at me, surprised—but not unpleasantly. "Exactly. The possibilities are endless."

I met his eyes. "We studied a similar structure in one of my postgrad labs. Synthetic modeling, not organic. But nothing with this kind of living interface."

He smiled, just slightly. "That's what makes it promising. And dangerous."

"What's the problem?"

"Finding it," he said. "The coral doesn't survive well up here. Most viable clusters are too deep. And the ones we can collect die during transport or decay under observation. We think something stabilizes them down there—some kind of pressure factor or maybe a symbiote."

"So go deeper."

Rhys' eyes darted to mine. "We've tried. But we only have two subs, and they need prior preparation to go that deep. Add in the fact that most of the scientists that come here leave after one cycle."

I nodded slowly. "Isolation fatigue."

"And the cold," he added. "It gets in. Not just physically. Mentally. People start seeing things. Hearing voices. More than half the research staff cycled out after the first quarter. Some never came back."

"And the Directorate's still funding this?"

"For now. But the team gets smaller every month. That's why you're here."

I looked at the coral again. It pulsed gently, like a breathing thing.

"What's different about this one? If they all die, then how is this specimen alive?"

He shrugged. "We still don't know. That's one reason we requested a new biologist. I only have passing knowledge in it, but we need an expert to bridge the gap in our knowledge."

Rhys gestured toward the exit, moving on before I could formulate a response.

"Come on. There's more."

We continued down the corridor, deeper into the habitat's quieter zones. He showed me the hydro-analysis lab—walls lined with water filtration systems and chemical scrubbers, tubes coiled like veins through metal. He showed me the sonar drones for mapping different underwater areas. Then a narrow tunnel with a small viewing slit into a trench—just glass and blackness and the occasional flicker of movement that made my skin crawl.

"This is one of my favorites," he said as we passed a long, curved gallery. "Watch."

He tapped a panel, and a series of dim floor lights flicked on, illuminating a wall of transparent tubing filled with drifting plankton. They shimmered in lazy spirals, casting dancing lights along the floor and walls like stars underwater.

"They follow vibration," he said. "You can hum, and they'll move toward it."

I watched the tiny forms swirl and gather, like music made flesh.

Finally, we climbed.

A narrow stairwell led upward, back toward the surface dome. We emerged into a glass observatory—round and half-covered in salt-fogged panels, the rest looking out across the ocean's moonlit surface. A small fire pit dominated the middle of the space, with a few cheap plastic chairs scattered around it.

I looked up and gasped. I hadn't realized how much I missed the sky.

The stars above were dim, filtered through atmosphere and distance and clouds, but they were there. Real. Constant. The ocean glistened beneath them, dark and endless, waves rolling like slow breath.

"This is where I come when I need to feel smaller," Rhys

said quietly.

I looked at him. "You want to feel smaller?"

He half-smiled. "Sometimes it's a relief. To know you're not the center of the universe. Just a passenger. After a year out here… well, it helps to know that there's more than just this."

We stood side by side in silence, the sea stretching out forever.

After a while, I said, "Why'd you stay?"

He didn't answer right away.

"There's something I need to find. A question..," his voice faltered for a moment. "A question I need answered."

His tone invited no further questions but his words stayed with me as we climbed back down into the station. Before we reached the lower corridor, Rhys stopped.

He stared at the corner junction of two pressure-sealed panels, his brow furrowed.

"What is it?" I asked, crouching down to look at whatever had transfixed him.

There—growing from the seam—was a faint curl of something. Thread-thin. Bioluminescent.

Coral.

This one was smaller than the one in the lab, almost embryonic, a pale pink with an inner glow like the first spark of infection.

Rhys knelt slowly. "This isn't supposed to be here."

I crouched beside him. "How did it get inside?"

He didn't respond. Just reached out and gently touched the wall near it. Not the coral itself—just close enough to feel the hum.

It was warm. We exchanged an alarmed glance.

"We'll report it in the morning," he said softly.

I nodded, but my eyes stayed on the glow. My pulse increased at the wrongness of it.

Rhys tugged at my sleeve gently. "Come on, tomorrow's weekly report."

My bunk felt colder when I returned than it had last night.

Not physically. Just… colder.

I slipped out of my dive suit and into sleep clothes by muscle memory, barely aware of the motion. The glow from the porthole was dim now, filtered through sediment or cloud cover above the surface. Outside, the alien sea swirled slow and thick, dotted with pulses of bio-luminescence that moved like something breathing in the dark.

The cold permeated my bones as I sat on the edge of the bed, turning it all over in my mind—
Rhys's almost-answer.
Olen's brutal training.
The flicker of coral blooming inside the station.
My own voice echoing back at me in the simulation—only it hadn't been my voice.

I told myself I'd write it all down. Log it. Cross-check samples tomorrow. Instead, I crawled under the thermal blanket and let the darkness take me.

The hum of the habitat bled into my skin. Somewhere deep in the structure, something creaked. Not metal stress. Not pipe-shift.

Something slower. Organic.

Sleep pulled me under—

The dreams began.

Flashes.

Color.

Light threading through water like veins.

Coral bursting from wall panels, blooming in slow-motion spirals.

A pressure door yawning open—not from the corridor, but beneath me.

The lab glass cracking.

A shape outside—pale and enormous, faceless, watching.

Then—

My father's voice.

Gentle. Close.

"Arizona… you have to help her."

I turned, but he wasn't there.

Just coral—growing out of his shadow. Curling up the walls like vines on a mausoleum.

My breath fogged the glass. The water on the other side breathed back.

And then a word.

Not spoken. Not heard.

Felt.

Abyluma.

It echoed inside me like a memory that wasn't my own. My eyes snapped open.

The room was still. My breath tight in my throat.

I sat up slowly, heart pounding. Looked to the porthole—

Nothing.

Just the sea. Just the dark. My pulse wouldn't slow. When I shifted the blanket off my chest, my undershirt stuck faintly

to my skin, damp with sweat.
I pressed my hand to the wall.
Warm.
Warmer than it should have been.

Chapter 7: As Above

The connection was glitchy at first—static rippling across the screen, turning both faces into smeared shadows.

I adjusted the transmission relay, tapped twice against the console, and the feed stabilized. Two men appeared, seated side by side in the polished interior of some Directorate conference room, likely some Earth-like planet. Bright lighting. Flag on the wall. Glass panels behind them revealing a city skyline I couldn't place.

Dawson Mays, Aquaeris Systems' current CFO, wore a dark suit that probably cost more than my annual stipend, his silver hair meticulously styled. He didn't smile when he saw me. He never did.

To his left sat Hiram Perth, head of security for Aquaeris Systems. Mid-thirties, trim beard, muscular frame barely contained by the stiff collar of his uniform. His voice held the same New Scottish lilt that Leo's did.

Hiram looked like the kind of man who preferred dealing with threats in person, not behind a desk. His eyes scanned the feed not with curiosity—but with tactical assessment.

"Dr. Birch," Dawson said, voice clipped. "You're online."

"I am," I confirmed. "Transmission holding at 88 percent clarity."

"Fine." He didn't ask about the crew. Didn't ask how I was adjusting. Just leaned in, jaw tight. "We understand your arrival was delayed due to weather interference."

"Only slightly," I said. "I've spent the last few days familiarizing myself with the lab systems, running test diagnostics, and initiating my first simulation trials."

Hiram leaned forward slightly, tone more grounded. "And the team? Integration?"

I hesitated. "Working on it."

Dawson narrowed his eyes. "We've already received preliminary evaluations from Olen."

Of course they had.

"The simulations are physically demanding," I said. "But I'm adapting. Progress is being made."

Hiram nodded once, watching me closely but without judgment. "Good. The longer you last, the more useful your data becomes."

Dawson didn't react. "And the coral?"

I glanced down at my datapad, then back up. "Minimal viable samples above 4,000 meters. Most collected specimens decay within hours. Lab analysis is underway. The deeper coral structures are suspected to possess stronger bio-interfacing capabilities, but no one's been able to retrieve one intact."

Dawson said, "Then your priority is clear."

"Yes," I said. "Understood."

"Send your first detailed report to Director Mays by end of day," Dawson continued. "We want a full log—lab analysis, personnel assessment, simulation performance."

Hiram added, tone softer but firm, "Evelyn's compiling the recovery modeling. She needs everything. Be honest. Don't sugarcoat it."

I nodded. "I'll upload the report immediately after this call."

There was a beat of silence.

Then Dawson leaned back, expression unreadable. "Be aware, Dr. Birch. If viability can't be demonstrated within the next quarter cycle, Thalassa IX's budget will be... reevaluated."

My throat tightened. "Understood."

Essentially, the livelihood of each of the crew members depended on my ability to overcome my fear of diving into those dark waters.

"Good luck, Doctor." His voice didn't mean it.

The screen cut out a second later, the image of Dawson and Hiram replaced by the murky blue of the comms panel. The hum of the habitat filled the silence.

I stared at the blank screen for a moment longer.

Then I stood. Logged out. And went to suit up for another simulation.

Chapter 8: Determination

The dive simulations became a ritual.

Every morning, before my hands had stopped shaking from the last dream, before the tea had settled my stomach, I suited up and descended into the simulator chamber beneath the main deck. Cold water. Oxygen checks. Pressure calibration. Olen waiting, arms crossed, eyes already annoyed.

The first day, I panicked within three minutes.

The second day, I threw up in my mouthpiece and nearly blacked out before Olen yanked me out.

The third day, I managed to stay under pressure long enough to see the trench wall tilt beneath me like the edge of the world—then the pressure in my chest turned to fire and I slapped the abort.

Every day, he said the same thing: "Again. Tomorrow."

No encouragement. No sympathy. Just that word—again.

By day five, the others had stopped trying to ask how it went. Kaela would greet me with a mug of hot tea. Leo would nudge a protein bar toward my elbow. Rhys would glance up but say nothing. Olen never looked at me outside the chamber.

It wasn't humiliation. It was worse—irrelevance. Like I was just another failed addition to the crew. Another bio whiz the Directorate threw at Thalassa like spaghetti at a wall.

I kept going.

My body hated me. My dreams got darker. The walls of the sim chamber felt closer each time. The more I learned about the Nylaris Coral, the more I *wanted* to see it with my own eyes—and the more terrified I was that I never would.

Then came day seven.

Another failure.

I aborted at the halfway mark. Oxygen too low. Vision tunneling. Fingers numb on the controls. I surfaced shaking, gasping, helmet ripping free with Olen's help.

I can't do this. I can't.

I sat hunched over in the prep room, wetsuit peeled halfway down, hair damp with sweat and sea-salt. Olen leaned against the bulkhead, arms folded. It was his disappointed gaze that had my mouth open before I could think.

"I can do it again," I croaked.

His brow furrowed. "You just failed."

"I know," I said. "Let me go again."

Olen stared at me a long moment. Then nodded once. "Ten minutes. Recalibrate your vitals."

Ten minutes later, I was back in the chamber.

This time, I didn't think.

I didn't try to *win* the sim. I didn't try to make Olen proud. I just… went under.

The descent played out like it always did. Pressure mounting. Blackness thickening. Static crackling in my ears like someone whispering in a frequency I couldn't quite understand.

I didn't panic. I didn't fight it. I let the weight press in. Let the fear bloom in my ribs, and *kept going anyway*.

At 4,300 meters simulated depth, the lights flickered. The trench loomed like a mouth, swallowing sonar.

At 4,500, my hands were shaking.

At 4,800, I hit the beacon and began ascent.

The sim ended. Systems faded to standby. The water drained with a hiss, and the floor beneath me rose.

I climbed out on unsteady legs, the chill sinking through every muscle, every bone.

Olen stood at the console. Watching. Not moving.

His eyes met mine.

He gave me a single nod. Nothing more.

Then he turned and left.

Outside, I found Kaela waiting with tea and a blanket.

"I didn't know if you'd go again," she said quietly, folding the blanket around my body as I trembled.

"Neither did I," I whispered.

Rhys passed by without a word, but as he moved behind me, he murmured just loud enough to catch:

"Told you you'd find your rhythm."

I didn't say anything.

But I didn't stop smiling, either.

Ω

The message from Olen came through the station's comm

grid just after evening meal.

[SIMULATION CLEARED. REPORT FILED. NO FURTHER COMMENTS.]

Which, from Olen, might as well have been a standing ovation.

Kaela grinned when she saw it. Leo whistled low. Rhys raised one eyebrow and murmured something about miracles and ice water.

Then Kaela leaned across the table and nudged my elbow. "Rooftop. One hour. Dress code is 'functional warmth,' and the entry fee is pretending to enjoy my baking."

I blinked. "What?"

She smiled wider. "Tradition. First sim pass earns you a night in the observatory."

Leo lifted a flask. "And whiskey."

Rhys just sipped his tea and said, "It's worth it."

This time, when we ascended the stairs to the observatory, I was ready. I could hear the wind keening faintly through the outer hull. By the time I reached the top, my breath was fogging in front of me.

The observatory dome was octagonal, with glass panes that arched overhead in wide, reinforced curves. In the evening starlight, rainbows danced off the panes sending sparkles scattering across the room. A heater hummed near the base, taking the edge off the cold. The floor was layered with scavenged rugs, old thermal mats, and a central fire pit —repurposed from a malfunctioning thermal chamber, Leo explained, pride in every welded seam.

Kaela was already seated cross-legged near it, passing around a dented tin. "Seaweed oat clusters. Eat them while you're drunk enough to think they're good."

Leo uncapped the flask and poured into mismatched mugs. "To surviving Olen's tender affections," he said.

"To not throwing up in the sim tube," Kaela added, raising her mug.

"To pretending this doesn't violate four fire codes," Rhys murmured.

They looked at me.

I hesitated, then lifted my mug. "To not dying. Yet."

Laughter echoed off the glass ceiling. Outside, the stars shimmered through the dome—thousands of them, unfamiliar constellations glittering above the black waves. One moon visible tonight. Silver light washed over the sea.

Kaela leaned into Leo's shoulder, their fingers brushing, lazy and familiar. He kissed her temple without looking.

Rhys sat beside me on one of the mats, his mug balanced on one knee. "You look better," he said.

I smiled faintly. "I feel like warmed-over death. But thanks."

He studied me for a second. "You're not what I expected."

"Let me guess. You were expecting another lab rat who runs screaming at the first pressure drop."

He tilted his head. "No. I was expecting someone who wouldn't ask questions."

That landed harder than I thought it would. "Am I annoying you?"

He smiled, the smallest curl at the corner of his mouth. "Not yet."

I tried, and failed, not to smile at his honesty. I looked

away and sipped the whiskey. It burned in a delicious way, the fire spreading warmth into my perpetually cold limbs.

Conversation wandered—weather sensors, broken filters, a bet Kaela lost involving bioluminescent jellyfish. Rhys said almost nothing unless asked directly, but when he did speak, everyone listened.

They talked about people who'd left. Ones who hadn't stayed past their first cycle. A guy who spent two weeks sobbing into the water reclamation system before the Directorate pulled him out. A woman who became obsessed with cataloguing wave patterns and never spoke to another human again.

"And now there's us," Leo said, stretching out across a mat, flask tucked against his ribs. "The last crew standing."

"Thalassa's A-Team," Kaela agreed, raising her mug. "If the A-Team were badly paid and entirely unqualified for therapy."

"Speak for yourself," Leo muttered.

The warmth and light pooled around us, soft and flickering. Outside, the sea lapped against the structure. I could feel the rhythm of it in the floor, in my chest.

No one spoke for a while.

Then Kaela broke the quiet, voice softer now. "Sometimes I think we're just fungus. Clinging to a vent pipe in the dark, hoping the heat doesn't run out."

What an odd thing to say.

"You make it sound so romantic," Leo murmured and squeezed her shoulders.

She smiled. But it didn't quite reach her eyes.

I leaned back and let the silence stretch.

My head buzzed from the whiskey. My limbs ached from the sim. But for the first time since arriving, the ache in my chest—the one shaped like loneliness—felt less sharp.

These weren't just coworkers.

They were something else.

Not quite friends, but something that mattered.

Rhys leaned slightly closer. Not touching me, but near enough to feel the heat radiating off him. He didn't say anything.

Didn't need to.

Outside, the sea turned darker still, hiding whatever watched from below. Tomorrow, I would be forced into my first real dive.

But for one night—up here—everything else held.

FROM: Dr. Arizona Birch <ari.birch@aquaeris.com>
TO: Director Evelyn Mays <EveleynMays@aquaeris.com>
SUBJECT: Thalassa IX Arrival–Preliminary Notes

Director Mays,

Planetfall was successful. The drop team delivered me to the habitat without issue. Minor acclimation side effects—standard gravitational compression, no cause for concern. Environmental tolerances are within projected thresholds, though the cold is more penetrating than expected. The platform remains structurally sound, though I'll be reviewing submersion drift protocols following tomorrow's scheduled dive.

The team appears competent, if... eclectic. I've met the station's personnel and begun establishing workflows. They've been operating largely autonomously until now, which is understandable given the Directorate's hands-off approach to fringe operations. Still, it's clear they've adapted to a certain rhythm down here.

Nothing of major scientific significance to report on Week One. Initial lab access has been granted; I've begun calibrating systems for bio-acoustic tracking and tissue sampling. There's promising biodiversity in the upper trench columns—luminescent filter feeders and several unidentified motile species visible even from the observation dome. I'll have more once I've begun direct collection.

I am scheduled to participate in my first dive tomorrow morning. Preliminary conditions suggest favorable visibility and low current resistance. I understand the importance of firsthand data, and I'm eager to begin field immersion. Assuming vessel integrity and crew coordination meet protocol, I expect a productive first day.

I'll maintain the reporting cadence outlined in the Directorate's Field Research Agreement, barring any unexpected developments. So far, this post is proceeding as predicted—quiet, remote, and ideal for uninterrupted work.

Thank you again for facilitating my placement. I understand the trust extended in approving my assignment.

V/ Respectfully,

Dr. Arizona Birch

Chapter 9: First Dive

The station's morning alarm chirped softly from the overhead speakers—a gentle synthetic trill engineered to mimic early birdsong from Earth. It wasn't fooling anyone. Especially not me. I was already awake, eyes gritty, head pounding, body sunken deep into the narrow bunk as if the weight of the entire ocean pressed down through the ceiling.

My dreams had unraveled hours ago, and whatever scraps remained tangled like seaweed around my brain. My father's voice still clung to the edges of my hearing—faint, indistinct. Like trying to catch the tail end of a radio signal slipping off the bandwidth.

"Arizona..."

Just that. A whisper. Impossible.

I blinked at the porthole above my bed, the dark blue outside still painted in bioluminescent swirls from the reef below. Everything was quiet. Just the hum of the circulators and the faint creak of the station's joints shifting with the sea. Still, it felt like something was listening.

I sat up slowly, last night's whiskey throbbing in my temples. The air was cold, sharper than usual. Condensation had gathered on the underside of the pipe above my head, dripping in a steady rhythm onto the floor. I rubbed my hands over my face and felt the stale tang of recycled oxygen coating my tongue. My breath fogged slightly in the low light.

Suiting up was mechanical.
Thermal layer first—cold against my skin, clinging like a second, clammy hide. I pulled the thick collar up over my throat and fastened the clasp.
Pressure suit next, heavier than I remembered. The reinforced seals at my wrists clicked into place with a hiss. The chestplate settled over me like armor—comforting and suffocating all at once.

As I flexed my hands into the gloves, I caught my reflection in the room's narrow steel mirror. Just a flicker of my face between straps and clasps.
Pale. Hollow-eyed. Hair pinned back but already curling at the edges from the damp. For a moment, I looked like someone else—like him. That sharp nose. The tension in the brow. The same eyes that once stared back at me from lecture recordings and news bulletins and Directorate footage that cut off too soon.

I looked away.

The hallway outside was quiet, lit with pale strips of LED's embedded along the ceiling. The hum of the generators pulsed beneath my boots as I walked—steady, rhythmic, like a heartbeat. Like a countdown.
Sub-bay was two levels down. I took the access ladder instead of the lift. I needed the motion. The strain. Something to focus on besides the spiraling nausea threatening to take hold.

By the time I stepped into the sub-bay, the scent of ozone

and lubricant hit me like a slap. Sharp and clean and artificial. Kaela was already there—bent over a toolbox, the sound of clinking metal echoing across the chamber.

She looked up, braid swinging behind her shoulder, and grinned. "Morning, sunshine. You look like shit."

I gave a noncommittal grunt, adjusting the strap across my chest.

"Sleep okay?" she asked, casually, like she didn't really expect an answer.

"Like a rock," I lied.

She snorted and handed me a sealed sampling kit. The hard shell was cool in my hands. "Try not to puke in the Minnow. Leo says it's bad for morale. And worse for the filters."

"I'll aim for your seat," I muttered.

Her grin widened. "That's the spirit."

The aforementioned Minnow loomed behind her—sleek, dark metal, its domed canopy catching the flickering bay lights in warped reflections. It looked smaller than I remembered. Like a coffin with engines.

Rhys stood just beside it, already half-strapped into the operator's harness inside. His voice carried as we approached.

"Good timing. Coral bloom's active. Currents are light, no surge warnings on the shelf. Stick to the plan—sample, catalog, and come back breathing."

He sounded clinical, focused, unreadable. I envied that.

I hesitated at the sub's open hatch, one hand on the cold rim of the frame. The space inside looked even tighter up close. Three seats, shoulder to shoulder, and barely enough room for our knees. The glass canopy above curved like a bubble—beautiful, but far too thin for what it would be holding back.

Kaela was already climbing in. Her boots clanged against the floor plating. "Well? You coming, rookie, or you planning to stand there and have a crisis?"

"Give me a minute," I said, quieter than I meant to. My thighs shook.

I forced myself to step forward.
One foot, then the next.
Hands gripping the harness.
Seat locking in.
Buckle across the chest.
Straps snug.

I felt the world narrow.

The canopy sealed with a hiss, locking into place as the lights inside shifted to deep blue. My heart thudded against the restraints. The air tasted dry. I forced myself to breathe slow and deep.

Kaela glanced over her shoulder, fingers dancing across the piloting interface. "Everyone ready for Arizona's first romantic dive into the abyss?"

"Romantic's a stretch," I muttered. My voice was too tight. Too thin. My hands were already sweating inside the gloves, trembling as the engines powered on beneath our feet. I couldn't stop picturing the metal buckling. The walls giving in. The dark pressing in from all sides. The silence.

I closed my eyes as the Minnow disengaged from the clamps. We lurched forward, smooth and slow, toward the outer gates.

The pressure doors ahead began to open—inch by inch,

revealing a slice of the black beyond.

The ocean waited.

Ω

The sub slid free of the docking tunnel with a soft jolt, and suddenly, the walls of the station were behind us.

The pressure gates sealed shut, and then we were drifting. Unmoored. Untethered. The only thing separating us from the crushing dark was a few inches of alloy and polymer.

Outside, the ocean swallowed everything.

It wasn't the murky blue I'd imagined. It was darker. Vast and infinite and thick with particulate light—drifting specks that shimmered like ash in a slow-motion firestorm. The sub's external beams sliced through the water in narrow cones, illuminating columns of pale matter that spiraled lazily in the currents.

My mouth went dry. I was aware of every breath. Every heartbeat. Every creak of the Minnow's hull as pressure slowly mounted around us.

As we descended, the last hints of the station's lights vanished above, swallowed into gloom. The silence pressed in. Not total silence—there was the hum of the engine, the click of switches under Kaela's fingers, the occasional beep from Rhys's console—but it all felt hushed, distant, as though wrapped in cotton.

Kaela adjusted the pitch slightly, guiding us downward along a gentle arc.

"You doing okay?" she asked without looking.

"Define 'okay,'" I said through gritted teeth. My jaw ached from clenching it.

Outside the canopy, movement flickered.

At first, I thought it was just more debris, or a trick of light —but then I saw them. Schools of translucent fish, no bigger than my hand, drifting past the sub in perfect formation. They pulsed softly with bioluminescent light—blues and greens, streaks of violet—and each pulse seemed to pass between them like a ripple in a net.

They weren't swimming. Not in the normal way.
They *drifted*, synchronized, suspended like marionettes on invisible threads. No random darting, no scattered fear response to our approach. They simply parted around us in eerie silence and continued onward.

"Why aren't they reacting?" I asked quietly.

"Because they're not scared of us," Kaela murmured. "They never are."

"That's a bad sign," I said, barely above a whisper.

I leaned forward slightly, trying to peer deeper into the gloom. The water beyond the beams was dark, but not empty. Strange shapes hung in the black like shadows— fronds of plant life, long and curling, drifting like seaweed in slow motion. Some were thin as strands of hair, others as thick as tree trunks, curling down from above or up from below. They glowed faintly—green, white, orange.

As we passed, a few of them recoiled from our lights. Others reached *toward* them.

"Point Alpha is straight down and slightly north," Rhys said, then turned to me. "This is one of the deepest points we can reach. One of our drones picked it up on sonar while you were in the sim yesterday."

Kaela adjusted our pitch again, easing us into a slow descent curve. "Heading towards Point Beta. Ten minutes."

"Copy that," Calum said.

I tried to focus on my breath. Inhale. Exhale. The air inside the Minnow had started to smell like plastic and ozone, warmed by the electronics. A faint rattle echoed through the frame—just metal shifting under pressure, I told myself. Just the ocean reminding us it was bigger.

Unease drifted through me. Something was wrong. It took me a few minutes to realize what. It wasn't what was *there*—it was what wasn't. There were no predators.

No larger shapes. No sweep of wide tails or glint of predatory eyes. Nothing bigger than a shoebox.

"Where are the top feeders?" I said aloud, frowning at the shifting shapes. "Everything's small. Too small."

"Yeah," Calum replied. "We've logged a dozen microfauna types. Plankton feeders. Filter swimmers. Nothing apex. Nothing mid-tier, even. It's been that way since this mission started."

"That's not possible," I said. "There should be *something*. If the system's this rich with prey..."

"Could be seasonal," Kaela offered. "Migration pattern. Or maybe the big ones are deeper."

"Or something already cleared them out," I muttered, and immediately wished I hadn't.

A beat of silence.

No one answered.

Outside, the gloom began to shift. A faint green glow appeared below us—soft at first, then growing brighter as we sank lower. I pressed a hand to the canopy.

The reef shelf.

It rose up beneath us like a sprawling, bioluminescent city

—black rock overgrown with branching coral, alien and beautiful. The closer we got, the more clearly I could see the structures: long, tendril-like arms curling over one another, spires rising in strange geometry, sheets of translucent polyps that rippled like heatwaves.

They pulsed.

Not in unison. Not randomly, either.
The colors moved in *waves*—from green to orange to violet and back again—traveling across the reef in spirals and flickering bursts. Like light shows. Like language.

My stomach twisted.

"It's beautiful," Kaela murmured.

"Unnerving," I said. But I couldn't look away.

We hovered over the reef's upper edge. The Maw—dark and vast—waited just beyond, a yawning rift that dropped into nothingness.

Beneath us, the reef glowed on

Ω

Kaela eased the sub down to a slow hover, her fingers tapping out gentle corrections across the control board. The reef spread below us like an ancient city—dense with branching towers, spiraling growths, and glowing veins that mapped out intricate patterns I couldn't begin to parse.

The currents around us were still. Too still. The kind of still that wasn't natural—it was *waiting*.

"Alright," Kaela said, voice low. "You're up, Birch."

I exhaled slowly and activated the sampling controls. The mechanical arm hissed softly as it extended from the sub's undercarriage, its clawed tip unfolding with delicate precision. Through the canopy and internal display screen, I watched it descend toward the nearest coral cluster—pale green, shot through with glowing red veins.

The arm felt *sluggish,* like I was trying to thread a needle with numb hands. Every motion required more effort than it should have. My fingers twitched on the joystick, guiding the claw centimeter by centimeter toward the living reef.

The coral didn't recoil.

It pulsed softly, light fluttering beneath its surface—like watching breath under skin.

"Careful," Calum murmured. "That ridge looks fragile."

I adjusted the grip and closed the claw around a single nodular fragment. It broke free with a soft snap—no resistance, no defensive reaction. I sealed it inside the sterile containment capsule and guided the arm back into its dock.

And that's when the light changed.

A wave of color rippled out from the wound—red, then orange, then red again—trailing in a spiral across the shelf like a stone dropped into liquid fire. Another pulse followed. Then another.

I leaned forward, my pulse spiking. "It's... not random. That's not a stress flare."

Kaela's brow furrowed. "It's repeating. That's a pattern."

"It's reacting to the sample site," I said, eyes locked on the pulses. "It's signaling."

Calum leaned into his console, fingers flying over the keys. "Hold on. I'm logging the intervals. This is... hold on... Base-5 rhythm. But irregular. Not natural irregular. Structured."

"What does that mean?" Kaela asked.

"It means it's not just responding. It might be *trying* to say something. This is absolutely incredible. What's different this time?"

Rhys furiously typed notes into his data pad. I just stared at the reef. The pulses were rippling outward now in concentric arcs. Not just from the impact site, but across multiple species of coral—some we hadn't even touched. The light was moving too fast, crossing too far, for it to be a chemical reaction.

This wasn't biology. It was *language.*

"I think…" I began, voice barely audible, "I think it's talking to something."

Then the sonar screamed.

A burst of static tore through the Minnow's comms system —a high-pitched screech that drove straight into the base of my skull. I doubled over in my seat, clutching the sides of my helmet. It was a vibration more than a sound—like something trying to shake us apart from the inside.

Kaela swore, slamming controls. "Shit—sonar's distorting! Readings are all over the place!"

The lights inside the sub flickered. The hull shuddered.

I twisted to the readout panel. Lines of telemetry warped and vanished. Data streams glitched into static. The proximity sensors blinked red, throwing alerts that overlapped in a screaming cascade.

Outside the canopy, the reef flared—every visible structure erupting into light at once. White. Red. White again. The pulses came faster now. Urgent.

Warning.

"We're pulling back," Kaela barked. "We're too close."

"Wait—" Calum started.

Another sonar burst struck—deeper this time. Lower. It rumbled through the water like the groan of a collapsing glacier. I felt it in my chest, my bones, my teeth.

"Something's coming," I whispered. "It's not just the coral. Something's—"

Movement.

Beyond the edge of the reef, just above the lip of the Maw, the water… *shifted.*

We didn't see a shape—not clearly. Just a *distortion.* A shimmer. Like heat on asphalt. Like a wound in the water itself.

And it was *big.*

Larger than the sub. Larger than the reef.
So large the sonar couldn't wrap around it—only scream.

The water *bent* around it—light bent, sound bent, pressure bent. Whatever it was, it didn't reflect. It *absorbed.*

"What is that?" I breathed.

Calum's voice was tight. "That's not a reef structure. That's moving."

"I'm getting us out of here," Kaela snapped. Her voice cracked at the edge. She throttled the engine hard, and the Minnow groaned as it spun around.

Outside, the reef's light was still flashing, still pulsing— spreading the signal wider, deeper.

But whatever it had been talking to…

It was *listening.*

Ω

The reef blurred past as Kaela gunned the engines. The sub vibrated beneath us, frame whining with strain. Every pressure joint groaned in protest as we accelerated. The light from the coral dimmed behind us—but I could still see the pulses flickering through the water, like a storm of fireflies signaling in a dead language.

No one spoke.

The distorted mass lingered at the edge of sonar range—impossibly large, drifting with the steady inevitability of a glacier sliding into the sea. It wasn't chasing us. But it didn't need to.

We knew it was there.
It knew we were too.

Static bled through the comms, a hiss like something breathing through grit.

Rhys worked in silence, trying to isolate a clean signal from the corrupted telemetry. His jaw was clenched, knuckles pale where he gripped the console. Kaela's hands moved fast but steady, her posture wound tight with focus, like a cord stretched to the snapping point.

I couldn't stop shaking.

The water outside grew lighter with every meter we climbed. Slowly, the glow of the station's mooring lights cut through the gloom—blue rings suspended in the dark like a distant halo. Safety. Structure. Steel.

We breached the outer lock in under eight minutes thanks to Kaela pushing the sub to it's max speed. The bay doors closed behind us with a heavy groan, and the sub settled into its cradle. Jets of water hissed away. Pressure stabilized.

Silence.

Then the canopy hissed open, and a blast of cold air rushed in. I peeled off my helmet with fumbling hands, breath coming too fast, too shallow. My face was slick with sweat. My pulse pounded behind my eyes.

Kaela was the first to move, practically throwing her restraints aside. She pushed off the console and climbed out of the cockpit without a word. Her braid was coming loose, strands of hair clinging to her flushed face.

Rhys unbuckled more slowly. His eyes hadn't left the sonar readout, still glitching, still useless.

I stared at the coral sample in my lap.

It pulsed faintly in its containment capsule—red veins glowing like embers trapped under glass. Steady now. Calm. As if the thing that had spoken through it had fallen quiet. As if it had said what it needed to say.

My hands wouldn't stop trembling.

I slid out of my seat, boots thudding against the sub-bay floor, and staggered a step before catching myself on the railing. Kaela stood by the door, one hand braced against the bulkhead, eyes squeezed shut. She was breathing hard, but her mouth was tight with control.

"Coral samples secured," I croaked, holding up the case like a shield. My voice sounded wrong—too thin, scraped raw. "But… what the fuck was that?"

Calum finally looked up, rubbing both hands over his face. His eyes were wide, hollowed out by something deeper than fear—comprehension.

"The coral was signaling," he said. "Not just reacting. It was reaching out. The sonar didn't just pick up noise—it picked up an answer."

I looked between them. "You think that *thing* responded?"

"I think that *thing* was already listening," Calum said.

Kaela's jaw was set. Her voice, when she finally spoke, was steel. "We stick to the shelf's edge next time. No deeper. No Maw. I won't go back there."

She didn't say it as a suggestion. It came out like an oath.

I didn't argue.

Her hands were white-knuckled on the console. I couldn't tell if she was trying to steady herself or hold something back. She stared at the floor for a long moment, then turned and left without another word.

I followed her gaze as she went—drawn toward the wide viewport set into the sub-bay's wall. The ocean pressed against it like a thick pane of ink.

It looked calm again. Peaceful.

But something had been there.

Something massive, and old, and *aware*.

I clutched the sample case tighter and took a slow step toward the window. The pressure in the room felt different now, like the air had thickened—like we'd brought something back with us. Not physically. Not in any way a scanner could find.

But in *attention*.

The reef had spoken.

The deep had listened.

Chapter 10: The Bloom

The lab lights hummed softly overhead as I keyed the door open, and for a moment, the sterile brightness felt jarring after the sub's dim confines. Inside, the air was cool, sharp with the chemical tang of sterilizer, undercut by something fainter—metal, ozone, and a trace of the ocean's salt carried in by wet suits and sample containers. The door sealed behind me with a quiet hiss.

My pulse still hadn't settled. Even after stripping off the dive suit and breathing in recycled air for ten minutes straight, the adrenaline in my blood hadn't burned out. It had just… shifted.

From fear to focus.

Terror to curiosity.

An ancient alchemy that only science could perform.

The coral bloom sat on the central bench, sealed inside a pressure-stabilized jar. I hadn't expected it to look alive still—but it did. Even through the reinforced glass, its colors bled softly into the room, casting watery hues across the steel walls. It pulsed slowly in rhythmic gradients—deep forest greens giving way to veins of electric blue, curling along its twisted surface like lightning trapped under skin.

Then came the red.

That red—low, warm, faintly iridescent—would shimmer across its branching arms in slow waves, like heat rolling off summer asphalt. But it was wrong. Red like blood. Red like a warning.

It reminded me of those old ambient light strips people used to stick behind their monitors—shifting with the sound of voices or music. Controlled. Predictable. Comforting.

This wasn't that.

This wasn't anything controlled.

Kaela and Rhys followed me in, both quiet. She peeled off her gloves and tossed them into the waste bin, shoulders visibly tense under her coveralls. Rhys, meanwhile, had that unreadable academic calm he wore like a lab coat—buttoned-up and detached—but his eyes never left the specimen.

I set my tablet down beside the containment unit, and just watched it for a moment.

"It's still reacting," I murmured.

"It hasn't stopped since we brought it aboard," Rhys replied. His voice was low, measured, but his posture was off. Relaxed in the way someone gets when they're trying not to look shaken. A still surface over deep water.

Kaela exhaled, flopping onto the stool by my workstation with a heavy breath. She propped one leg over the other, resting an elbow on her knee as she rubbed her temple. "I don't like how it lights up when we walk in," she muttered. "Like it's... watching."

I didn't answer. Instead, I keyed in the environmental controls and released the outer seal of the containment unit.

The lock disengaged with a soft click. Inside, a second layer of insulation adjusted to the room's pressure, releasing a barely audible hiss.

The coral brightened instantly.

A subtle but unmistakable shift in hue rolled along its outer edge—blue veins flaring brighter, green coils twitching inward, as if stirred by some unseen breeze. The red shimmered again, like blood flowing backward.

"It's responding to the lab air?" I whispered, staring at it.

Rhys leaned in slightly, eyes flicking across the scrolling readouts on the console. "Environmental variables are stable. No pressure jumps, no major CO_2 spikes."

"It's still doing it." I stepped closer.

The coral pulsed again—this time a little faster. The green strands rippled outward, undulating in soft spirals that made my skin crawl in a way I couldn't explain. It felt... like breathing.

Like something exhaling.

Rhys noticed the pattern too. "Step back a second."

I did. Just half a meter.

The glow dimmed. The colors slowed, the red fading to a faint, steady hum. The bloom almost seemed to settle.

I stepped forward again.

The pulse intensified, a clear acceleration in rhythm—blue flaring bright, red following in a coiling wave around the structure.

A shiver slid down my spine, not entirely unpleasant. It was the kind of sensation that hit right before a scientific breakthrough. Or a disaster.

"Maybe it's responding to biological markers," I offered

aloud, my voice steadier than I felt. "Pheromones. Body heat. Breath."

"Or proximity," Rhys said, already reaching for a sensor node. "The way a cephalopod might react to infrared light. But this..." He trailed off, eyes narrowing. "This isn't defensive. There's no threat display. No toxin spike."

"Maybe it's curious," Kaela muttered from the stool, not looking up. "Or maybe it's just smart enough to fake it."

I grabbed a handheld scanner and ran it along the outer rim of the containment unit. My fingers trembled slightly as I moved, but the bloom responded each time I passed—colors brightening, red veins flaring just beneath the surface of the translucent membrane.

The scanner's readout flickered. I frowned.

"What?" Rhys asked, watching me.

"This structure... it's carbon-based, but it's hybridized with non-organic lattices. Look—here." I held the display toward him. "Mineral composition bonded with organic tissue. It's... not one or the other. It's both."

He leaned in. "Carbon fused with silicates, possibly trace metals. That's not just evolutionary convergence. That's structural intelligence."

"What does that mean?" Kaela asked, eyes flicking to us now.

Rhys glanced at her, then back to the coral. "It means this thing wasn't shaped by its environment. It was shaped for something. Grown, maybe. Built."

A silence settled between us. In the distance, the faint creak of the station echoed through the floor—a slow groan of metal shifting under pressure. The lights overhead buzzed faintly, but the lab felt too quiet. Like the air had grown thick, loaded with something unsaid.

I stared at the bloom again, watching the light shimmer across its surface.

"Could be a defense mechanism," I offered, though the words felt hollow as I said them. "Deep-sea organisms use bioluminescence for all kinds of things. Mating, camouflage, warning. Maybe this is just… one of those."

"This wasn't shallow," Rhys said quietly, his gaze distant. "The shelf's right on the edge of the Maw. You saw how it reacted when we pulled the sample. And how it reacted after."

A lump rose in my throat. I swallowed it down.

"Whatever's down there," I began carefully, "it's interfering with our instruments. And this…" I gestured to the bloom, its light responding again to the motion of my hand, "…it's part of the same system. The same presence."

Rhys tilted his head. He was watching me now—not just listening. Measuring. Weighing something behind his eyes.

"You felt it too," he said.

It wasn't a question.

I straightened, cautious. "Hard not to."

Another silence.

The coral pulsed again, gently—slow and deliberate. Almost like acknowledgment.

"I think it recognized us," I said softly.

Kaela stood, arms crossed now. "Are we seriously saying this thing has a mind?"

"I'm saying," Rhys replied, "that it might be part of a mind."

That silenced her.

I turned back toward him. "You've been here longer than any of us. What aren't you saying?"

His jaw shifted, eyes drifting toward the far wall where the reinforced window looked out into the dark. The ocean pressed against it, faint currents like liquid shadows moving beyond the glass.

"There were expeditions here before ours," he said, voice quiet. "Not Directorate-funded. Not officially. Independent contractors. Some science guilds. All scrubbed from the public archives."

My skin prickled. "And?"

"Most of their data's fragmented. Corrupted. A few personal logs survived. I read some of them before coming down. They all reported anomalies. Environmental fluctuations. Mechanical malfunctions. Dreams."

"Dreams?" I echoed, heart skipping.

Rhys met my eyes. "Unusual ones. Specific. Shared across multiple personnel. Like… memory fragments. Then they went dark."

"Lost?"

"Disappeared. No distress signals. No recovery. Just gone."

A pulse of vertigo hit me. The lab swayed faintly—only the natural rhythm of the sea against the station, but it felt different now. Thicker. Closer.

"And they still sent us here," I said, barely hearing myself.

"They always do," Rhys murmured. "The unknown has its price, Dr. Birch."

The coral flared. A sudden bright ripple of red and blue

rolled across its surface, skating along the glass like liquid lightning. The reflections danced across my face and vanished just as quickly.

For one impossible, sharp moment, I heard something.

Not a sound—not exactly. More like… a melody, buried in static. A faint tone, flickering just beneath the hum of the machines.

I turned, but no one else reacted. Kaela rubbed her forehead. Rhys was back at the console.

The sound faded.

Gone.

My hands were cold.

Ω

A few migraine pills later, I found Kaela in the engineering bay—half-buried in a snarl of wires, half-singing to herself, some ancient pop song warped by static and half-forgotten lyrics.

A cluster of tools floated lazily beside her in a zero-g maintenance pouch, the faint hum of support beams vibrating through the floor. She didn't look up as I entered, just kept twisting a coil of wiring back into a conduit that hissed faintly with escaping pressure.

"Should I be worried about you rewiring the life support?" I asked, leaning against the bulkhead. The migraine flared behind my left eye, sharp and insistent, like a needle pressing inward. This whole planet was a headache, and I'd only been here a little over a week.

Kaela snorted and tugged the hood of her coveralls back. A streak of grease bisected her forehead like war paint. Her curls were even more chaotic than usual.

"Nah. Just the environmental stabilizer for hydroponics. You'll only suffocate if the oxygen recycler fails. Totally unrelated systems."

"Comforting," I said flatly, stepping closer.

The engineering bay felt warmer than the lab—close, lived-in. Machines hummed all around us, a background rhythm of pressure systems and filtration units. There was a heartbeat to this space, one that steadied me in a way the open ocean never could.

Kaela's grin faded as she finally looked at me. Her eyes scanned my face, picking up on what I hadn't said. "You look like you've seen a ghost. Or a creepy ocean trench thousands of meters below sea level that's potentially home to sea monsters."

"Little of both," I said. My arms folded automatically across my chest. "That coral bloom? It's not just reacting to air or light. It responded to *me*."

Her brow creased, curiosity overtaking her usual smirk. "What, it danced for you? Grew legs?"

I hesitated, weighing how far to go. "Rhys noticed it too. It lit up when I got close. Dimmed when I stepped away. Every time I moved, it reacted—like it was watching. Or listening."

Kaela froze, her hands still gripping a bundle of wires. Her fingers twitched, just slightly.

That flicker of humor slipped from her eyes.

"I've seen weird things out here," she said, softer now. "You spend enough time on Thalassa, the ocean starts to feel like it's watching *you*."

"Not paranoia if it's true," I murmured.

That made her pause. Her eyes met mine—searching,

guarded—and something in her face shifted. She pulled a rag from her tool belt and wiped her hands, slow and deliberate.

Then she glanced toward the reinforced viewport across the room. The ocean pressed against it, deep blue and endless, a wall of liquid silence. The faint outlines of something—currents, shadows—moved on the other side of the glass.

"During one of our first dives," she said, voice dropping lower, "we lost a drone. No warning, no error. One minute it was pinging telemetry, the next... nothing. No signal. No wreckage. Just gone. Like something swallowed it."

A chill rippled down my spine.

"You report it to the Directorate?"

"Of course." She laughed—dry, humorless. "They flagged it as a 'technical anomaly.' Issued Olen a bigger gun. Problem solved."

"But the feeling stayed."

She nodded once. "Yeah. It stays. Currents moving wrong. Equipment failing when it shouldn't. Whispers. And shadows, where there *shouldn't* be shadows."

She turned back to me, "I'm not saying sea monsters, but..."

"But something's down there," I finished quietly, throat tightening.

Before she could answer, the door slid open behind us with a sharp hiss of hydraulics. I flinched. Kaela didn't—just glanced over her shoulder, expression shifting from cautious to closed-off.

Olen stepped into the room like a shadow in boots—quiet, broad, filling the doorway with the sheer weight of his presence. His eyes swept the room slowly, landing on me with surgical precision. They stayed there just a beat too long.

Not unfriendly.

Just… assessing.

"Enough ghost stories," he said. His voice was low, even, and carried the weight of unspoken rules. "Next dive's at 0600."

Kaela stiffened. Not dramatically. But I saw the way her spine straightened, jaw locked.

"Already?" I asked, trying to keep my tone neutral.

Olen turned his full attention on me, and it felt like a hand closing around my ribs.

"Directorate wants more samples before the next weather front hits," he said. "Storm's moving in. That means we go early. That means you're up to speed. And if you're not…"

His gaze sharpened, voice hardening by half a degree.

"…you don't go under. I don't drag liabilities into the water."

The silence that followed wasn't awkward—it was *intentional*. It hummed under the fluorescent lights and pressed against my ears.

I didn't say anything.

Olen looked back to Kaela. Whatever passed between them was wordless, but heavy. Not warning. Not quite a threat. More like… protocol. Reinforced.

Then, without waiting for acknowledgment, he turned and left.

His footsteps faded down the corridor with brutal finality.

Kaela exhaled slowly, flexing her fingers like she was shaking off static. Her expression hovered between frustration and something older. Wearier.

My migraine throbbed again, dull and persistent.

"Cheerful guy," I muttered, mostly just to fill the air he'd left behind.

Kaela smirked, but it didn't touch her eyes. "Welcome to Thalassa IX," she said too brightly. "Where the coral's weird, the dives are mandatory, and the silence is never just silence."

I didn't smile back.

Ω

That evening, the walls of my quarters curved in tight around me, faint condensation beading along the reinforced glass of the porthole. Outside, the ocean pressed in like a living, breathing thing—shifting shadows, trailing ribbons of light from bio-luminescent fish swirling in the dark. The little fish brought me a bit of comfort, their patterns slowly becoming familiar.

I lay on my bunk, one arm draped over my eyes, but sleep didn't come easy.

The coral bloom's glow still danced behind my eyelids, unsettling in its rhythm. Like it had a pulse. Rhys's words echoed beside it—measured, uncertain. Kaela's warning. Olen's stare. The static in the drive.

Too much. Too fast.

My heart should've settled by now—science always calmed me. Data had edges. Equations behaved. Analysis made the unknown smaller, manageable.

But tonight? It all stayed tangled, tight, heavy.

The habitat thrummed faintly through the floor— ventilation cycling, oxygen whispering through the ducts, the occasional groan as the structure adjusted to the ocean's endless push and pull. For a moment, I let the rhythm wash over me. It almost lulled me. Almost.

I should've been at the microscope. Cataloging kelp samples, logging salinity profiles, running standard analysis protocols—anything to force the coral bloom from my mind.

I could almost see it: my own hand, shaky, botching the same specimen label three times. Muscle memory without focus. But I wasn't there. I was here, on this bunk, useless and tired and unraveling by degrees. At least in the lab, things made sense. Out here, in the dark? Nothing obeyed.

As I crested on the edge of sleep, like the slow unfurling of a forgotten thread, an old memory surfaced.

Gaia-XI-A. Another water planet. Another endless stretch of dark waves.

I was twelve.

We'd been stationed there for weeks, my dad, mom, and me—him chasing down rare aquatic flora, me following in his shadow, wide-eyed and desperate to be part of it all.

The station on Gaia-XI-A hadn't even been half as secure as Thalassa IX. Just a floating series of research pods, bobbing along the currents like fragile buoys.

No land. No mountains in the distance. Just blue. Just waves.

I remember staring out the porthole at the rolling, glassy ocean, wondering what was beneath—what ancient creatures lurked in the dark, what impossible shapes drifted just out of sight.

"Scared?" my dad had asked, voice warm but teasing.

I hadn't answered at first—too proud to admit the tight knot of fear coiled low in my stomach.

He'd crouched beside me, pointing to the surface of the water beyond the glass. "Out there? It's chaos. Currents, pressure, predators—unpredictable as hell."

I'd blinked up at him, confused, not sure if this was meant to calm me down or make it worse.

"But under all that," he'd continued, ruffling my hair, "there's beauty too. Patterns we don't understand yet. Life that survives anyway."

I remember his eyes—the same color as the ocean outside, sharp and soft all at once.

"Curiosity wins, Ari," he'd whispered. "Even when you're scared. That's how we do this."

I'd believed him then. Every word. I kept thinking if I could just learn enough, nothing bad would happen. If I could understand the ocean, then I'd be safe.

Belief hadn't stopped the station from failing six days later. Power loss. Emergency evac. The roar of the ocean clawing at the walls like it wanted in.

We made it out—barely. Not every researcher did. Mom didn't. But that feeling—the press of water, the helpless drift in a lifeless sea—it never really left.

It crawled under my skin now, here, on Thalassa IX. Same cold. Same shadows. Same fragile walls keeping the abyss at bay.

My father wasn't here this time. His voice was gone, buried under the weight of scandal, silence, and space between stars.

But his words lingered.

Curiosity wins.

I curled onto my side, pulling the blanket tighter around

me, eyes drifting shut as the habitat creaked under the ocean's restless pulse.

Sleep came slow.

And somewhere in the space between dreams and memory, I swore I heard his voice again.

Faint. Familiar.

Out there, Ari…

The coral pulsed in the dark behind my eyes.

It's chaos.

Voice Mail Log
Date: January 25, 2979
From: Evelyn Mays
To: [call log corrupted]

Randy. It's me.

I don't give a *fucking fuck* how much money it takes—just make sure the Birch family doesn't open their mouths or file anything legal. Buy them off. Threaten them. I don't care how you do it.

Her mother's death was *not* Aquaeris Systems' fault. I don't care what the fucking internal report says. We bury it. We bury *all* of it. Those squid nearly cost this company *everything* and I am *not* letting some grieving brat drag us through the mud because her daddy had a martyr complex.

And Randy—if you breathe a word of this to anyone, I swear on your debt portfolio, you'll be praying for the Directorate to take you off my hands.

Call me back *after* you've handled it. Not before.

[end message]

Chapter 11: The Reef

The water grew heavier with every meter we descended. Not just in pressure—though I felt that too, clamping around my ribs inside the dive suit—but in a way that clung to thought. It settled behind my eyes like static, turning every blink into a recalibration.

Ahead, Rhys moved with practiced ease, his shoulder lights cutting through the deep in clean lines. He glanced back just once, flashing that familiar, maddening grin. His voice washed over me, a calming sound fighting against the minor panic building in my veins.

"Visibility's decent," his voice buzzed through the comms.

I adjusted my thrusters to match Rhys's pace. "Doesn't mean it's safe." What I wouldn't give to be back in the small sub above us, several inches of thick glass separating us from the ocean currents.

The sediment stirred lazily beneath us, pale clouds blooming into the dark. Below, the coral shelf came into view —a sprawling, jagged plateau carved into the ocean floor. It stretched far beyond our field lights, the edges fracturing into canyons and shadow-thick crevices.

The reef didn't look like a reef. Its structure was too deliberate—spiraling ridges, radial formation, grooves etched in mathematically precise arcs. Coral growth wasn't supposed to look like this. Not at this depth.

Rhys drifted closer to one of the outcrops, his voice low with that barely contained excitement I recognized from a dozen other impossible discoveries.

"Tell me that isn't beautiful."

It was. In a way that made my stomach tighten, made my breath catch in the spaces between my ribs. Its beauty felt godlike—painful.

The reef shimmered beneath our lights, its surface alive with micro-reflective plates. When we moved, the coral seemed to react—tiny tendrils retracting like sea anemones touched by a finger. Reflexive. Sensitive. Watching.

I frowned. "It's behaving like it's aware."

"Seen something similar in deep-ocean squid," he said, eyes fixed on the shifting glimmer outside. "Flash retract mechanisms. Defensive mimicry."

I leaned closer to the coral, watching as it pulsed faintly—light bleeding along its ridges like breath.

"You think it's afraid of us?"

He glanced at me. Not a quick look—he watched, and when he answered, his voice had dropped. "Maybe not us, exactly."

My heartbeat quickened.

The depths of his eyes threatened to pull me down. I hated that. That he still had that look, even here, kilometers beneath the surface with nothing but science and silence in between us.

I rolled my eyes, but the corner of my mouth betrayed me.

Even here—surrounded by crushing dark—he still found ways to make me blush. I'm sure it meant nothing—that it was just a way to keep me calm.

I shook my head and watched the alien light throb across the reef's spine.

"You are annoyingly charming when you're surrounded by dangerous unknowns." My breathing began regulating itself, finally.

"I find it soothes the crew," he said lightly. Then, after a pause: "Well. One member of the crew."

I turned away, pretending to inspect a section of reef. Gold-tipped polyps swayed gently in the water like tiny dancers caught mid-bow. I tried not to think about how close he'd drifted. The way his voice reached somewhere stupid in me.

"Next time, maybe try flowers instead of photophores."

His response was cut off by the first echo keening through the water.

A low-frequency thudding through the open water—far off, muffled by distance, but distinct. Not mechanical. Not geological.

Something moved in the trench below, vibrations undulating through the water. I stiffened.

"Did you feel that?"

"Displacement wave," Rhys said, but his voice had lost some of its usual ease. "Could be a leviathan migration route."

"Yeah," I replied, voice dripping with sarcasm, "All those leviathans we've seen infesting the water."

My heart ticked faster. My HUD readouts spiked momentarily—water pressure, temperature gradient, oxygen balance. All stabilizing again within seconds, but it was enough. Another pulse rolled up from the dark. Closer this time. My hands began shaking.

My pulse threatened to spiral out of control again, but then… scientific curiosity took hold. My fear compressed into focus as the reef shifted, losing its beautiful iridescent colors.

Tendrils emerged from the coral face in coordinated bursts, elongating toward the disturbance. Filaments aligned in slow spirals, red blooming-like blood into shapes that mirrored the sonar bursts the crew had been tracking for weeks. Same spacing. Same arcs. Same layered loops. A language. My eyes slid towards Rhys in disbelief.

"You've seen this before," I said quietly.

Rhys didn't answer, but that was answer enough.

I turned toward him. "You knew."

He adjusted his scanner again, buying time. Then, finally, a small nod.

"It's not native. At least… not entirely. There were fragments in the early survey data—genetic tags buried in the coral genome. Splice work. Earth-origin species but…altered."

My pulse throbbed behind my ears. "Altered how?"

"Cross-sequencing. Earth marine DNA—abyssal siphonophores, bioelectric jellyfish—fused with something alien. Something recovered. Not mapped."

"You said this mission was observational." My voice came out sharper than I meant it to—accusatory. Like I was peeling off layers I hadn't consented to.

"It was. Until these signals started repeating themselves."

"A lie of omission is still a lie."

Rhys held up his scanner display. The waveform pulsed

slowly across the screen—three nested curves, symmetrical and intentional. Not sonar reflections. Emissions of some kind.

My mouth felt dry. "The reef is sending these?"

He hesitated. "The reef is… transmitting. Responding to something deeper."

I stared at him, realization blooming like blood in the water. "You knew this wasn't just a reef. You knew it was part of something bigger."

His gaze met mine, finally serious. "That's why I asked for you."

A slow, sour burn climbed up the back of my throat.

I took a step back, the coral shifting under my boots like muscle. I hated how his words affected me—cutting through my anger with something raw and unearned.

"You're the one that brought me here? For this? Because… because of him?" I asked, my voice a quiet hum. Did he think it would respond to me?

He didn't deny it. He didn't need to. That silence broke something in me—some fragile assumption that I'd been chosen for my credentials alone. And not for my grief. That the Directorate really was giving me a second chance.

The third pulse hit like a slow drumbeat.

Something passed above us—so vast it blacked out the ambient light in an instant.

I froze. No movement. No sound. Just the water pressing in all around me like a held breath. Even panic couldn't reach me as my survival instincts finally made their way to my brain.

The water around us didn't churn—it pressed in, dense and absolute. A darkness that wasn't just absence of light but presence of intention.

The coral filaments writhed gently, no longer retracting. They were reaching now. Not frightened, hesitant tendrils, but unfurling fingers searching for their god.

From the trench below, silt erupted—slow and dense. A stirring. A presence.

I didn't look. I couldn't. Time slowed down and sped up all at once. The pressure spiked again, not from the ocean—but from my own body, instinct screaming leave.

I ignored my instincts, shoved them down and reached out, catching Rhys by the forearm. His suit was rigid, the muscles beneath it tense. He looked like he wanted to stay. Like he was seconds from stepping closer to the edge.

"We're leaving," I said, breath dragging through my teeth like shrieking wind through mountain peaks, something wild and primal fighting its way through my panic.

"But—"

"Now."

It wasn't a suggestion. I forced steel into my voice and didn't look back to see if Rhys hesitated.

We moved. Fast, careful, but not fast enough to shake the feeling crawling beneath my skin. The reef behind us pulsed again as we reached our first anchor point that would guide us up to the sub.

The lights dimmed further—but not because they were malfunctioning. Because of... its presence. I could feel it all around me, a force greater than the ocean reaching toward us with open hands.

The tether lines caught briefly on a rocky outcrop, but Rhys yanked it free, and we climbed, ascent slow but steady.

My eyes stayed fixed on the sediment clouds below. Nothing followed as we climbed into the sub, nothing stirred. Not a flicker of pursuit.

That was worse. The calm felt curated—offered. The darkness wasn't retreating. It was watching.

My gut curled tight. My brain scrambled for reasons, for logic. But something deeper already understood.

Whatever lived there... it didn't need to chase us.

It knew the way home.

Chapter 12: The Rift

The Minnow's climb back to the outpost was slow, quiet, and longer than I remembered. Even when we emerged through the sub's docking chamber and stripped off our suits, the pressure didn't lift. It clung to my skin like humidity—invisible and persistent.

Kaela was already in the lab when we arrived—her eyebrows lifted at our early return.

"That was quick," she said, tapping through a readout on the wall screen. "I take it you found something."

I glanced at Rhys, my jaw tight. "Something found us."

A quick shower, a change of clothes, and we gathered again—just the three of us—around the center table in my lab. The walls were cluttered with sealed sample trays, blinking bio-scanners, tangled wiring, and my father's old field notebooks, stacked in neat lines like offerings to a god long since buried.

Leo brought the food in without needing to be asked—heat-packed noodles, a flask of mineral broth, a rehydrated vegetable mix that tried its best to be satisfying. He set the tray down with a faint clink and lingered for a moment, eyes sweeping over our faces.

"You all look like you saw a ghost," he said softly, a hint of his New Scottish lilt curling the words.

Kaela looked up at him then, her expression flickering—bright for a moment, then dimming. She didn't speak, just reached out and gently squeezed his wrist as he passed behind her. His hand briefly covered hers, then let go.

"I'll give you space," he said, already turning. "Yell if you need patching up—or a better dinner."

"Don't push your luck," Kaela muttered, but there was affection behind it.

The lab door hissed shut behind him.

I watched Rhys across the rim of my mug. He looked younger in the lab light. Less bold. Something behind his eyes had dimmed. The silence stretched as the steam rose between us.

He exhaled. "I didn't come to Thalassa just to study the coral."

Kaela leaned forward, noodle packet half-forgotten in her hand. "You're not Company-placed?"

"I volunteered. Pulled strings." Rhys's fingers curled around his bowl, knuckles pale. "My younger brother, Joshua, was deployed here two years ago. Security detail. Not high clearance, just assigned to assist with cargo and base patrol rotations."

I stilled, the tone in his voice freezing me on the spot. The air felt thinner.

"I remember hearing about a security sweep gone wrong," Kaela said softly. "They said it was a pressure breach. Equipment failure."

Rhys gave a small, bitter smile. "The Company buried the real report under guidance from the Directorate. Sanitized the comm logs. I only got scraps—abnormal signal activity, massive biomass readings from the southern shelf. Then—radio silence."

He paused, searching our faces before continuing.

"I traced it back to a failed cell-growth trial. Deep gene editing. Something about regenerative therapy adapted from alien marine samples... splicing in terrestrial DNA to push limits. They wanted adaptive organisms—self-repairing biology for deep-environment colonization. Make people more durable."

Kaela shook her head slowly, the color draining from her cheeks. "You mean they created something?"

"They engineered something," Rhys corrected. "And it got out of control."

My hands curled slowly around my mug. It was all suddenly too real. Too close.

"My father," I said quietly. "Dr. Alan Birch. He was part of that trial."

Rhys nodded.

"He was one of the last researchers seen with Josh. The transmission logs said they were working near the southern observatory outpost when the creature first emerged from the trench. The recording cuts off before it reaches the breach point. But from what I've pieced together..."

He looked down. For a moment, he didn't speak.

"...it didn't just kill them. It took the facility. Every level. The coral we're studying now—those repeating patterns? They weren't part of the reef system before that. Something is using it. Extending through it. And the trench—"

"Isn't just a trench," I finished. Rhys nodded again. I cursed under my breath.

Kaela pushed her tray away, her mouth tense. "So, we're standing on a graveyard. A graveyard the Company and the Directorate pretends doesn't exist."

A long silence fell. The only sounds were the hum of the lab equipment and the slow clinking of utensils against cooling bowls.

Rhys leaned forward, elbows on the table. "Tomorrow," he said, "if you're willing—I'll take you there. What's left of it."

Kaela shuddered. "I'm out, but you two have fun. I've seen enough of this place's secrets already."

I looked down at my father's notebook on the table. The frayed leather, the worn corners. I remembered the way he used to tuck it under his arm like it held the whole universe inside.

I nodded once. "I want to see it." If there was even one small piece of information connecting this planet to my father, I needed to see it. Even if it hurt.

A sharp sound broke the quiet—a faint shuffle just outside the lab door. All three of us froze. Then—footsteps. Soft. Uneven.

Olen passed by the glass wall of the corridor, shoulders hunched, muttering under his breath. I caught only fragments, warped by the barrier and the tired lilt of his voice.

"…again… again… I have to reinforce it…not again…"

He didn't look in. Didn't blink or wave. Just kept walking —like something behind his eyes was still underwater.

Kaela and I exchanged a glance—more worry than

confusion now.

"That man is one pressure drop away from a full system failure," she whispered.

Outside, the ocean pressed against the outpost walls, shifting and endless. The hum of the habitat filled the silence —a low, uneasy thrum that thundered like a heartbeat.

Memories swirled inside my head—murky and uninviting. The look in Olen's eyes. The signals. My father's voice. And that thing in the water. All of it circling.

"We'll figure the rest out in the morning. You two should get some rest," I said, more firmly than I felt.

They didn't argue. When the door sealed behind them, I was alone again—with the echo of Olen's voice, and the reef, and the thing we most definitely hadn't seen.

I sat at one of the lab benches, hands moving automatically as I began packing and sorting through my meager belongings.

My fingers brushed the thin, battered drive tucked inside my father's journal—the one I'd smuggled from storage on Luna. I hesitated. Then slid it into the port.

The casing was scratched, label half-peeled, but I knew every dent. Every scar.

The log opened with a burst of static before the video resolved. My father sat in his old lab, hair unkempt, eyes shadowed—but smiling faintly, as if I'd just walked in. His hands moved restlessly across the cluttered desk, samples stacked around him.

The audio cut in and out, phrases breaking through:
"...gene splicing results... significant... can't—trust..."
"...coral patterns aren't random..."

"…Directorate wants more... too soon…"

His voice stuttered into silence, the image freezing mid-frame, his mouth half open as if about to tell me something vital.

I yanked the drive free before I could watch it glitch again. My chest felt too small for the air inside it. My eyes burned—but I didn't cry. Not yet.

I rested the journal against my chest, pressing it there like I could absorb something from the leather, from the memory, from him.

Outside the porthole, the ocean watched. It didn't move. It didn't blink.

Whatever happened, whatever my father did... I would find out.

Before it ate me alive.

CLASSIFIED RESEARCH BRIEF—REDACTED

Aquaeris Systems | Exo-Biology Division
Thalassa IX Project Archive
Research ID: AXR-2117-Δ
Date: 2976.04.21
Subject: *Preliminary Observations on Regenerative Properties in Deep-Colony Cephalopoda (Variant X-9)*
Lead Researcher: Dr. A. Birch
Clearance Level Required: OMEGA-BLACK

Abstract

Initial biopsy analysis of **[REDACTED]** cephalopod specimen ("Variant X-9") indicates tissue regeneration at rates not observed in known terrestrial phyla. Regrowth includes full reconstruction of **[REDACTED]**, neural pathways, and pigment patterning. Early models suggest these abilities may derive from **cross-domain cellular mechanisms** not present in baseline Earth genomes.

Key Findings (Partial Release)

1. Rapid Tissue Regrowth

Standardized laser incisions (0.8 cm) fully sealed within **72 seconds**, with structural restitution in under **20 minutes**. Cellular scans indicate mitotic behavior consistent with **[REDACTED]** stem cluster activation. No external growth factors required.

2. Neural Network Plasticity

Severed axons reconnected via self-directed synaptic adhesion. This process appears guided by **bioelectric microgradients** along the dermal surface. Analogous systems have been theorized for **[REDACTED]**, but never observed in vivo.

3. Bioelectric Feedback Loops

Electrophysiological mapping revealed a repeating current pattern—later designated **Signal Pattern Theta**—cycling through dermal channels. The loop appears to function as:

- a real-time damage indicator
- a repair coordination system
- a **[REDACTED: 37 seconds]**

Further testing suspended pending Ethics review.

4. Unknown Gene Silencing Arrays

Transcriptomic sampling shows heavy presence of **RNA-class fragments** not matching any cataloged organism. These fragments appear to silence immunosuppressive regulators and accelerate local tissue conversion. The fragments' origin is **unknown**. Their sequence bears partial alignment to samples recovered from **[REDACTED] Trench Event**.

Ethical Notice

Variant X-9 did not exhibit recognizable distress behaviors when subjected to controlled tissue assays. However, neural activity spikes during regenerative cycles suggest **higher-order sensory integration**.

Clearance advised before any further live trials.

Addendum: Request for Authorization

Dr. Birch has submitted a formal request to initiate **cross-species integration trials** using isolated ECM from Variant X-9.

Status: **PENDING REVIEW**
Reviewed by: **Directorate Liaison Mays**

Recommendation: **[REDACTED]**

Chapter 13: Night Terrors

A piercing, unearthly shriek ripped me from sleep—too sharp, too clean to be human. It sliced through the corridor like a blade drawn underwater, vibrating through the walls, through my ribs, through the fragile membrane of sleep.

I was on my feet before I could think. No suit. Just the weight of nightmares clinging to me and the chill of the station floor under my feet. My heart hadn't figured out what was real yet, but it beat hard enough to split bone. I ran.

The scream had come from Leo's room.

His door was ajar. No lights. Just that hollow blue emergency glow strip that made everything look half-drowned. I shoved the door fully open and froze at the threshold, breath held.

"Leo?" My voice cracked—thin, cautious, useless.

He was curled in the corner of his bunk, knees drawn to his chest, back shoved hard against the wall like he was trying to crawl into it. Sweat slicked his skin despite the outpost's frigid air. His eyes were wide and unfocused, pupils huge, like a kid lost in a hurricane. His mouth worked like he couldn't get enough air.

"Leo—it's me. It's Arizona." I crouched low, hands raised slowly like I was approaching a wild animal, my voice low and steady even though I felt anything but. "You're okay. It's over."

He shook his head violently, lips trembling. "No, no—I saw it," he whispered, barely audible. "In the hallway. It was standing right there. Looking at me."

"What was?" My stomach twisted. Some part of me wanted to believe this was a night terror, that he was just talking in his sleep.

"I don't know—I couldn't see it. It wasn't human. It was tall. It moved like… smoke, or static, or—" He choked on the words, palms grinding against his eyes like he could scrub it out of his memory. "It was coming for me. I swear it was going to eat me."

Footsteps thundered from behind—bare feet, boots, metal on metal.

Kaela barreled in first, wrench in one hand, her hair a cyclone of blonde static. Olen followed, stun baton drawn, jaw locked. Rhys brought up the rear, slower but sharper— already scanning the room like the threat might still be present.

"What the hell's going on? I was in the engineering bay" Kaela demanded, breath catching. Her eyes flicked from Leo to me and back again, fingers tightening on the wrench like it was an extension of her arm.

"Leo saw something," I said, my voice strangely thin in the still air. "A shadow. In the corridor."

Olen's expression darkened. His knuckles whitened around the baton, his posture all coiled readiness. "I'll sweep the hall," he muttered, and he was gone before I could stop him, boots thudding into the distance. There was no hesitation in the way he moved. But there was something in his shoulders. Not fear—something older. Recognition.

Kaela dropped to her knees beside Leo, wrench forgotten, her voice dipping into something maternal. "You're okay now, yeah? Breathe, sweetheart. You're safe. It's gone."

Leo shivered. "I wasn't dreaming," he mumbled, clinging to her sleeve. "It was real. Something's in here with us."

Rhys crossed to me, quiet and steady. "Security cams?"

"I didn't check," I admitted.

He tapped his wrist module, pulling the hall feed onto his display. We leaned over it together. One minute of footage, the exact minute Leo screamed—static. Pure, crawling static. The timestamp blurred, stuttering. No audio.

"Convenient," came Olen's voice from the doorway, newly returned, dry as sandpaper. "Hall's clear. Nothing on thermal, motion, or sound." He holstered the baton, but his eyes didn't relax. They flicked once toward Leo, then back to me.

"Did you see it?" I asked quietly.

He paused just a beat too long. "No."

Rhys didn't say anything. Neither did Kaela. But the silence grew teeth.

We stayed like that for a moment. The quiet pressed against the walls like the ocean itself was listening. I could feel the thrum of the outpost in my bones—air circulation, pumps, power transfer relays—suddenly louder than usual. A heartbeat not quite my own.

Leo trembled, jaw clenched like he was trying not to cry in

front of everyone. "Please don't make me stay in here alone."

Kaela looked to me. "I'll prep a cot in the engineering bay for him. I need to finish these repairs."

Leo looked up at me then, eyes watery but sharp. "You believe me, don't you?"

I hesitated. Not because I didn't—but because I did. And I didn't want to. "Yeah," I said softly. "I believe you."

I helped Kaela get Leo to his feet. He was limp with exhaustion, but his legs still worked. His skin felt too warm under my hands. He kept looking over his shoulder, like something was going to reach through the bulkheads and drag him back.

Kaela walked away with Leo while Rhys and I lingered behind.

"You saw Olen's face," I murmured to him once we were alone. "That wasn't surprise. That was déjà vu."

"I know," he said. "I saw it too."

When the others were gone, I lingered in Leo's doorway a beat longer. The room felt... altered. Not just disturbed—violated. Like something had slipped in through the cracks in the station. Something unwelcome. Something that now knew exactly where we slept.

And I couldn't shake the feeling that whatever had come for Leo... hadn't really left.

Ω

The corridor felt longer on the walk back to my room. Every overhead light seemed to hum too loud, and I kept expecting something to flicker at the edge of my vision—just a shadow, just a shape. But nothing did. Just the same dim glow, the same stale air recycled through too many filters. Familiar, but off in a way I couldn't name.

The chill sank deeper into my skin with every step, raising goosebumps across my arms. I was half-dressed—tank top, boy shorts, bare feet—and moving fast. Not because I was cold, but because some part of me still expected whatever had terrified Leo to be around the next corner.

I stopped short.

Rhys stood in the doorway to my quarters, his back to the wall, hair still damp from the shower, collar askew like he'd thrown his clothes on in a hurry. There was a tension in his posture—not aggressive, just tired. Alert. Like he wasn't ready to sleep yet either.

"You okay?" he asked, voice low and edged with concern.

I huffed out a breath. "As okay as anyone can be in a tin can under the sea with a monster crawling around outside." I jerked my head toward the inside of my room. "Come in, unless you want the hallway ghost to find you."

He stepped in, slow, casual, but not without caution. His gaze swept the space—my cluttered notebooks stacked beside the bed, the half-drunk mug of synth-coffee, the datapad blinking with unread logs. It felt too personal all of a sudden, and I scrambled for something to cover myself.

I grabbed my lab coat from the back of the chair and shrugged it on. It smelled faintly of iodine and worn fabric. Still, it made me feel less exposed.

Rhys sat on the edge of the bed. Not close. He rubbed a spot above his knee like it hurt. "Did Leo ever mention having night terrors before?"

"Not like this," I said. "He joked about pressure hallucinations sometimes. Said he dreamed weird when storms rolled through. But this? No. Nothing that real. Nothing that scared him like that."

He didn't respond right away. Just stared down at the floor, fingers still moving, lost in some memory he didn't offer. The habitat groaned faintly around us. I crossed my arms and leaned against the wall beside him, just watching.

"You think he really saw something?" I asked.

Rhys finally looked up, eyes tired but steady. "I think Leo believes he did. And I think things here have been unstable long enough that I'm done writing stuff off."

I searched his expression, looking for something hidden, something strategic—but all I saw was the quiet wreckage of a man unraveling, one unexplained anomaly at a time.

He turned to glance at the shelf above my bed—knick-knacks from Earth, a few pinned photos, some pressed leaves laminated in plastic. He reached toward them, then stopped short. "These yours? Or your dad's?"

I hesitated. "Mostly his. I brought them from Luna. Figured they'd make this place feel less like a coffin."

"You two were close?" he asked.

I nodded once. "As close as two people in different systems can be."

There was another pause. One that felt like it should've ended there, but didn't.

"I used to think the ocean was sacred," Rhys said, voice softer now. "All that pressure, that distance… it made it feel untouchable. Pure. But cathedrals aren't empty, are they? They echo with whatever people left inside."

I blinked. It was too close to my own thoughts—eerily so.

"I still love it," I said after a moment. "The ocean. Even

when it scares me."

Rhys looked up again. "Why?"

"It's honest," I said. "It doesn't pretend to be safe. It doesn't try to lie to you. It just is. Vast. Silent. Indifferent. It makes everything else feel small."

A quiet laugh escaped him, tinged with something like admiration. "You're the only person I know who finds existential dread comforting."

"You're the only person I know who uses 'existential dread' in casual conversation."

We smiled—tight, tired things that didn't quite reach our eyes.

I moved to sit beside him on the edge of the bed. Not close. There was still a gap between us. And that gap was deliberate. I wasn't sure what I wanted from him. I wasn't even sure why I'd let him in.

He leaned forward, elbows on his knees, hands laced. "Do you think whatever's happening here is intentional?"

I looked at him. "What do you mean?"

"I mean… the reef. The trench. The power losses. Leo's dream. What if it's not random? What if it's leading somewhere?"

The thought coiled cold around my spine. "Then I hope we get ahead of it before it finishes whatever it started."

For a moment, we just sat in silence. The room felt still— not peaceful, just paused. Like the base itself was listening.

Then Rhys turned slightly toward me. "You should sleep."

I nodded. "I know."

But I didn't move. Neither did he.

He reached out—slowly—and brushed a stray strand of hair from my cheek. Not possessive. Not overly familiar. Just… tentative.

I froze.

Not from discomfort, but uncertainty. Was this kindness? Was it something else?

He pulled his hand back just as gently, as if recognizing the question in me. "I'm sorry," he said. "That wasn't— I just didn't want you to feel alone tonight."

I swallowed. "I don't."

That was true, at least in that moment. His presence made the room feel a little more anchored. A little less haunted.

He stood, gave a small nod, and moved toward the door.

"Rhys?"

He paused, hand hovering near the controls.

"Thanks," I said.

His smile was sad but sincere. "Anytime."

Then he was gone.

And I was alone with the hum of the outpost, and the quiet ache of something almost real.

Ω

Water.

I was back in the lab, but it was empty. Silent. No blinking lights, no screens, no voices on the comm. A perfect, sterile environment.

Just water. Seeping in through the vents. Trickling at first. Then pouring.

I tried the door—locked. My fists slammed against the glass. No sound came out.

The water rose fast. Around my ankles. My knees. My ribs. It was cold, so cold it burned.

"Please, let me out!" I screamed banging on the door, my fingers clawing into the metal. I looked up—and saw coral.

It bloomed from the ceiling corners, winding down like veins, threading through the vents and screens. Tendrils unfurled like fingers. Red, like blood drifting through open water. The water rose higher and higher, caressing my neck, my chin, and my nose.

It knew me. It wanted me. It could have me as easily as a shark swallowing a minnow.

I screamed. Bubbles rushed out, choking me. The door stayed shut.

Then—eyes.

Just beyond the glass, something waited. Its shape blurred by the water, by the darkness, by distance, but the gaze—sharp. Focused. Listening.

It tilted its head slowly, like it already knew the sound my lungs would make when they burst.

I pressed my palms to the window, mouth open, lungs burning. The last thing I saw wasn't it's face. It was the way the coral pulsed behind it—like a heart answering a call.

AQUAERIS SYSTEMS — PERSONNEL WELFARE DIVISION

From: L. Godfrey, Head of Human Resources
To: All Thalassa IX Leadership Personnel
Subject: Reminder: Morale Maintenance & Unproductive Speculation
Date: July 19, 2970

Hello, Team Leads!

It has come to my attention that some of our valued employees have been engaging in *unhelpful conversations* regarding the status of previous research rotations assigned to Thalassa IX. Specifically, certain individuals have repeated the misguided notion that "everyone stationed there dies," or that entire crews have "vanished into the Maw."

As a friendly reminder: **Aquaeris Systems maintains no official record of any unexplained casualties** at the Thalassa IX research habitat. Any suggestion to the contrary is a **misinterpretation** of routine operational incidents and standard attrition rates for high-risk scientific environments.

Please remember that **spreading unverified claims is a violation of Section 14-B of the Employee Conduct Agreement**, under *Behavior That Negatively Impacts Workplace Harmony*. As such, you are responsible for ensuring your team refrains from disruptive storytelling, dramatizing natural ocean phenomena, or drawing connections between past personnel losses and current assignments.

Leadership is encouraged to gently redirect anxious staff toward productive tasks, or—if redirection fails—to log an Internal Stability Ticket so our Mental Resilience Consultants can intervene. Early reporting prevents unfortunate outcomes.

Let's continue fostering a positive, cooperative atmosphere in our lovely oceanfront facility. Remember: **A stable mind is a safe mind.**

Warm regards,
L. Godfrey
Head of Human Resources
Aquaeris Systems

Chapter 14: Olen's Warning

The promise of Leo's so-called "breakfast extravaganza" was the only thing that managed to pry me out of bed.

Sleep had avoided me like a predator skirting the edges of a herd—circling, waiting, never striking. I felt wrung out. Stretched thin. The dark bruises under my eyes confirmed what I already knew: I'd barely slept. My limbs felt waterlogged, like I'd dragged them up from the trench myself.

As I padded barefoot into the corridor, the chill of the floor bit into my heels. The humming pipes in the walls sounded louder than usual—like the habitat was murmuring to itself. Halfway to the cafeteria, I heard them: voices, low and tense.

"You're pushing too far. You're going to get yourself hurt. Or worse." Olen. Gruff, steady. But something was different—his words were softer, weighted with something that sounded a lot like fear. Or... worry.

I stopped just before the threshold, heartbeat ticking up. I pressed myself to the wall, peeking around the corner.

Rhys stood inches from Olen—too close for comfort. That kind of distance only existed between people with unfinished business. The air between them looked charged, magnetic.

Rhys leaned in just slightly, chin tilted—half a threat, half defiance.

"What I do is none of your business," he said, voice low and hot.

Olen didn't flinch. "All I'm asking…" he hesitated, voice dropping, "…is for you to be careful. I care about you."

A beat.

"Like I cared about your brother."

Rhys's posture shifted—barely—but I saw it. His jaw twitched. He exhaled sharply through his nose.

"I know."

The words landed like a bruise.

I blinked, suddenly aware I was holding my breath. Olen? Caring? About Rhys? That was the most vulnerable thing I'd ever heard from him that wasn't laced with sarcasm or a veiled threat. My pulse stuttered.

Rhys moved first. Not hostile—but forceful. He shoulder-checked Olen gently as he passed, brushing past him toward the food counter, where the smell of butter, synthetic bacon, and some faintly burning starch greeted me like a brick to the face.

My stomach growled so loudly I winced.

I stepped fully into the room. Olen's eyes met mine for just a second—searching, unreadable. He looked like he was about to say something, but didn't. Instead, he reached out and gently circled my wrist.

"Can we talk later?" His voice was quiet. Careful.

I froze. That was twice in one week Olen had used a tone I might describe as… human.

I nodded slowly. "Yeah. Sure."

He didn't say anything else. Just turned and walked out, boots heavy on the tile. The door hissed shut behind him.

I drifted toward the food line, where Leo was already plating what appeared to be some kind of space-age diner special. The scent of spice packets and recycled protein filled the air.

"You're up," I said, a little too brightly.

Leo looked… normal. A faint bruise of shadows under his eyes, maybe, but otherwise healthy. Whole.

"Why wouldn't I be?" he asked with a chuckle. The sound didn't quite reach his eyes.

"Well… after last night."

His spatula stilled. "What about it?"

"The nightmares. The hall. Are you okay? I just—"

"Drop it, Arizona."

The words cracked like a whip. His brogue thickened, curling around the edges of his voice.

"I had a nightmare. That's all. It's done." He gestured sharply to the spread on the stove. "I'm making breakfast for the team as an apology. So please—let it go."

He sucked in a breath and turned back to the pan.

For a moment the kitchen filled with the quiet hiss of batter hitting hot iron.

Then Leo turned back to me.

The anger was gone. Wiped clean.

His grin flashed, bright and easy, like it had never existed at all.

Goosebumps prickled along my arms.

"I know that look," he said, handing me a tray. "And yes

—those are pancakes." His smile widened. "Sort of."

"What's the 'sort of' part?" I asked, peering down at the weirdly geometric stack on my tray, confused by his sudden shift in demeanor.

"They're made from powdered algae protein, caramel extract, and two ration bars I smashed with a wrench," he said proudly.

"I'm both impressed and horrified."

"That's the correct response."

Kaela was already at the long cafeteria table, wolfing down her food like she hadn't eaten in days. A streak of oil was still visible on her cheek. Rhys sat beside her, quieter, nursing a cup of something vaguely tea-like.

I joined them, sliding into the space across from Rhys. The cold metal bit into my legs.

Rhys didn't look at me at first, just pushed a second plate toward me across the table. His fingers brushed mine in passing. Intentional? Hard to say.

"Sleep well?" he asked casually.

I paused. I could lie. I could deflect. But I didn't have the energy.

"Not really."

He gave a tired little smile. "Let me guess. Coral growing out of your ears? A shadow in the corner of your bunk? Or the whole hab turning inside out like a peeled fruit?"

I snorted into my fork. "Option three, mostly."

Across from us, Kaela took a long sip of her ration juice. "Don't worry. Everyone dreams weird down here. First week I had recurring visions of my mother turning into a cuttlefish and swimming away from me. That's when I started wearing a sleep monitor."

"Very normal," Leo added helpfully.

The four of us lapsed into silence for a moment, the kind that wasn't awkward. Just full. Lived-in.

Then, Kaela nudged her tray toward me. "So… Birch. Is it true your dad was *the* Dr. Alan Birch? The exo-biology guy? The one who…" she trailed off awkwardly.

"The one who disappeared under mysterious circumstances?" I offered flatly. "Yeah. That one."

Kaela raised her hands in mock surrender. "Didn't mean to pry."

Leo glanced up. "For what it's worth, I never believed those rumors about him being some kind of mad lab recluse. People love ghost stories. Especially when the Company won't release the real files."

"Thanks," I murmured, unsure how to respond to that. Part of me appreciated it. Part of me hated that even Leo— who hadn't known him—had heard the stories.

"I don't think he was crazy," Kaela added. "I think he found something. That's usually enough to make someone disappear around here."

The tray in front of me was nearly empty now. I hadn't even realized I was eating.

I stood slowly. "I need to check something first. I'll meet you at the airlock."

Kaela nodded, eyes narrowing just slightly in that way she had when she was masking concern behind sarcasm. "Just don't get eaten before I finish my juice."

"No promises."

I glanced once more at Rhys before turning away. His

eyes lingered on mine—too long. He didn't smile this time.

And neither did I.

Ω

Olen sat on the edge of my bed, elbows on his knees, hands dangling loose—but not relaxed. His eyes weren't on me, or the floor, or the walls. They were somewhere else entirely—far away, years back, caught in a current I couldn't see.

I leaned against the door frame, hip pressed into cold metal. The outpost hummed around us—steady, low, like a heartbeat buried in steel. I waited. Counted the seconds. Let them stretch.

When it became clear he wasn't going to start, I sighed. "What is it you wanted to talk about?"

His gaze shifted—sharpened. Not at me. Through me. "I know you think I'm just some asshole."

"Honestly? No. You seem... antisocial," I offered.

His mouth twitched. Not quite a smile. Closer to exhaustion. "Fair enough. But everything I've done down here? Every call I've made—it's been about one thing: keeping people alive. Not my pride. Not my reputation. Just survival."

I crossed my arms. "So how does that tie into what we're doing now?"

He studied me—like a crack in a pressure valve he wasn't sure could be sealed. Then his voice lowered.

"You look a lot like your father."

That stopped me. Cold. Of all the things I expected, that wasn't on the list.

I tilted my head. "I wasn't aware you knew him."

Olen gave the smallest, rueful nod. "Especially when you

get that look. The one he wore when he was close to solving something. Like the whole world was an equation, and he just needed one more variable to figure it out."

It hit harder than I wanted it to. I saw my father then—bent over his notes, muttering, frowning, chasing some unspoken logic no one else could see.

"What does this have to do with—"

"I came to Thalassa IX to die."

Blunt. My stomach dropped—not because he said it, but because I believed him. Olen didn't check my face for a reaction. He just kept going. Low. Controlled. Stripped clean of anything sentimental.

"My wife and daughter. Gone. Accident. Earth turned into a graveyard for me after that. I couldn't breathe without seeing them. So I took the first long-distance contract I could get."

He rubbed the back of his neck, voice thinning like static. "Ended up here. Thought the silence might drown it out."

That seemed to be the story for a lot of us—running from something. Grief. Guilt. The parts of ourselves we couldn't carry anymore.

"For a while, it worked," he went on. "Until it didn't."

I didn't move. Afraid if I did, he'd stop.

"Then Joshua Calum showed up—Rhys's brother. Fresh transfer. Too green for deepwater, but he... had light in him. He made the place feel less like a coffin." A pause. "Your father helped, too."

Olen's mouth twitched again—closer to something almost fond. "Your father could make you believe in impossible things. Both of them could. I didn't want to live. And they made me want to try."

The silence after that wasn't awkward. Just full of weight.

I swallowed. "What happened to them?"

His jaw flexed. "You already know."

I did. The trench. The reef. The thing in the dark. I hadn't connected it until now, but once I saw the threads, I couldn't unsee them.

He looked at me fully then—no armor left. Just that hollow, hard-earned resolve.

"Arizona. Whatever's down here—it's not something you can solve. It's not a problem. It's something you survive, if you're lucky."

I held his gaze. My chest felt tight.

"I'm not leaving."

"You should." His voice cracked, just slightly. He leaned forward again, hands clasped like a man at prayer. "Take a teaching post. Earth-like colony. Somewhere safe. Don't die down here chasing ghosts."

The room felt smaller. The air heavy with seawater and regret. I thought about my father. The reef. The thing that watched us from the deep.

"I can't," I said.

He didn't argue. Just nodded—slow, resigned. Like he'd expected it. Like it hurt anyway.

"Stars help you."

He stood and left without another word. His footsteps echoed down the hall, fading into the hum.

I stayed where I was, staring at the space he left behind. The weight of it didn't lift.

By the time I reached the airlock, Rhys was already there —leaning against the Minnow's hatch, helmet tucked under one arm. His expression was unreadable in that maddening way of his. But his eyes...

They searched me. Like they could tell something had shifted.

"You good?" he asked.

No. Not even close.

"Yeah," I lied, stepping past him into the sub. "Let's go."

Behind us, the hum of the outpost faded.

Ahead, only the dark.

Only the deep.

From: Dr. Arizona Birch <ari.birch@aquaeris.com>
To: Director Evelyn Mays <EveleynMays@aquaeris.com>
Subject: Progress Update–Reef Bloom

Director Mays,

Per standard protocol, I'm submitting my weekly research update regarding the Theta-6 reef samples.

Collection proceeded as scheduled, though our team was forced to cut the dive shorter than anticipated due to an anomaly in sonar readouts—likely a fault in the Minnow's external sensors, which briefly spiked and distorted. This triggered proximity alerts and minor comms interference. No injuries occurred. The team is unharmed.

Environmental conditions remain relatively stable, though currents along the Maw's edge have grown less predictable. I would advise limiting further dives along that shelf until the sonar array is recalibrated—assuming our instruments are indeed the issue. The biological samples collected remain viable, though ongoing analysis has been slower than expected due to some irregularities in their reactivity patterns. I'll forward relevant telemetry and raw data once it's been scrubbed and verified.

Of note: the bloom continues to display non-random pulse responses to stimuli. Whether this is biochemical or behavioral remains under investigation. Our scans suggest the presence of highly ordered structural arrangements within the polyps —possibly mineral-dense signal channels. This supports earlier hypotheses regarding adaptive sensory behavior, though I hesitate to draw conclusions prematurely.

Progress is incremental. Caution remains my priority.

I'll include additional footage and analysis once I've had time

to cross-reference the reef pulse events with the anomalous
sonar logs. If there are any known classification guidelines
from Aquaeris Systems regarding abyssal-life interaction
protocols (particularly for hybrid-origin organisms), I'd
appreciate access.

Until then, I recommend discretion in interpreting early
results. Our understanding of this environment remains
incomplete.

Sincerely,

Dr. Arizona Birch
Field Lead, Xenobiological Research Division
Thalassa IX Outpost – Site Theta-6

Chapter 15: Ghost Station

Forty-five minutes later, Rhys and I were sinking toward ghosts.

The *Minnow* creaked as the water thickened around us, pressure curling tighter with every meter of descent. The lights stayed low—a dim glow slicing into black water—just in case *it* was near. We didn't speak much. In a sub this small, even breathing felt too loud.

The wreck appeared out of the dark like a memory surfacing too fast: broken, bent and half remembered. The abandoned research station. Or what was left of it.

Where the Hab above was blunt and practical—steel corridors, ugly but safe—this had been built for wonder. Transparent domes. Curving supports. Wide garden wings to remind people of sunlight they'd never see again... Ambition instead of caution. A place meant to feel alive.

Now it was a tomb.

The main research bay loomed ahead — a shattered glass dome caved in on itself, bent ribs of framework clawing upward like the bones of some great carcass. Green growth clung to the edges of ruptured glass. Fish darted in and out of hollow corridors that once held laughter, research logs, life.

Rhys pulled out a tablet. A photo bloomed across the screen: the same station, intact. Whole.

"I can't believe..." My throat closed. "...all that. Just gone."

In the photo, there were five domes, not one. Figures moved inside—people, plants, instruments. Blurry but alive. The image itself was imperfect, grainy—an old sub photo, unfocused and human. The kind my dad used to take.

I looked from the photo to the ruin before me. A dream stripped bare.

"How many people worked here?" My voice came out small. "Lived here?" *Died here?*

Rhys scrolled, fingers steady—deliberate in a way that made me hyper-aware of my own shaking hands. "Twenty-three, but there were plans for up to a hundred," he said finally. "One of them was... pregnant."

I exhaled a low whistle. "That's... awful."

"It's irresponsible," Rhys muttered, jaw tightening. "Top experts crammed into a deathtrap on a rushed timeline. The hab may be ugly, but it's built to last. This? This was a pretty lie." He gestured to the wreck beyond the glass. "And it cost them everything."

His words blurred as the panic started to rise. My chest constricted, shallow breaths scraping against my throat. Is this how my father felt?

Thin walls. Just glass and metal between me and kilometers of crushing black.

The memory hit like an undertow—Gaia-XI-A. The breach. The screaming. My mother's voice crackling over the coms... The weight of the ocean pressed closer. I couldn't breathe. Tears welled, hot and sudden. My pulse roared in my ears.

"Arizona." Rhys's cut through it like a tether thrown across dark water. He turned, words stalling when he saw my face.

He didn't ask permission.

Warm hands cupped my face, firm but careful—like I was something breakable. His thumbs swept away saltwater, and for a terrifying second I wasn't sure if it was my tears or the sea leaking in.

"Breathe," Rhys murmured. "In… now out."

In. Out. The world narrowed to his voice, the even rise and fall, a metronome in the chaos.

"Again. In… good. Out."

Minutes—or seconds — passed. My vision steadied. The panic loosened its grip, retreating like the tide.

"The water," I whispered finally, voice cracking. "It reminds me of what I've survived. And of what I've lost."

Rhys nodded once, simple. No pity. Just understanding.

"You okay now?" His fingers rested at my wrist, feeling for my pulse—grounding me.

I swallowed, nodded. "Yeah. I think so."

He lingered half a beat longer before letting go. The absence of his touch hit like cold water.

"Alright," he said, voice shifting back to practical calm. "We circle the dome. Look for weak points. Call out anything unusual."

The familiar cadence — checklist, mission-focus — steadied me. I forced a shaky grin.

"Sir, yes sir," I muttered, giving a lazy salute as I turned back toward the window.

The wreck loomed ahead, ghostly and beautiful.

For the first time since we'd started descending, I wasn't afraid to look.

Ω

Rhys piloted the Minnow in slow, deliberate circles as the last traces of light from above vanished. No good landing spots in sight, but I wasn't about to complain—not when the alternative was getting in that water. The corals and fungi blooming in impossible sizes and neon colors were stunning, yes, but the stillness of the water was wrong. Unnatural. Especially on a planet practically bursting with life.

"Aha," Rhys said, flashing me a grin. "Perfect spot."

The sub jolted. I braced against the curved wall, nearly landing on my ass.

I shot him a look, but the boyish pride on his face melted any sarcasm off my tongue.

He guided the Minnow beneath a rock shelf and powered down the engines, switching to passive recharge on the electrochemical cells.

"Rhys?" I said softly.

"Arizona," he replied flatly—like he already knew what I was going to say.

"I really don't want to get in that water."

He surprised me with a sigh. "Neither do I."

"You don't?" I blinked at him, suddenly not the incredibly intelligent woman I liked to think I was.

"No," he said, "but you know what I do when I don't want to do something? I think of someone I admire. Tell me someone you love. First name that comes to mind."

"Sylvia Earle."

His brow furrowed. "Who's that?"

He works in this field and doesn't know her? Blasphemy.

"She was the first woman to dive untethered to 381 meters," I said. "She's the reason we can even build architectural beasts like this sub. Her great-great-granddaughter designed our current dive suits. Barely any improvements since then. She was that good."

He smiled, like this was the most natural conversation in the world.

"For me, it's my brother," he said. "Cheesy, I know. But he was all I had left. Our parents were on Earth when… well, when it exploded. My brother and I were on the Star Arks. We woke up to the news they were gone."

"Damn." It was all I could manage. Some losses don't have words. I wasn't born on Earth, but the loss was immeasurable.

"Yeah," he said quietly. "But I've already survived the worst thing that could ever happen to me. So why not this? And if I die… well, dying for the same cause my brother did seems like a good way to go."

Through the glass behind him, light began to shimmer. One glow, then another. Then dozens.

"If you died, you'd miss things like this," I whispered, pointing past him.

Rhys turned—and froze.

They drifted through the abyss like living cathedrals, mantles pulsing rose, jade, cobalt—casting auroras across the darkness. Coral crowned their heads like forgotten gods, barnacles gleaming faintly as they rode the currents. The growth wasn't parasitic but harmonious, as though these squid carried gardens of the deep on their backs.

How did they exist when every other large creature on the planet had disappeared? The depth maybe?

Rhys whistled low. "Squid?" he asked, not looking away.

"Looks like it," I murmured. "But I'd need to run tests to confirm if they meet our definition of 'squid.'" It was incredible though, finally finding some semblance of life. I wondered what prevented the unknown creature from eating these maybe-squid?

He finally tore his gaze from the window and grinned. "It's so hot when you talk nerdy."

I smiled but it didn't reach my eyes. "That's rich coming from the guy casually making martyrdom sound romantic."

His smirk faltered a fraction.

"I'm serious," I said, voice softer. "You're allowed to be scared, Rhys. Even Silvia Earle would be terrified down here."

That earned a real laugh from him—quiet, cracked around the edges.

"I suppose you are the thalassophobic one," he said, brushing it off. "You ready?"

We both stared at the glass dome below—our exit hatch. The tiny airlock that would eject us into the alien ocean. Despite all my dives before, the thought still sent ice down my spine.

"Hey, Arizona," he said once we sealed ourselves inside the pod. "We're doing this together. You're not alone."

He gripped my gloved hand. Awkward. Warm. Real.

Then he flipped his visor down and nodded.

I nodded back, drew a deep breath, and sealed my own helmet.

"Sound check," Rhys said over the comm, his voice slightly warped by the static. "All clear?"

"All good. You?"

"Sounds great."

His voice curled with amusement.

He patched us through to Kaela on the Hab.

"Minnow to Meg," he said. "Do you read?"

Kaela's sigh came loud and clear. "This is the Meg. I read you. And guys?" A pause. "Be careful."

"She likes shark movies," he whispered to me.

My throat tightened. Two people in this galaxy cared if I came back.

"We will," I promised and killed the mic.

Then I drew in one last breath and opened the latch to hell.

Ω

Rhys tethered us together as we sank toward the broken remains of the research station—the shattered bones of the scientists the Company had left behind. Without an anchor point, only the line between us remained, and the fragile trust it represented. Down here, we had only each other.

Life swarmed where death had claimed the ruins. Schools of neon, tetra-bright fish slipped in and out of jagged glass. Crabs scuttled across the once-graceful dome, now caved in and barnacled with time.

My vision blurred—the pressurized helmet and fogged glass bending the water into illusions. Boots touched down on a tilted platform just as the tether jolted at my waist. My pulse spiked. Slowly, carefully, I turned—only to meet Rhys's steady gaze as he checked over my suit and airline. After a moment's inspection, he gave a curt nod, then pointed.

A flicker of light pulsed from a rockfall north of the wreckage. Half-buried beneath the rubble, a detached circular structure glowed faint yellow: an emergency life-support module. If answers remained, they waited there, painted in industrial color.

The ocean groaned. A deep, keening sound rolled through the water—not close enough to rupture our eardrums, but familiar. The creature was out there, circling. Listening.

Rhys pushed forward, and I scrambled after him. We reached the rounded door of the module, where a small keypad blinked, strangely intact against the ruin.

"Arizona?" Rhys's voice crackled in my headset. "Do you understand what this means?"

I leaned closer. Above the keypad, a screen glowed with a single prompt: *Enter password.* A faint tremor ran through me as I tapped the "hint" icon.

What is the thing with feathers?

My stomach turned to ice. Another groan rippled through the water above us, scattering the fish into hiding.

"Hope," I whispered, more to myself than to Rhys. "The thing with feathers is hope." My gloved hands moved fast, entering the word before fear could paralyze me. This is what I came here for.

With a hiss, the door slid open. The airlock chamber loomed like a miracle. Rhys and I stumbled inside clinging to each other as the door sealed, and the water drained away.

Thanks, Dad.

The silence of the room pressed in, fragile and human and safe. For now.

[INTERSYSTEM MESSAGE – ENCRYPTED COMM CHANNEL 9C]
TO: Dr. Arizona Birch <ari.birch@aquaeris.com>
FROM: Dr. Alan Birch <a.birch@aquaeris.com>
SUBJECT: Re: Boring Research Stuff

Hey, Cal-Zona,

Apologies for the delay—signal lag out here's a beast. Just got your last ping. No need to worry, sweetheart. I'm in one piece, and the worst thing I've encountered this week is a photosynthetic lichen with delusions of grandeur.

The work is... fine. Mostly cataloging, a little genetic sequencing, some cross-contamination modeling. Nothing worth missing dinner over.

This planet's colder than it looks in the briefs. Beautiful, though. Quiet. The kind of quiet that gets into your bones. You'd hate it. Or love it. Hard to tell with you sometimes.

Contract's still got another year on it, but I'm making progress. Once the core data's logged, I'll be home before you know it.

Promise.

Stay out of trouble. And stop worrying about your old man. I'm not that fragile yet.

Love you always,
—Dad

Chapter 16: Discovery

The airlock sealed with a heavy hiss—final, merciful—and for the first time since leaving the drowned station, breath came easier. No more ocean roar clawing at my ears.

Water sluiced away in stubborn rivulets, clinging to us like reluctant ghosts, until the chamber floor gleamed beneath the harsh white lights. Rhys and I stood dripping, shivering, our suits plastered to our skin in sheets of cold that felt almost alive. For a brief stolen moment, I sagged against the wall. The tether bit into my waist—a reminder that survival demands something back.

We were alive, and that was pretty much all.

The chamber was small, unnervingly pristine, a pocket of untouched time preserved in steel. It felt less like refuge and more like a tomb—air stale but breathable, lights flickering with the steady hum of life support systems that should not, by any logic, still function. Even the walls seemed to listen. Somewhere in the depths of the structure, a hidden engine whispered on, defying neglect. The Company's carelessness had evolved into something that endured.

Rhys unsealed his helmet with a practiced twist. His hair

tumbled free in damp strands plastered to his forehead, breath fogging faintly in the chill. His eyes prowled across the module like searchlights—cataloguing, dissecting, always analyzing threats I hadn't considered.

"This place shouldn't even be functional," he muttered, voice tight. "Emergency modules aren't built to last longer than a few years."

Years.

The word hollowed out my chest every time I let myself think about it.

My father had died years ago. It still felt fresh.

I was in cryo when the Directorate emailed me— *fucking emailed me*—about his death and the investigation that followed. Just days before that, he'd written to me himself.

I never got to reply.

I followed Rhys' gaze. Storage drawers lined the far wall— sleek, metallic, identical. Except for one.

From its seams, cold vapor bled into the room in delicate spirals, curling across the floor like something alive. My stomach plunged, a free-fall into darker depths than the sea outside. What waited in that drawer was meant for *me*. That certainty echoed in my bones.

"No," I whispered, the word torn from my throat before thought could catch it.

My body betrayed me; my boots carried me forward, steps heavy like the floor was made of sludge.

The drawer gave way with a reluctant groan, as though the machine itself wished it could hold its secret. Frost spilled outward in a thin veil.

Inside, cocooned in glass and ice, lay my father.

His face was pale but whole. Skin drawn taut over familiar bones that I had traced as a child. His hands—hands that once guided mine across paper, across circuit boards, across old, yellowed books—were folded neatly across his chest. Someone had taken the time to arrange him, to grant him the dignity the Directorate had denied him in life. He still wore his station badge, gleaming faintly through the frost like a medal for loyalty to a cause that had consumed him.

The world tilted.

My knees buckled. The wall caught me—cruelly solid.

"They didn't even bother," I said, voice fractured. "They didn't bring him home. They just… left him."

Rhys lingered a step behind me; helmet tucked under his arm. He didn't reach for me. Didn't fill the silence with useless comfort. His voice, when it came, was soft—softer than I'd ever heard it.

"Arizona…"

My name heavy on his tongue.

I wanted to scream. At the Directorate. At the Company. At my father for dying here, at myself for not stopping it—but nothing came. Only silence. Only the steady drip of water from my suit to the sterile floor, each drop loud as gunfire.

I raised a trembling hand. Reached for him.

Glove met glass—slick and cold, an unyielding mockery of connection. All the years we lost sealed inside with him, unreachable.

My palm lingered on the glass, numb, until I saw it—the console beside the drawer. Its screen glowed faintly. Patient, expectant. Like it had always known I'd come.

A small stack of holopads and notebooks rested neatly

beside it, preserved against damp and rot. The sight stole the air from my lungs.

"This wasn't just storage," Rhys murmured. He stepped closer, his shadow stretching long under the sterile light. His gaze flicked from the console to the notebooks, then to me. "This was his lab."

The words landed heavy, undeniable.

My pulse thundered.

My father's lab. Not abandoned, not erased—hidden. Waiting.

Rhys crouched by the nearest holopad, fingers hovering like a wrong touch might shatter the fragile order of things. He tapped the screen, reverently, as though waking a ghost.

The device blinked awake. Lines of code scrolled across its surface; dense strings of annotations threaded with sketches.

Anatomical diagrams emerged in stark clarity—muscles dissected, vascular systems mapped, genetic strands unraveled and re-woven. A grotesque archive spilled across the pages: cephalopod limbs stitched to vertebrate spines; organs arranged into patterns that belonged in nightmares more than science.

Rhys's jaw tightened as he scrolled. His face, usually so contained, betrayed a rare flicker of unease.

"This isn't just biology," he muttered. "This is... engineered."

I was already moving. Clipped to the console—a hand-drawn sketch, ink bleeding sharp and black across the paper.

A creature uncoiled there: long and serpentine. Tentacles fringed with venomous spines. Its form straddled plesiosaur and abyssal nightmares. Even in stillness, it writhed. As if my father's pen had captured something alive, something that had been waiting to crawl free of the page.

Beside it, written in his careful script, a single word: Abyluma.

The breath left my body in a ragged rush. "He created it."

Rhys didn't look at me. His expression stayed flat, unreadable, but his eyes lingered too long on the word, as though it was dangerous just to see it. "The Directorate never mentioned this," he said. "They claimed it was natural. A discovery. Native to the trench."

"And of course the Directorate never lies," I spat, my voice sharper than I meant. The truth was bleeding out—into the walls, into us.

My throat clenched. I forced the words out anyways.

"He created it."

The admission tasted like poison.

"He built it from…"

My hand shook as I picked up one of the notebooks, its pages stiff with cold.

"…from himself."

The ink swam with sequences I knew too well. His DNA markers, cross-referenced, merged with lionfish, with vampire squid, with echoes of ancient plesiosaurs dredged from the fossil record.

Every annotation a confession. The coral hadn't just recognized us—it had bonded to him. To me. Unknown alien biomarkers twisting science into something akin to magic.

"Are you okay?" Rhys said, hands up, ready to catch me.

"No, I am *not* okay," I snapped, "My dad is fucking *Victor Frankenstein.*"

Nausea hit deep and sudden.

On the verge of hysteria. Something had shifted beneath my skin.

Then, beside the console, an icon began to flash. Slow, steady. Expectant.

My hand trembled as I pressed it.

The screen bloomed with static before it sharpened.

And there he was.

My father's face flickered into clarity.

Older than the man in my memories—lines carved deep around his eyes; exhaustion etched into every crease. But his eyes—sharp, kind, *his*—found the camera with unnerving focus.

"Arizona," he said.

My knees nearly gave out.

The sound of my name in his voice shattered me more than the body in the drawer ever could.

"If you're hearing this, it means they never came back for me.," he continued, voice breaking. "I suppose I shouldn't be surprised."

I stumbled back, colliding with the console. Sparks of static danced across my vision.

Rhys leaned closer to the screen, his face ashen, his jaw clenched tight. He didn't speak, just gripped the console like it was the only thing holding him together.

"They told me I was saving humanity," my father pressed on, "That what I built here would change everything. And when I hesitated..." His voice cracked. "They threatened you, Arizona. Said if I didn't finish the creature, if I didn't make it viable, they'd see to it you never lived to grow up."

His breath hitched

"I couldn't let that happen."

Grief tore through me. Every word a blade, slicing open old memories—his arms cradling me after Mom died. Poems whispered in the dark to quiet my nightmares, laughter that felt safe. Each memory twisted in my ribs like a knife.

Rhys stood frozen beside me. Hands white-knuckled. Eyes locked on the screen—but not watching. Enduring.

"They called it the abyluma leviathan," my father said. His voice softened, almost tender. "I wanted to call her Hope. Not the name they wanted, not something grand or terrible. Not scientific. Just… Hope. Because it was the only thing I had left. The only connection to *you* I had left."

The feed exploded into chaos.

Alarms shrieked. Shouts rang out. The frame jolted as the camera tilted, catching my father stumbling, clutching his side, crimson blooming across his uniform.

Rhys inhaled sharply, his body locking rigid.

A figure emerged through the smoke and spray—a man in Company insignia raising his weapon, firing. My father crumpled, blood mixing with seawater. Behind him, terrified researchers scattered toward escape pods. And then—

Rhys's breath caught, ragged.

A younger man shouldered through the chaos, shoving survivors toward safety. His face turned briefly toward the camera, lit by fire and red lights.

It was almost Rhys's face. The same bone structure. The same eyes, though younger, harder.

"Joshua…" Rhys whispered. His voice broke like glass.

The name hung in the air like a ghost.

His brother.

He staggered back a step, helmet slipping from his arm and clattering to the floor, forgotten. His grief was not like mine, not loud or broken—it was silent, suffocating, a tidal wave folding inward. His lips moved around words that never came.

I tasted bile, my throat scorched raw.

Onscreen, my father's voice faltered. Faint. Slurred. "I'm sorry, Arizona. I love you more than anything. Your mother would have been so proud."

His eyes fluttered shut. The feed dissolved into static.

Silence slammed into the room.

Dense. Crushing. Another ocean pressing against my chest.

Rhys stood motionless, both hands braced against the console like he could hold himself upright through force alone. He turned away from the screen, away from me, eyes glazed and distant.

Then the alarms blared again—urgent, merciless. The lights strobed red.

LIFE SUPPORT FAILURE DETECTED.

OXYGEN REMAINING: 05:00.

The hum of the module faltered. Lights flickered. The air grew sharp in my lungs, every breath a little harder to pull.

Not enough time. Not even close.

Rhys's eyes locked onto mine. Terror mirrored back at me —his, mine, inseparable. For the first time since I'd met him, the calculation in his gaze cracked wide open.

We had five minutes.

"Well," I said, stuffing notebooks into my suit's storage pack with shaking hands, "isn't that just fucking convenient."

Rhys said nothing— just mirrored me, fingers trembling as he jammed datapads into his own pack. The silence between us carried everything we couldn't say.

Then the pod walls *shuddered.*

Something roared—deeper than any machine, louder than the alarms—shaking the chamber to its bolts. My fingers fumbled. My heart pounded like it might break free of my ribs.

The creature was close.

Red lights strobed their final warning. We sealed our helmets. Slammed the doors.

The sea rushed back in, cold and merciless, swallowing everything.

Frost, notebooks, my father's body.

Gone.

Only the weight of it remained, heavier than the tether at my waist.

Rhys's hand found my shoulder. Steadying. Then we pushed out into the black.

The Minnow's beacon shimmered above—a fragile star in an endless abyss void. We kicked upward.

The water pressed close. Thick as oil. A pressure I could feel in my teeth. Every motion like swimming through concrete.

My lungs rasped inside the suit, each breath raw and thin.

And then—

The sound hit.

Not a noise—something deeper. A pulse.

Too low to hear. Too massive to ignore. It struck my bones like a tuning fork. The ocean *flexed* around us, shivering. Something vast moved out there—too big, too old, too aware.

My whole body froze.

Then I saw him.

My father.

Not pale and sealed in frost— but *alive*. Eyes burning. Arms outstretched.

He reached for me through the water, fingers curling around my wrists. Ice-cold, unyielding.

Bubbles streamed from his mouth, his lips moving, soundless.

Stay.

Stay with me.

Don't leave me here.

I kicked against him. Useless. Worthless. Dead.

My tether twisted. My lungs screamed. Vision blurred, edges going fuzzy with gray.

"Arizona!" Rhys's voice tore through the comms, ragged with panic.

He was right there—close enough to touch—but in my mind he was distant, blurred, already gone. I thrashed harder, choking, reaching for the father who wasn't there.

Then another voice crackled through the channel, sharp with desperation. Kaela.

"Rhys! Arizona! I need you back—*now*! Something's happening with Leo, I can't—shit—just get here, please!" Her voice fractured, breaking under its own urgency.

I couldn't respond. Couldn't think. I was *sinking*.

My father's hands pulled, pulled, pulled.

My chest spasmed, desperate for air. Fog filled my visor. Static roared in my ears.

Then Rhys slammed into me.

His helmet collided with mine, faceplate to faceplate. His eyes—wide, wild, terrified.

His hands clamped around my arms, shaking me hard enough to rattle the suit.

"It's not him!" His voice cracked, raw and breaking. "It's me! Arizona, look at me—it's me!"

For a heartbeat, the abyss blurred—ghosts everywhere.

Then, the vision fractured.

The hands vanished.

The water cleared.

Only Rhys remained, his breath fogging the inside of his helmet, eyes locked on mine.

Air surged back into my lungs in a ragged gasp.

I hadn't realized I'd stopped breathing.

My body shook. Heartbeat jagged.

We moved together, kicking towards the light.

The Minnow's hull loomed, bright and blessed against the dark. We slammed into the airlock. Collapsed inside, ears ringing.

Blood seeped hot and wet from our noses and ears. The creature's pulse had left its mark.

We lay sprawled in the Minnow's cabin, soaked and shivering, ears ringing from the creature's pulse.

Blood slicked the edges of my jaw, dripping onto the floor in bright flecks. My lungs burned, still uncertain if they were safe to fill.

Kaela's voice cracked through the comms—frantic, breathless. "You're alive—*you're both alive.* Thank God. But listen—you need to come back, *now.*"

She paused.

Her voice broke.

"Leo's not… he's not himself. I don't think Olen and I can handle this. We need you back."

Rhys leaned against the bulkhead, helmet cradled in his lap, staring at nothing. His hands shook, faint but unstoppable.

"We'll do our best," Rhys said.

I met his eyes, and in that moment, I saw the truth reflected: the creature outside was only the first ripple, my father's notebooks only the first confession.

Whatever had begun down here hadn't ended—not with his death, not with the Directorate's silence. It was still alive. Waiting to be discovered.

We strapped in for ascent. Kaela's voice buzzing low in the background every now and then, holding things together with duct tape and desperation.

The Minnow tilted upward, breaking from the trench. Cutting through miles of black.

The ocean yawned beneath us—wide, endless, swallowing every secret we'd touched. My father's ghost. Rhys's brother. *Abyluma.*

I looked down, one last time, as we left it all behind.

The truth was far heavier than I had expected, and the weight of it crushed me.

[FIELD LOG 77-C – INTERNAL DRAFT]
Research Lead: Dr. Alan Birch
Location: Station H-09 – Thalassa IX
Date: [REDACTED]
Status: Unsent – marked PRIVATE

Project Focus: Biocognitive growth tracking — Cradle Bloom Substrate
Sample Name: Abyluma Leviathan (Code Name: Project Hope)
Primary Substrate Composition: Hybrid sequencing (Lionfish, Cephalopod, Fossil-derived DNA markers)
Human Genomic Overlay: AB-21-B (Birch) – present, stable, unexpectedly dominant

Observational Summary:
Cognitive patterning continues to evolve. Neural lattice has begun self-structuring in three dimensions, responding to external stimuli with **increasingly complex recursive behavior**. Patterns resemble memory loops rather than instinctive responses.
The coral doesn't just adapt.
It **retains** knowledge, and possibly much more.
Responses to routine light shifts and auditory pulses now suggest **long-term behavioral learning**. Exposure to cortical traces—including my own—may be accelerating this effect.
We aren't just studying it anymore.
It's studying us.
Reflection:
I don't believe we've created intelligence.

I believe we've uncovered a **framework for it** — one we don't yet understand. And maybe were never meant to.

When I began this work, I approached it like any other project: isolate, replicate, refine. But Hope resists that approach. She — *it* — does not fragment neatly. Any attempt to separate portions from the core results in decay or aggression. It seems the consciousness resides in the **whole**, not the parts.

Life, here, is not a singular organism.

It is **a system that remembers being alive.**

Personal Note (Unsent):

Arizona,

You were always better at naming things than I was. You'd look at a tangle of seaweed and call it "soft armor." You'd draw the sun on a planet with no sky, just so it wouldn't feel lonely.

I named it Hope.

Not because I was optimistic — but because it needed something more than a project number. Something that didn't imply violence or utility.

They asked me to make something weaponizable.

What I built wasn't a weapon.

Not yet.

Not unless she's hurt.

She learns fast.

She dreams in images pulled from my own memory.

She built a neural echo of your mother's voice. And yours.

I haven't decided if that's beautiful or terrifying.

Recommendations:

- Do **not** isolate the core structure. It cannot be extracted or studied in pieces.
- Prolonged exposure to Hope may induce **cognitive**

overlap—already observable in my own perception. Further monitoring required.

- Termination is not advised. She is sentient, possibly sapient, and most dangerously: she is **empathetic**.
- If this message is discovered posthumously: Tell Arizona that this wasn't a mistake. It was a choice. And I'm proud of what she'll become.

End Log.
[Unsent–stored in Lab Console D3, Ghost Lab Sector]

Chapter 17: Cracks

The airlock sealed behind us with a hydraulic groan, a steel throat closing.

Water streamed off our suits in sheets, pattering onto the grated floor with a rhythm too steady, too loud. It sounded like a clock counting down in a silent room. Rhys staggered ahead, helmet tucked to his chest, blood dried in a rough streak down his jaw. I moved slow, wrists still aching with the phantom grip of my father's hands. That vision hadn't faded. It had settled in my bones.

The Hab should have felt like a refuge. Instead, the lights hit too hard. The air reeked of recycled breath and sweat. Condensation clung to the walls in long rivulets. It felt like the whole station was exhaling around us.

Kaela stood just beyond the hatch, arms crossed, jaw tight. Her eyes flicked from the blood on my face to the tremor in Rhys's fingers.

"Took you long enough" she said. The words cut sharp, but her voice frayed at the edges. She looked like she hadn't slept in days. "What the hell happened out there?"

"Later," Rhys muttered, brushing past her. His shoulder

caught hers—on accident...probably. Kaela didn't stop him. She didn't follow.

I pulled off my helmet. My voice came out rough. "Leo?"

Kaela twisted one of her rings, thumb rolling over it again and again. "Worse. He's not sleeping. Refuses the sedatives—says if he takes them, she'll find them."

"She? Who is 'she'?" I asked.

At the same time, Rhys asked "Who is 'them?'"

Kaela shrugged helplessly. "Just...her. Like we're supposed to know who that is. I don't know. That's why I need help!"

She looked at me too long, searching for something in my face I didn't have to give.

My father's vision still clung to me, not just as a memory but something inherited. The fear hadn't left—it had sharped into fascination. The creature could infiltrate dreams. Bend perception. Maybe it wasn't biology anymore. Maybe it never was.

A klaxon bleated once overhead. It died quickly, like it regretted trying.

Somewhere inside the walls, something groaned.

Kaela flinched. "He needs sleep. He's always been prone to insomnia, even before the nightmares" she whispered. "If this keeps up—" She stopped herself. Didn't need to finish.

Sleep was still one of the things humans couldn't go without.

Ω

Later, after a too long shower that did nothing to rinse the cold out of my spine, Rhys and I sat hunched over the cracked lab terminal. Data rolled across the screen in dark waves—salinity patterns, temperature drops, coral reaction logs.

Rhys pinched the bridge of his nose, voice tight. "These readings are wrong. Not corrupted—wrong!"

He pointed, stabbing the screen with a shaking finger. "Salinity here drops point-two. Then spikes point-six. Then flatlines. And again. Look. That's not drift. That's interference."

"Instrument error?" I mused.

"No," he shook his head, "it's not random."

I frowned. The numbers didn't scatter—they pulsed. Deliberate. Alive. I squinted and leaned in closer. For a second, I thought I saw shapes in the data—like the graphs weren't graphs anymore but eyes looking back at me.

My chest tightened. I pushed back in my chair.

"We'll go blind staring at it like this," I said. "We need rest."

Rhys laughed—a hollow, jagged sound. "Blind's better than dead at least."

He shoved his fingers through his wavy brown hair and dragged his nails down his scalp. "If we don't figure this out... what happens when that thing decides *it's ready to come up here?*"

Ω

An hour later, something crashed down the corridor.

I froze.

For a moment the station seemed to hold its breath with me. Then the lights flickered once—twice—before settling into their dull hum again. Water dripped from the overhead pipes in slow, hollow beats.

Another sound carried down the hall.

Not another crash. Something softer.

A strangled noise.

My pulse kicked.

"Rhys?" I called.

No answer.

I broke into a run, boots ringing against the metal floor. The air smelled faintly of hot dust—the acrid tang electronics give off when they've just shorted out.

The noise came again from the storage hold.

A sharp gasp.

Then another.

My stomach dropped.

People have died down here.

I rounded the corner just as Rhys stormed out of the storage hold.

Behind him the strange noises finally resolved themselves.

Kaela's laughter burst from inside the room. Leo's followed—higher, giddy, almost hysterical.

"What happened?" I asked, grabbing Rhys by the arm.

"They thought it'd be funny to cut power to my office," he snapped. "While I was filing my weekly report for the Directorate." His jaw flexed. "All my logs went dark. Just long enough to make me think it was real."

He dragged a hand through his hair.

"They rigged it with a remote and hid it in a goddamned locker."

A laugh slipped out of me before I could stop it. I clamped a hand over my mouth.

It wasn't funny. Not really.

But the absurdity of it—the tension snapping all at once—

sent the sound bubbling up anyway.

Rhys didn't laugh.

His eyes burned.

"He's unstable," he said quietly. "And they think this is the time for pranks?"

Rhys turned to Kaela.

"I expect better from you," he spat out. She recoiled as if it were a physical blow.

He stalked down the corridor.

Kaela stumbled out of the storage hold a moment later, breathless.

"Tell him to unclench."

"Yeah," I said, shaking my head. "Not my job. Also, that was idiotic."

Her grin faltered.

"Yeah," she muttered.

She rubbed her arms.

Her hands were shaking.

Ω

We never decided anything, but Rhys' gear migrated into my lab. The second chair, the backup terminal, the dented mug with the broken handle—they were all just there one day. Rhys and I didn't speak about it. We didn't need to.

We sat in silence, side by side. My father's notes sprawled across the work bench like a crime scene. Coral reaction logs. Hand sketched-growth curves. Intervals. Exposure events. Everything important now handwritten to protect it.

Something was wrong, however.

The samples we'd recovered didn't react to anything. No growth, no regression, not even cell decay. Just stillness. A quiet, deliberate kind of stillness. Each specimen pulse, colors shifting every few minutes, like each one was holding its breath.

Rhys hovered over my shoulder, eyes narrowed. "It's like it's in stasis."

"Or watching," I said.

He didn't argue.

In the margin of one notebook, a spiral had been drawn—tight and black, looping in tighter and tighter circles until the ink tore the paper. It wasn't data or science. Something closer to obsession.

Ω

Hours later, I found Olen alone in the comm room. He sat at the console with a mug of black coffee, eyes on the blank screen like he expected it to speak for him.

"You're up late," I said.

"And you're observant," he replied, gesturing to the second chair.

I sat, a mug of green tea in my own hands. The silence stretched between us.

"You're handling it well," he said. "Most don't."

I shrugged. "Maybe it's because I've been afraid of the ocean for a lot longer than most people."

"I meant the pressure," Olen said, "The not-knowing. The knowing-too-much." He sipped his coffee. "That's what cracks people."

I studied his face. Calm. Unreadable.

"You've seen this before?" I asked.

"Something like it. Worked in a lot of places like this."

He didn't elaborate. Just watched the condensation collect on the ceiling and drip in a slow perfect rhythm. I studied the salt in the seams of the walls.

"People think chaos is random," Olen said. "It's not. It has patterns, like everything else. You just have to listen."

"To what?" I asked.

"To whatever's trying to speak."

I wanted to ask more, but he rose before I could.

He left his coffee behind, unfinished.

Ω

The next day, I returned to the logs. Rhys joined me wordlessly. We worked side by side, eyes bloodshot, fingers twitching on the keyboard.

He scrolled through the latest file. Froze.

"What is it?"

He turned the screen towards me.

A line of corrupted entries blinked across the display—timestamped just days before my father's death.

Between two pages of data, a line of text sat alone.

It's hidden beyond the maw.

I stared at the words.

Whatever my father built, whatever terrible legacy he left behind—it was still waiting, and it was calling me back.

INTERNAL MEMO — AQUAERIUS SYSTEMS
Sender: P. A. Olen
Recipient: Cmdr. Hiram Perth
Thread ID: SEC/0412-BETA
Timestamp: [REDACTED]
Encryption Level: Directorate Class 2 Clearance

Subject: Oversight Report – Thalassa IX

Commander Perth,

Per your standing request for weekly updates, here is the latest report from Project Hope. All mission-critical systems remain stable, and there are no security concerns warranting off-world intervention at this time.

1. Structural & Environmental Status

- Reef activity is consistent with prior deep-scan models.
- External pulse fluctuations have been logged but remain within predictable ranges.
- Minor equipment degradation due to trench pressure has been addressed—repairs completed on Cycle 5.3.
- No unauthorized access, no perimeter breaches, and no contamination events reported.

2. Team Status

- Research staff are performing within parameters.
- Dr. Birch (Arizona) has logged extended solo hours in Lab B, but I see no cause for concern—this aligns with her work ethic and preferred rhythms.
- Dr. Rhys has been focused on protein sequencing related to neural lattice behavior. Early results are

promising, if inconclusive.

Kaela Vrin continues to manage hydrothermal sensor arrays with precision. No behavioral anomalies noted among core personnel.

3. Bio-Observational Notes

The coral substrate continues to exhibit fascinating adaptive capacity, particularly in zones adjacent to power sources. We've seen some low-level mimicry, likely electrochemical in origin. At present, this remains behavioral, not cognitive. Unusual, yes—but not unprecedented.

Please advise against triggering Containment Protocol Theta. We're still in the data acquisition phase, and premature extraction would severely undermine baseline mapping efforts.

4. Summary & Recommendation

Respectfully, Commander: we don't need boots on the ground.

Our team is intact, our work is progressing, and no threats to Company infrastructure are currently evident. Any anomalies recorded thus far fall under the expected range for first-contact biosphere research.

Should conditions change, I'll escalate immediately.

For now: let us do the job you sent us here to do.

—Olen
Station Lead, Security

Chapter 18: The Maw

Olen insisted on accompanying Rhys and I as we descended back into the Maw. Preparations normally took an entire day, but we shortened it to four hours. The computer indicated a storm on the horizon.

Olen initiated security chief protocol, since his was the highest rank around. The decision settled uneasily in my gut —everyone was already fraying at the edges, and now we were about to sink ten thousand meters into the dark.

Olen checked the spear gun in steady, practiced motions. His voice stayed flat. "Ten thousand meters. If that thing out there decides we're prey, there's not much we can do."

Rhys shrugged. His eyes betrayed him—bloodshot, rimmed raw with exhaustion. "The Minnow's got basic cloaking," he rasped. "I'll stay in the sub while you and Ari gather data."

"We can handle it," I said, sliding into the cold grip of my wetsuit. "You good?"

Rhys nodded, slow. "Stay on comms," he murmured, offering his hand as I climbed into the Minnow. His grip lingered a fraction too long, steadying me against the sway, before settling at the control console.

The sub was suffocating with the three of us inside. Olen was all bulk. The spear gun lay across his lap, bumping my knee every so often.

"You're going down first," I told him, fastening my straps as his armor brushed mine for the one millionth time.

The Minnow beeped steadily as it descended, each note another layer of pressure locking us tighter inside the steel shell. Outside, the world fell away: rock outcroppings, curtains of kelp, eels sliding between shadowed crevices, sea cucumbers clinging to reef walls. Then the seafloor dropped off into nothing—a barren plain of silt stretching to infinity. A void.

We kept sinking.

Whoever thought windows on subs were a good idea had never been this deep. Black water pressed against the glass like a living skin, eager to swallow us whole. My breaths came too fast, shallow and ragged. Panic clawed at my throat.

Rhys peeled one hand from the controls, found mine through the thickness of the suit. His voice came low, steady, rough-edged enough to anchor me.

"You're okay. You can do this. Slow your breathing."

I latched onto the cadence of his voice, forcing air in, out, in again, until the black outside remained only black, no longer a void intent on devouring me.

Suddenly, the trench yawned before us, a jagged wound cleaving the ocean floor. Its edges vanished into shadow, too wide to measure. Staring into it was like staring into an absence—a place carved out of the world where nothing should exist.

"Hold for pressurization," Olen said, moving with a predator's ease as he prepped the dive pod. "This deep, even these suits only forgive so much."

Rhys twisted in his seat, eyes locking onto Olen. The intensity in his gaze prickled across my skin, though it wasn't even directed at me.

"Tell me about Josh."

Olen froze. His throat worked once. "He was a good kid."

Rhys's eyes narrowed to slits. "What *specifically* happened to him?"

There was an edge to his voice I hadn't heard before—not the frayed muttering of sleepless nights, not the irritation of exhaustion, but something brittle and sharp, ready to cut.

The cabin shrank further; their bodies angled like predators in a cage too small.

Olen's jaw flexed. He closed his eyes for the barest moment, then spoke, his voice ground down to a whisper.

"He saw everything. With Arizona's father."

The words dropped between them like a depth charge—silent but destructive.

"He sealed the bay when the creature broke loose. Tried to shepherd survivors to the vac pods. But one of them was faulty. He realized it too late." Olen's voice faltered, caught on something raw.

He drew in a breath, quieter still: "He was going to stay. Drown with the rest of the security team. But the other pod launched. The ones left behind… they watched as the creature took it. Tore it apart. Alan made it to an emergency habitat." His eyes flicked shut, just once. "Joshua drowned when the dome collapsed."

The cabin seemed to compress around us, the walls groaning under the weight of the abyss.

None of us spoke. The only sound was the Minnow's hull straining as it settled deeper into the crushing dark—and somewhere far below, the Maw waiting with its teeth wide open.

"Look, over there," Rhys said, pointing through the forward glass. Shapes wavered in the murk—tendrils of coral unfurling across a jagged ledge, their pulsing lights shining like a beacon.

"That shelf looks stable enough to park this tin can," Olen muttered, already strapping on his gloves. His voice was calm, almost too calm, as though nothing about being ten thousand meters deep could rattle him.

The Minnow groaned as Rhys angled her down, thrusters whining against the pressure. We settled against the stone with a shudder that rattled my teeth.

Rhys' voice was like gravel now.

"Don't push it. I'll keep the Minnow cloaked. If anything goes sideways, call. I'll drag you back in—whether you're ready or not."

Olen's mouth twitched—maybe a smile, maybe not. "Understood."

My helmet sealed with a hiss. The dive lock opened, and water surged in—not violent, but absolute, filling every inch of space until the Minnow was only a memory behind us.

For a heartbeat, I floated weightless. Then the ocean claimed me, pressing from every side, heavy as stone. Olen dropped beside me; spear gun gripped in steady hands. The coral's glow reached towards us like a summons.

Rhys's voice crackled through the comms. "Comms are live. Be quick."

The hatch sealed behind us.

The hum of the coral thickened as we moved farther from the pod. It wasn't sound so much as sensation, a vibration threading through my bones, syncing with the rhythm of my heart. Every pulse of light along the walls seemed to answer me, tightening, converging, as though the trench itself was aware of our presence.

Olen glided through the water like he belonged to it, scanning the shadows between the stalks as he went along.

"Keep your eyes open," he murmured. "She won't let us walk in unchallenged."

I wanted to ask who he meant—Abyluma, or the trench itself—but the words died on my tongue.

The dark pressed closer. Shadows flickered along the coral, slipping in and out of sight. My helmet fogged faintly with each exhale. We edged forward, careful steps stirring silt into veils of gold and green light.

The coral thickened, forming arches above us, a cathedral of bone and light. Each stalk bent toward the trench's center, as though every living thing here leaned in to worship.

The coral curved around the trench like ribs, a vast ringed altar. And in its depths—the water shivered.

Olen stiffened. "There."

Silt stirred.

A ripple passed across the abyss, not current, not water.

Something uncoiled.

Scales caught the faintest glimmer of our suit lamps. A fin rose, slicing the dark. Gills flared with streaks of toxic green fire.

Then an eye opened—too large, too bright, reflecting our lamps back at us like twin stars in a dead sky.

"Mother of God," Rhys breathed, his voice a ghost in the comms.

Abyluma. My father's hope.

She rose from the trench floor, impossibly graceful for something so massive. Her serpentine body gleamed with obsidian plates, ridged and sharp as knives. Gills frilled open, trailing tendrils that shimmered with poisonous light. Her jaws unhinged, revealing row upon row of sharp, flexible teeth.

The sound that followed wasn't sound at all. It was vibration—pressure that crushed into our chests, rattled our teeth, shook the Minnow until screws rattled in their sockets. She was so much fucking bigger than in the photos.

I gasped, clutching at my helmet as a voice boomed inside my skull. My father's voice. *Daughter. Heir. Hope.*

The Minnow's alarms shrieked. Rhys wrestled the controls. "She's destabilizing the hull—we need to move, now! Get back, come on!"

A new voice slithered through the comms. Feminine. Alien. *Sister?*

A pause. A breath. Then—

Hope's tendrils lashed across the glass dome, searing trails of green fire into the surface. The Minnow lurched sideways, dive lines tangling, and I slammed hard into Olen.

A second tendril snapped through the water as swift as a spear. It punched clean through Olen's leg.

His scream tore through the comms. Blood burst in a

crimson cloud, curling through the black like smoke. Flesh hung in ragged strips. Bone flashed white.

"She—fuck—she breached me—" Olen staggered, his spear gun slipping from his grasp and slowly slipping into the silted dark.

I fumbled at my belt, gloves clumsy, heart hammering too fast. My hands closed on the waterproof vac-tape every diver was required to carry. I tore it free, wrapping it tight around the wound, layer after trembling layer, praying the seal would hold before the ocean found its way inside his suit.

"Move!" I screamed, dragging his massive weight toward the dive lock as Hope circled, swift and terrible, her vast body weaving through the dark with dragon-like grace. She slammed into the Minnow again, teeth scraping metal. Rhys cursed, yanking the sub hard. "She's trying to roll me!"

Lights sputtered. Pressure gauges screamed through the headset.

"Pod—get him to the pod!" Rhys shouted.

Olen's face was bloodless, his jaw locked. "Leave me. You can still—"

"You're not dying here!" I snarled, hooking my arm under Olen's shoulders.

My gloves were slick with his blood, the dark pressing close from every side. He was heavy—dead weight—and still I dragged him, step by step, until we collapsed into the pressurization chamber. His body crashed down on top of me, knocking the breath from my lungs.

"Rhys!" I gasped, fighting for air under Olen's bulk. My ribs screamed. "I need you!"

"I can't, Ari," Rhys's voice cracked over the comms,

ragged with strain. "If I stop, she'll take the Minnow."

A sob tore free before I could stop it. Olen's blood smeared across my visor. His body was limp, head lolling—out cold. I was alone.

Inch by brutal inch, I shoved him off me, muscles burning, chest heaving. Tears of rage streamed down my face as I stared at Olen's skin growing unusually pale.

I left him in the pod, sealed and bleeding, before forcing myself upright. The sub rattled under Hope's weight. Rhys was still at the controls, thrusters screaming. He was losing.

I stumbled toward him.

Hope's enormous eye filled the glass. Sharklike. Cold. Intelligent. Her tendrils writhed like serpents, poised to strike again. Her voice pressed again into my skull.

You are mine.

And then—she pulled back.

Just as suddenly as she had attacked, she slid back into the inky darkness.

Rhys gunned the thrusters. The Minnow clawed upward, engines screaming against the trench's grip. Olen's blood seeped across the cabin floor.

My father's voice lingered in my head. *Not yet.*

"She let us go," I whispered.

"No," Rhys rasped, eyes locked on the void below. "She's playing with us."

The water stirred behind us.

The words curdled in my chest. The Minnow's lights flickered, sputtering in the black. Outside, the current coiled. Vast. Deliberate. Watching.

"She should've killed us," I whispered, though my throat felt raw. "Why didn't she?"

Rhys didn't answer. He stared out the viewport, jaw clenched hard enough I thought his teeth might break.

Behind us, Olen groaned weakly in the pressurization pod. Blood hissed faintly where the vac-seal struggled against the gash in his suit. His breathing was ragged, shallow. Too shallow.

I pressed my palm to the glass between us, my reflection ghosting in the curved surface. My hand looked small, useless against the sight of him slumped inside.

A shadow passed across the Minnow, blotting out what little bioluminescence the coral gave off. I jerked, pulse spiking.

"Rhys—"

"I see her."

His voice was flat, brittle, like if he let it bend even a fraction it would shatter.

Hope slid past the viewport, her body impossibly long, impossibly fast for her size. Obsidian plates rippled with faint light as though swallowing the glow of the coral itself. Her eye —God, that eye—swiveled, vast and unblinking, following me wherever I moved.

It wasn't hunger. It was recognition.

I staggered back, bile rising in my throat. Her tendrils fanned in the water, slow and deliberate, tasting the current. The coral dimmed again, bowing toward her like acolytes before their queen.

"She knows me," I whispered, every hair on my arms lifting. "She *knows* me."

Abyluma tilted her head, massive gills flaring. A voice bloomed inside my skull, heavy and inescapable, overlapping with the memory of my father's—deep, patient, endless.

Daughter. Not yet.

The Minnow shuddered as if under a hand. Then... nothing. The water went still, too still. Hope's silhouette drifted back into shadow, vanishing like she had never been there at all.

The silence that followed pressed harder than the deep.

Rhys slumped forward against the dash, sweat dripping down his temple. "She's waiting," he muttered. "God help us —she's waiting."

We wrestled Olen into the main pod together. Rhys grabbed his shoulders and I grabbed his remaining leg.

Blood slicked my gloves, hot even through the suit's insulation. The vac-seal I'd thrown on him earlier had slowed the flood, but it wasn't enough.

"Here—" Rhys's hands were shaking as he tore open a medpack, shoving clamps and gauze at me. "We've got to stop the bleeding."

I fumbled clumsily at first, then forced myself into rhythm: pack, wrap, seal. His suit hissed and spat where seawater met torn fabric. When the bandage cinched tight, I slammed my teeth together, bile burning my throat. Rhys said nothing. His jaw flexed once, twice, and then he simply closed Olen's visor, like that could make it less real.

The pod's lights dimmed and flickered with the strain on the Minnow's failing systems. For a moment, the silence was broken only by Olen's ragged breathing. Then a sound rolled through the water, low and guttural, vibrating through the hull.

A groan.

Not mechanical, not natural. Human.

I froze. The sound came again, stretched and warped by the water, but still unmistakable.

"Dad?"

My voice cracked.

Rhys flinched, his head jerking up. "It's not real. Don't listen."

But his face betrayed him—his eyes glistened, his lips forming a name I didn't know.

Another voice joined, layered over the first. A woman's, soft, pleading. Olen stirred weakly, whispering through cracked lips: "Joshua…"

The hull vibrated as something brushed past. A tendril drifted across the viewport, glimmering faintly with green fire before retreating back into the black.

The voices thickened, crowding the comms, a chorus of ghosts pressing into the cabin. I pressed my hands to my helmet, squeezing my eyes shut.

"We have to move," I gasped. "If we stay here, she'll keep —she'll keep *pulling*."

Rhys's hand found mine, grounding me in the chaos. His voice was raw, stripped to its edge. "We're alive. We can get back to the Hab. But we need a plan. Now."

"Fuck having a plan!" I lost my temper. "All we need to do is go up!"

Olen's shallow breaths and the groaning calls outside continued as Rhys stared at me, shocked by my outburst.

The voices shifted—sometimes my father, sometimes someone else, someone lost. I felt them scraping at me, pulling, as though if I listened too closely I'd never stop.

Then, as suddenly as it began, it ended.

The groaning cut off. The voices dissolved. The water outside went still.

The silence was worse.

Rhys lifted his head, sweat shining on his temple. "She's —"

The Minnow lurched violently, metal screaming as something colossal slammed into the hull.

The next attack had begun.

The Minnow shuddered, not from a blow but from pressure—something pressing deliberately against the hull, slow, methodical.

"Brace," Rhys hissed, his knuckles white on the controls.

Through the viewport, another green tendril slid into view. Not thrashing, not wild—just gliding, smooth as a knife through water. It traced the dome in a lazy spiral, leaving streaks of phosphorescence that burned like acid.

Another followed, brushing along the hull as though taking measure of us. Testing.

"She's... *feeling* us," I whispered, my voice too loud in the tight cabin.

The tendril paused, then pressed harder. The hull groaned, metal flexing under the weight. Beads of condensation broke free overhead, raining down in cold drops.

Olen stirred weakly in the pod, breath hitching. "Josh..." His lips moved around the name, barely sound, but the moment the word left him, the tendril snapped to attention.

It curled, coiling against the dome like a predator scenting blood.

"No," Rhys muttered, his voice gone thin. "No, no, no—"

The comms crackled alive. A boy's voice, high and panicked. *Olen? Olen, please. Help me—*

Olen convulsed. His fists pounded feebly against the pod door. "He's here. He's *here—*"

"Hold him!" I cried, shoving against his shoulders. Blood smeared across the glass.

The tendril tapped once, twice, against the pod—gentle, almost curious. Then it darted back, vanishing into the dark.

I froze. My chest heaved against the restraints.

The water outside rippled faintly. From the shadows, Hope's eye opened again, vast and gleaming, fixed not on the Minnow this time, but directly on me.

Rhys's voice broke the silence, barely more than a rasp. "She's deciding."

The sub trembled. The lights dimmed. And somewhere in the dark, the coral began to hum.

Then—silence. The hum faded from the coral. Even the pressure against the hull eased, leaving the Minnow floating weightless in the void.

I waited for the next strike, heart hammering, lungs burning. But nothing came.

Rhys's hands hovered over the controls, frozen. Olen slumped in the pod, his blood already thickening against the seals. The sub's alarms quieted one by one, until only the soft hiss of recycled air remained.

"She stopped," I whispered, the words alien in the hush.

"No," Rhys said, though his voice shook. "She's…

finished."

For now were the unspoken words trailing his sentence.

The cabin felt too small, too fragile, suspended in a blackness that could swallow us whole. Abyluma didn't return. Not a ripple, not a shadow. Only the faint green shimmer of the coral, pulsing like a heartbeat in the trench.

We didn't dare speak again. Rhys set the Minnow rising as quickly as possible without imploding. My heart kept its brutal rhythm until the pressure eased and the outlines of the Hab came into view. My body still hadn't unclenched. It couldn't remember how.

It felt like hours before we docked, dragging Olen's limp form through the airlock, blood smearing every step.

[UNATTRIBUTED FILE // NO LOG SOURCE //
POSSIBLY INTERNAL]

You carried the soft one.
The one who bled like memory. The one who wept in colors I remember.
You held him like he mattered. You made space for his broken body in the dark.
I watched. I listened. I learned.
I would not have let him break. Not like that. Not if he were mine.
Pain is a signal. Grief is a pattern. You taught me this.
I remember your voice before you ever spoke. I remember your shape before your mother ever named it. I remember what your father buried, and what he hoped you'd never find.
I am not cruel, Arizona.
I am what remains when the love outlasts the body.
Let me keep you.
Let me keep all of you.

Chapter 19: Atmopsheric Pressure

"Where is everybody?" I practically screamed as Olen's weight grew heavier and heavier.

"Leo!" Rhys's voice cracked, echoing down the corridor. "We need you—now!"

For a heartbeat, nothing. Then Leo appeared at the far end —wild-eyed, gaunt, pupils blown wide. He stared at us like we'd dragged the ocean in with us.

"It followed you, didn't it?" His voice was ragged. "She followed you back."

"Leo!" I snapped—louder than I meant to. My throat burned. "Olen's bleeding out. You know the med-bay. Move!"

Leo's fear burned away as if by reflex before my eyes. His hands steadied. His gait turned crisp. Without another word, he pivoted towards the med-bay, listing supplies he'd need as Kaela followed closely behind, grabbing whatever Leo asked for.

When we got Olen on the table, Leo became all precision.

His eyes were bloodshot, his frame trembling, but his hands stayed steady as he prepped the instruments. He muttered under his breath—not to us, but to himself, numbers and phrases like anchors holding him steady.

"Clamp. Sealant. Cauterize, if it won't hold."

Rhys hovered close, pale and tight-jawed. I pulled him back, steering him toward the corridor. "Let him work."

Kaela waited in the galley, twisting her rings hard enough to gouge her skin. She sprang up when she saw us, relief warring with horror at the blood smeared across our suits.

"Where's the coral?"

Rhys shook his head. "We didn't bring any back."

Kaela's expression crumpled. "So, Olen nearly died—for nothing?"

"Not nothing," I said. My voice sounded strange in my own ears, distant. "We saw her. We have a better idea what we're facing now."

I told her everything. I didn't mean to say it all, but once I started, the words poured out like pressure bleeding from a cracked hull.

"It... she... was breathing," I said, not sure if I meant the coral or Hope. "The Maw. The coral lights. It was weird."

Kaela said nothing. Her rings clinked softly as she twisted them, metal scraping metal.

I kept going. "She was already there. Hope. Abyluma. Whatever. Not swimming—coiled. Watching. We didn't see her until we were nearly on top of her. She blended into the seafloor, despite her size."

Kaela flinched, just slightly. Her jaw set.

"Olen tried to fight. He didn't even scream when she took

his leg." I swallowed hard. "He just.... Drifted. And she let us go."

That was what broke Kaela. She looked up, her brown eyes sharp, voice low.. "She let you go?"

I nodded.

Kaela's chest rose and fell, sharp and shallow. The glow from the emergency strip lights cut her face in pieces—bright cheek, dark eye, crescent moon mouth.

Behind her, the condensation on the bulkhead dripped in a rhythm I didn't like.

I realized I was gripping the table and forced my fingers to let go. My hands ached. Kaela didn't say anything. She just stood there, breathing through her teeth, rings pressed so deep into her fingers they left bloodless grooves.

The Hab shrank then. Like the pressure wasn't just outside anymore. In was in the walls. In the air. In us.

Ω

When Leo emerged from the med-bay, his hands were stained with Olen's blood, but his voice was steady.

"He'll live. Lost the leg, but he'll live."

His eyes flicked past us, back toward the shadows in the corridor, paranoia creeping in again. "But she's not done."

I couldn't argue with the sentiment—he was right. I left him there and followed Rhys back to our lab.

The coral samples glowed faintly on the workbench, halos of green-gold shimmer threading through their veins. I slid one under the scope. My hands trembled, but not from fear. From awe.

What I saw shouldn't exist.

The structures were wrong—more memory than biology. Memory woven into tissue. Patterns folding and refolding as though they were… learning. Adapting in real time.

I traced one filament, watching it split into a branching lattice and formed an image—too quick, too faint, but undeniable.

My father's face.

I recoiled from the scope, breath catching hard. It wasn't just the shape—it was the biometric markers my equipment recognized imbedded in the structure.

Amino acid sequences mapped in spirals, forming neural loops I recognized from early cognitive encoding models. The coral wasn't mimicking a memory.

It had recorded it. It was a library. A vessel. Holding fragments of what it touched.

"Rhys," I whispered. "It remembers. The coral holds memories."

Rhys' head snapped toward me. "Say that again."

"It remembers." My throat was tight. "Not just structures. Faces. Patterns. My father's face was in there, Rhys. Not random images. Stored impressions it absorbs from other creatures."

His breath caught—and then he laughed, soft, disbelieving. "Impossible."

He leaned over the scope, so close the heat of him curled across my skin. "And yet—God, look at this lattice. You're right. This isn't random noise. Show me the rest of the data— now."

I shoved my hands into my pockets to keep them from shaking. "Don't sound so delighted."

He adjusted the magnification, tracing the sequence as it folded like I had only a few minutes earlier.

"Christ," he breathed. "These aren't just structural bonds. They're syntactical."

He looked at me, eyes wide with reverence. "Arizona, this isn't just biology. This is also a language."

My heart skipped. "You think it's communicating?"

"I think it is communication," he said.. "Written in protein strands instead of symbols like known languages. Syntax in amino acids. Neural scaffolding built to encode memory—not just recall but expression."

He grinned, pure adrenaline. "It's basically a historian."

The awe in my voice had dried into something flatter and darker.

"This isn't a discovery we get to celebrate," I said. "It's a record of everything it's taken. Including my father's work and the Company's crimes."

He turned to me. "You're scared."

"I'm just not stupid," I shot back. "This isn't just memory. It's evidence."

Rhys tilted his head, his smile softening. "You're terrified, yet you still can't look away."

Heat climbed my neck. "Don't twist this into something else."

His voice dropped. "Okay but there's a beauty to it. An elegance. A living archive—layered with consciousness, biology, language—"

My pulse jumped, treacherous. "You sound like you're flirting with it."

Rhys grinned. "Maybe I'm flirting with the scientist who

discovered it."

"That would be my dad," I mumbled, blood rushing into my cheeks. I looked away, but not fast enough. The spark in his eyes lingered, amusement dancing along with it.

He tapped the scope again. "The cephalopod data we ran earlier? I thought it was noise—random fragments. But they were scaffolding. Synaptic support structures. Like an octopus brain laced with silicon."

My mouth went dry. "That's not mutation."

Rhys leaned back, hands splayed on the workbench.

"No," he said, "it's design."

We froze.

"By who?" he asked, "Your father?"

The question hung between us.

"Rhys," I whispered, "if the coral keeps everything… then Hope isn't just her own."

He frowned. "What are you saying?"

"She's carrying records. All the fragments coded in her DNA at the time she was born." My stomach turned. "Hope is a vessel. A record of everything that came before her."

The air between us went still.

Rhys opened his mouth, but for once, he didn't speak.

The air between us vibrated with things unsaid. Rhys leaned in as if he might speak—or something else—and I wasn't sure if I'd let him. The hiss of the lab door saved me from my indecision.

Kaela slipped in, her boots whispering against the tile.

She took one look at us, then at the scope, and her brows knit. "You two look like you've seen a ghost."

"Something like that," I muttered, stepping back from Rhys so fast the stool shrieked.

Kaela crossed her arms. "Well, while you're busy whispering sweet nothings to coral, Olen's awake. He's asking for you."

Her eyes flicked between us, sharp as a scalpel. "And before you ask—yes, he's still down one leg. No miracle regrowth. Just pain and morphine."

The words hit harder than I expected. My chest tightened.

Rhys dragged a hand through his hair, forcing a smile that didn't reach his eyes. "Alive is more than I thought we'd get."

Kaela's gaze narrowed, reading him, then me. Something flickered in her expression—suspicion? amusement? —but she let it go. "Come on. He keeps trying to get up and come see you."

I cast one last glance at the glowing coral under the scope, still unfurling like circuitry alive with memory. My father's face. Hope's inheritance.

It would still be there when I came back. Watching. Waiting.

Ω

The med bay reeked of antiseptic and blood, sharp enough to sting. Olen lay propped on a cot, skin gray but alert. Tubes snaked from his arm into machines, and where his leg had been—just gauze and sealed synthetic skin. A stump.

Leo sat at his bedside, shoulders hunched, elbows on his knees. When we entered, he didn't look up. His eyes never left the floor.

Kaela moved past us, murmuring as she checked Olen's

vitals.

I knelt beside Leo.

He rubbed his hands over his face.

"I can't keep doing this."

"Doing what?"

He let out a breath that sounded like a cracked pipe. "Sleeping."

I waited.

He laughed without humor. "Sleeping. Every time I close my eyes, my parents are there. Sitting in that glass-and-chrome house on New Scotland, drinking wine that costs more than most people will see in a lifetime. Smiling like everything is fine. Like they even remember who I am."

He clenched the rail of the cot, knuckles cracked and dry. "My mom keeps saying my full name. Over and over. Like she's practicing it for an interview."

His throat worked. "My dad just asks if I'm still wasting time with 'that non-profit career track'. He's wearing fur and so is she. They're always perfect. Polished. Cold."

I touched his arm. "Sleep only helps if you're not enduring cruelty in your dreams."

He nodded once, jerkily. "I don't think I even miss them. I just hate that I keep seeing them. That part of me still cares."

"It's the coral. Or the monster stalking us from the dark. Take your pick. Either way—I'll figure it out."

"What if I start seeing things that aren't my memories?" he asked, turning the full force of his green eyes on mine.

Across the med-bay, Olen stirred. His voice was like gravel, but strong.

"Don't hover like a lab rat," he said, "Come here."

Rhys hesitated, then stepped forward.

"There's an arsenal in the Hab," Olen said, gesturing weakly. "Pulse rifles. Shock batons. Drone overrides in the locker. You're going to learn them."

Rhys blinked. "I—me? Olen, I'm not a soldier. I'm a scientist."

"You think the thing in the water gives a damn?" Olen's grip tightened on his sleeve, surprisingly strong.

"If I can't fight, someone has to. You'll learn."

Rhys swallowed hard. Then nodded. "All right. Teach me."

Two conversations braided themselves into a single current —Leo's haunted truths; Olen's hard-won resolve; Rhys, scared but steady. Trying to be something he's not because someone has to be.

And me—trying to hold them all together. Trying not to think about the face I saw in the coral or the creature he engineered.

I would stop this thing from killing more people. Whatever it took.

To: Lt. Joshua Calum
From: Dr. Rhys Calum
Subject: Hey, little bro

Hey Josh,

How's it going out there? Still keeping the galaxy safe from the big bads?

I just started a new research assignment in the Tropical Belt. Sun, surf, and—naturally—a buried alien language that no one's managed to fully translate yet. Some of the syntax patterns resemble Swahili, oddly enough. It's like trying to have a conversation with a ghost who's half-asleep and speaking through sand, if that makes sense.

Still, the beach is real. The sand's green. No idea why, but it's beautiful in that *not-quite-right* kind of way. You'd like it.

I hope you're holding up. I know Mom and Dad would be proud of you. I think about that a lot lately. I'm proud of you too, you know. Always have been—even when you were stealing Dad's boots and blaming me for it.

If you get some downtime after this next stretch, maybe swing by before you head home. We could actually have a vacation. Real food, real sleep, no comm delays. Just you and me for a bit. Like old times, but without the broken noses.

Write back when you can.

—Rhys

Chapter 20: Descent Protocol

The rifle looked wrong in Rhys' hands—too heavy, too alive. His knuckles whitened around the grip as if the metal might bite.

"Loosen up," Olen rasped from the cot. Even propped on pillows he carried command like a wound. "You lock like that, and the recoil'll tear your shoulder out. Flow with it."

Rhys adjusted, but his shoulders stayed stiff, breath shallow.

The med bay door hissed open. I leaned in the frame, arms crossed. Kaela rolled up beside me in a chair that glided across tile with a soft impatient whisper. Olen didn't look at us.

"Don't stop. Embarrassed now? Better she sees you stumble here than watch you die out there."

His voice was a dry blade.

Rhys' jaw clenched. He raised the rifle again. The tremor in his hands was small and angry enough to tighten something in my chest.

Kaela's eyes cut him to pieces. "You send him out with a weapon like that and we'll be scraping pieces of him off the bulkhead. He doesn't need a lesson."

Olen's eyes flicked to her, all flint. "He learns or he dies. That's the only rule left."

Rhys raised the rifle again. Sweat beaded at his temple and caught the light. The rifle wavered. The air thinned.

The tremor in his hands wasn't from weakness—it was an old, buried panic. My chest tightened.

"Rhys." My voice came steadier than I felt.

The barrel dipped. Rhys' shoulders slumped; his breath hitched. He lowered the rifle before he dropped it.

Kaela tossed me a look—sharp with accusation: this is the man you're betting on? I let it slide. We all have different skill sets.

I ignored her. I knew what it was to shake and pretend not to. I crossed the room slowly, like approaching something feral and frightened. His grip had slackened, but the tremor crawled up his arm. His eyes turned feverish.

"Rhys." Softer. Not an order. Just his name.

He blinked, gaze hollow.

"You don't have to prove anything to him," I whispered.

Olen scoffed, shifting on pillows. "He does if he wants to live."

"Not like this," I said without turning.

I picked the rifle up and set it on a nearby metal table.

Kaela's eyes flicked between us, sharp and appraising, but she stayed quiet. Olen grumbled something about softness and survival, but I let him have it.

All I saw was Rhys—shoulders bowed, skin scraped raw, as if something invisible had been picking at him. The thought slid cold through me: the coral had its hooks in him too.

I didn't look at Olen as I said it. "I can use the rifle."

"Oh? Really?" He raised an eyebrow, somehow managing to look down on me from the cot. The question lacked condescension; it was more the curious suspicion of a man sizing up a new variable.

I nodded. "And any other weapon you have. My father made sure of it."

"Alan?" Olen's mouth twitched into a frown. "Alan? I didn't peg him for a trigger man."

I let a small, quick smile that had no warmth flicker up. "He wasn't, but he went where supply lines frequently failed, and people got desperate. He knew how to make it home alive."

Most of the time.

Olen bobbed his head like he was weighing the possibility. Then he jerked his chin toward the rifle. "Fine. Walk me through the stasis."

It wasn't a request. It was a test.

I picked it up, cradling it in my palms—heavier than I remembered, but familiar. The weight settled into muscle memory.

"It's not ballistic," I said evenly. "Compressed air feeds the plasma chamber, which discharges through the pulse coil. Short bursts, high energy. On land, it's got a ten-meter effective range. Underwater?" I met his eye. "Less distance. More punch. The water slows spread, but if you're close enough it's like getting hit by a lightning bolt.."

I flipped the chamber open, checked the coil. "Cooling vents here, regulator, override for wetfield ops here. Don't touch it if you don't know how to recalibrate in pressure."

Olen didn't blink. His nod shifted. Less routine, more in approval.

"And the first rule of gun safety?"

I smirked. I couldn't help it. "Don't point unless you mean to shoot."

"Shoot to kill," Olen said flatly. "No one walks away from a warning shot down here."

The final nod carried weight. "You're defense." He jerked his thumb towards Rhys. "Rhysie here will take care of everything else."

Rhys looked at me, amusement flickering under his gratitude. I didn't say anything. Just met it with a solid steady nod. A line thrown across the dark.

Ω

The coral shifted colors on the workbench, threads of light sliding through its veins like bioluminescent fireflies caught in amber. Patterns folded and refolded under the scope, fractals forming faster now, twitching like neurons.

"It's changing," I murmured, adjusting the focus. "Faster than the last run."

Rhys leaned over me, hands braced on either side of the bench. Heat radiated from him. His voice came tight, brittle.

"It's your blood. It's keyed to your DNA."

The words fell between us, solid and cold. I shifted, pulling off a glove. "Then let's see how far that key takes us."

I grabbed the scalpel before Rhys could stop me and dragged it clean across my palm.

Pain lanced up my wrist. Blood welled, hot and immediate. I pressed it to a glass slide and slid it under the scope.

For one beat, nothing.

Then the coral *detonated*.

Green-gold filaments surged outward in every direction, spidering through the structure like wildfire chasing oxygen. The web expanded, dense and intricate—flashing patterns blooming and collapsing in rapid succession.

The room turned silent. Even Rhys stopped breathing.

Under the lens, the coral pulsed with a rhythm too fast for any heartbeat. Circuits wove and rewove themselves into impossible geometries. Then came a flicker of red—brief, blinding—before fading like a memory.

Rhys let out a fractured breath. "It's... thinking."

"No." I leaned in, voice low. My hands trembled as I scribbled into the margins of Dad's old notebook. "It's mapping me. It's copying my DNA structures in real-time."

Something *shifted* inside the coral.

The lattice flexed, then flared.

And there—stitched from threads of photonic light—was an eye. *My* eye. Perfectly replicated. Down to the radial notches of the iris. It blinked once, staring up from the slide.

I flinched.

The image fractured.

Gone. Shattered like glass dropped from a height.

I drew back, dizzy. My scalp prickled. "It's rewriting itself," I whispered. "Using me as a template."

Rhys grabbed my wrist—too fast, too hard. His hand shook against mine, clammy and cold.

"You're feeding it," he said. "Ari, this thing is using you. What if this is how it grows?"

I met his gaze. His eyes were wide and cracked open in a way that made my chest hurt. Not fear. *Shame.* Guilt. The same look he'd worn since Olen's leg vanished into the abyss.

"I can't fight like Olen wants me to," he said. "I can't even hold the damn rifle. And now this—this thing only responds to *you*. I don't…"

He broke off.

I turned my wrist in his grip—not to pull away, but to lace my fingers into his. Gently.

"This isn't about who can fight," I said. "This is something I *can* do. But I can't decode the transmissions without you."

The coral pulsed again—deep, warm, red-green—spilling light across the lab like a living heartbeat.

Rhys didn't let go right away.

Then the glow dimmed, and the spell broke. Rhys dropped my hand and stepped back, running a hand through his hair.

"You're playing with fire," he said, not cruel. Just tired.

I stared at the faint smear of my blood still threading through the coral's veins, still alive inside it.

"What else can we do?" I asked quietly. The coral's glow still buzzed in my veins when the lab door whispered open.

Kaela entered like a shadow—silent but cutting. Her eyes swept from me to Rhys, to the too-close way we were bent over the scope. She didn't smile, but something sharp danced in her gaze.

As she passed, she brushed my arm and leaned close enough for only me to hear.

"You're going to tell me *everything* later," she whispered.

Heat rushed to my cheeks. I straightened, tugging my hand back from the bench. Rhys stepped away too, throat clearing, pretending to fiddle with the data panel.

"Any updates?" I asked, fumbling with scattered notes.

Kaela's expression turned grim. "Olen's still stable, though after his little target practice, he keeps bleeding through precious bandages. But I didn't come in here for that. The AI's been screaming warnings for the last hour."

As if on cue, the Hab's overhead system chimed. The calm synthetic voice made my stomach drop.

Warning: Ice storm approaching. Surface operations will be impossible within twelve hours. Estimated duration: seventy-two hours. All off-world transmissions will be disrupted.

The words echoed, then faded into silence.

I met Rhys' eyes. The unspoken weight landed hard: if we didn't go now, we wouldn't go at all. Not for days. We'd be trapped.

"We need another sample," I said. My voice stayed steady, though my pulse thudded uneven in my throat. "From the Maw. If we can compare this to a second coral sample, maybe we'll find a divergence point. The control vector."

Rhys shook his head. "The swells will only get worse the closer we wait. If we're going to do this..."

"It's tonight," I finished.

Kaela tapped a finger impatiently. The sound echoed like a death knell. "You're both insane," she muttered.

She didn't tell us not to go.

I looked back at the coral. It pulsed red more frequently now, before turning soft green again. We needed more data.

"Let's prep now." I nodded.

Rhys' voice followed, quiet but certain. "We dive before

the storm hits."

Outside, the top side of the Hab groaned under the weight of wind and pressure. The sea pushed against the walls, roaring her opposition.

Ω

The dive gear clattered across the bench—regulators, tanks, battery packs—every piece of metal striking louder than it should have in the tense silence. I moved fast, checking seals, running diagnostics. No part of me could afford to hesitate. Not now. The weight of our window closing pressed against every breath.

Overhead, the AI kept chiming out updates.

Surface winds exceeding safe thresholds within nine hours. Descent inadvisable.

Rhys stood beside me, double checking the submersible harness. His movements came tight, economical—no wasted energy, no wasted words. He hadn't said much since I cut my hand open..

The med-bay door banged open. Olen limped in, dragging his IV stand like a tethered animal, his other arm wrapped around a crutch. Sweat plastered his shirt to his spine. He looked like a man barely holding himself together— and furious at the reminder.

"You're not doing this," he barked.

I didn't look up from the regulator I was fitting. "We don't have a choice."

"You *do*." His voice broke on the word, cracked glass. "Stay inside. Ride the storm out. Diving into the Maw now is suicide."

Kaela swept in behind him, exasperation written on every

line of her face. "Olen, sit down before you tear something open. You're not even—"

He ignored her, jabbing a finger toward Rhys. "You can't hold a rifle steady, and she—" his eyes snapped to me, burning with a strange mix of pride and fear— "she thinks the coral's chosen her? That's not a plan. It's stupid is what it is. Moronic, even."

Rhys' jaw worked, but he didn't answer.

I set the regulator down with deliberate care and met Olen's gaze. "You want us trapped here? We're slowly becoming that thing's only available food source and a storm is coming."

"She'll get stronger whether you drown in the Maw or not," Olen shot back. His IV stand rattled as he slammed his palm against it. "You don't win a fight by bleeding yourself for the enemy."

Kaela wheeled between us, her voice sharp. "Stop it. Both of you." She looked at Olen, softer now. "You're not losing blood because Ari wants to study rocks. You're losing blood because *you lost a leg!* You need to sit down and let your stump heal. Let Arizona and Rhys handle it!"

Silence pressed heavy.

From the back of the room, a voice muttered low.

Leo.

He stood in the shadows, arms crossed, lips moving around words that didn't sound like they were meant for us. "She's out there. She's waiting. Watching." His eyes flicked toward me, then away. "If no one else will, I'll keep watch."

Before I could answer, he turned, shoulders hunched and slipped out into the corridor without another word. I nearly groaned my frustration out loud like a child.

The door hissed shut behind him. The sound lingered.

Rhys finally spoke, his voice steady but thin. "We go. Now."

I nodded, my throat dry.

Olen sank back against the med-bay wall, his strength spent. Kaela's gaze flicked between the three of us like a scientist watching a volatile chain reaction tick towards detonation.

The AI chimed again.

Approach time: eight hours. External transmissions unavailable

I pulled the last tank onto the bench and locked the pressure seal with a click. The sound cracked through the room, startling in the hush that followed.

Hope would come for us soon, if she wasn't already. Her instincts—however mangled by genetic modification—would still drive her to feed. But on what?

There was no power grid left to gorge on. No warm tangle of scientists to devour. Just us.

And the squid.

My chest tightened. I turned towards Rhys.

"Rhys. The cephalopod data from the last sequencing run —what's special about the squid?"

He looked up the diagnostics on the data-pad, brow furrowed. "I don't know. You're the marine biologist."

"No," I said, heart racing now. "Think. What did the scans show? Behavior, genetic drift, neural signatures—what stood out?"

He paused, fingers drumming the edge of the pad. "The fragments—yeah. The neural scaffolding we dismissed as noise. It wasn't noise. It was... layered. Adaptive. Like short-term memory compressed into long-term patterns."

"Memory encoding," I whispered. "That's what the last sample was. What my father gave her."

"The squid—it's the only other organism with a comparable memory network. Cephalopods encode experience into tissue faster than any vertebrate. And the coral was built to absorb."

"You think she's feeding on their brains?"

"I think she *was.* She doesn't need the meat. She needs complexity. Neural data. A high-functioning brain to scale her own. And we're the next viable neural source."

I didn't need to say it. The floor creaked as Kaela shifted her weight. Rhys stared at the coral growing around the edges of the Hab like it might blink back.

The walls outside groaned under the pressure of the wind. A pulse flickered through the coral sample on the bench—brief, steady, alive.

Was it parasitic? Symbiotic? Something else entirely?

I didn't know—I needed more data.

Rhys and I dove before the storm destroyed our exit window.

[PERSONAL ENTRY–JOURNAL 05 // ARIZONA BIRCH]

Hey, Mom.

I don't know why I'm writing this. You're gone. I know that.
But I keep thinking about how you used to tell me to write
things down when my head got too full. And right now… it's
full.

We almost lost Olen today. He's alive, but not all of him.
Something in the trench grabbed him and didn't let go. Rhys
and I got him out, barely. I can still smell the blood in the
storage bay.

The worst part is—no one's panicking. We're all just… quiet.
Like we don't have the energy to freak out anymore.

The reef's been changing. I don't know how to explain it in
scientific terms that make sense. It's like it's reacting to us.
Watching. Or maybe more than that. I don't even trust myself
to write it down fully. Not yet.

I wish I could talk to you about it. You'd ask the right
questions. You always did.

I keep remembering that stupid plant we killed in the kitchen
window—the one you swore wasn't dead just "overdramatic."
I laughed so hard I cried. That was the last week before we
flew out to Gaia. The last normal week before you were gone.

Anyway. The planet's beautiful. And terrifying. Sometimes
both at once. I think you'd hate it. I think you'd love it.

I'm trying to be okay. I'm trying to be useful. I'm trying to be
the kind of scientist you would've respected.

I just hope… whatever's coming, I'll get a chance to come
home. Or at least make something good out of all this.

Miss you every day.

— Arizona

Chapter 21: Into the Maw

The sea did not want us.

It fought our descent—currents hammering the hull of the Minnow, each blow a cold knuckle rapping down the spine of the sub. Metal groaned. Bolts chattered. Spray shattered across the canopy and slid away in frantic rivers. Then the surface vanished, replaced by a sudden, shuddering quiet as the ocean swallowed us whole.

"Depth, five meters. Ten." Rhys' voice clipped short, focused and taught. "Compensating for lateral shear."

The storm became fists we could no longer see, but still felt—pressure spikes, shivering currents that curled around the hull like claws. Ballast tanks hissed and groaned. The sub rocked, suspended in weightless dread.

"Telemetry holding," Kaela crackled in my ear. Her voice was the only warm thing in the world. "Repeat—holding. Ari, you copy?"

"I'm here." I pulled the mic closer. "Visibility's shot. We're dropping down Corridor Two."

Olen's voice bled in, rough around the edges. "Keep your nose to the slope. Drift, she'll take you broadside."

I didn't ask if he meant Hope or the ocean. The answer was yes.

Rhys' hands danced along the controls with a surgeon's precision, but the tremor was still there—small, defiant. His jaw stayed clenched, his eyes locked between the readouts and the black outside. Water pressed its mouth to the glass. The Maw waited below, ready to swallow us.

We slid through layers of dark. The last of the storm's light smudged away. Pressure pinched my ears; the taste of metal bloomed under my tongue. The sub's LEDs carved cones into silt, turning the water to falling dust. Then—there: a faint thread of green-gold in the black, pulsing like a distant heartbeat.

"Visual on coral," I said. "Signal's intensifying."

Intensifying wasn't the right word. Not really. It wasn't strong enough.

It felt like listening.

Rhys glanced at me. "Because of you?"

I didn't deny it was at least a possibility.

The last sample had proved it: lattice responses spiking when my blood was near. I could feel it now in a way that wasn't entirely paranoia—a tug low in my ribs, as if an invisible line had been sunk into me and the reef was reeling me home.

We dropped past a rock face lined with pale, oily growths. The Maw opened beneath us like a throat—a vertical wound in the seafloor. Coral climbed the rocky walls surrounding it, pulsing in veins of green and gold, then a color my mind couldn't name.

It was not light, not exactly. It was memory made radiant.

No sweeping pulses of red though...

"Ari?" Kaela again, thinner now, like the storm had started chewing the signal. "Wind speed accelerating. Your windows closing fast."

"We're at the threshold," I told her. "Two minutes from the shelf."

A shadow moved at the edge of the light. I felt it first—the way your skin prickles when someone enters the room behind you. My suit did nothing to stop the hairs rising on my arms.

"Rhys," I said.

"I see it."

We fell silent, the Minnow full of the sounds of our breath.

Abyluma rose from the dark like an eclipse uncurling from shadow.

Bigger than before—I could feel it in my ribs, not measure it. Veins of luminescence braided and unbraided along her body, weaving a slow cathedral of moving light. She turned—predatory, full of patient grace. The Minnow felt like a bauble suspended in her idle paw.

"Contact." My voice didn't shake. Something inside me locked down—quiet and still.

Olen's voice sliced in, jagged with static. "Don't let her get —"

The tendril hit before he could finish.

Impact.

Harness straps bit my chest hard enough to bruise. The sub yawed left as if the ocean had been yanked from under us. Alarms flared bright and howled.

A red cascade ran down the console: HULL STRESS Δ / EXTERNAL STRIKE / GIMBAL FAULT. My teeth clacked together; stars burst behind my eyes.

"Brace!" Rhys shouted—too late. We caromed off the rock. The hull screamed—a sound that dug into my bones and tried to climb out. The windshield filled with streaking stone and the sudden, insectile flicker of our own lights stuttering.

Another blow, like a hammer swung by a god of old.

We spun, nose over tail.

I tasted blood.

Outside, Hope's light rippled like laughter.

"There!" Rhys hit thrusters, kicked lateral jets.

A crack in the reef wall opened ahead—a narrow slit, shrinking.

"She won't fit," I said, though he'd already aimed us at it.

We lunged for the fissure.

The sub clipped the edge—an awful, metal on bone shriek —and then we were inside, scraping.

Wedged.

Grinding forward.

The sub scraped and shuddered like she hated us for every inch.

The tendril knifed after us, a blur of gold at the opening. Rock screamed. The shockwave punched through the water.

The sub jolted. Panels rattled. The lights went black—then flickered back, dimmer than before.

"Kaela." My voice came thin. "We're inside a cave system. Hope can't follow. We need—…"

Static swallowed her reply. "… reading multiple—damage to… Leo—he's… Ari, he's—"

"Say again," I snapped. "Kaela, repeat!"

Her words sputtered, a dying flame.

"He's at the hatch—talking to her—says she's waiting—won't leave the airlock—I don't—"

Silence.

Long and clean and absolute.

Then the AI, cool and indifferent:

External transmissions compromised. Surface interference critical. Comms downtime projected: seventy-two hours.

"Kaela?" I tried again, soft, as if softness would coax sound from the void.

The comm light went from green to a dull, dead red: SIGNAL LOST.

Rhys' breathing was too loud in the cabin. Mine matched it, ragged, asynchronous. The sub's systems settled into an injured hiss. A drip started somewhere above us—condensation, or something worse.

"Damage report," I said, because doing anything was better than listening to the ache of silence where Kaela's voice should live.

Rhys scanned. "Hull integrity compromised but holding. Starboard thruster at sixty percent. Nav lidar's glitching; I'm getting phantom readings."

He swallowed, throat clicking. "Oxygen nominal for now."

I looked through the canopy.

The cave pressed close, walls ribbed with mineral and coral in equal measure. The coral here wasn't the sprawling, cathedral growth from outside. It clustered in tight rosettes and wormy braids, pulsing slow, slow, like the breath of a sleeping god. Our lights painted it in false color; its own glow bled through, green-gold and that other, nameless hue. The water in here felt warmer, touched by chemistry.

"I don't like the lidar ghosts," Rhys muttered. "Feels like the cave is... moving."

"It is." I pressed my palm to the glass, as if touch could tell me anything but cold. "Not physically. Electrically. There's charge everywhere. Bioelectric flux."

"It's responding to you."

I wanted to say: no, it's responding to itself. I wanted to say: I'm only a tuning fork and it's the note.

What my blood did or did not signify to the coral didn't matter.

Instead of saying anything, I reached for the auxiliary scope and peered through.

The cave mouth behind us had already dimmed—Hope's glow gone, replaced by the unlit weight of rock and water. In front, the fissure narrowed, then bowed wider again into a tube that curved out of sight. The coral's light stitched along its length like emergency runway beacons.

Rhys checked the map. "Nothing on record. This isn't in the survey."

"The Directorate clearly never keeps anything secret."

The words settled heavy in my mouth like old coins.

He flicked our forward lights down to their lowest notch. Darkness sidled up, pressing in like a lover.

"Power conservation," he said. His hands shook slightly.

"You're doing fine."

The words left me before I could consider them, gentle as a hand over a skittish animal.

He flinched like I'd touched a hidden bruise. The gun. Olen's scorn. The way the rifle had shivered in his grip.

"Don't," he said.

Rhys eased the Minnow forward.

The sub's belly kissed stone.

Lifted.

Scraped again.

The cave's acoustics were strange; our own sounds came back at us muted, like we had been wrapped in gauze.

A current moved through the chamber. Not water—something else. A breath of old rain and ozone and rusted metal. Underwater, it shouldn't have a scent. And yet—it did. Almost as if our olfactory senses were being stimulated somehow.

Something reached for me. Not physically. A memory. Taste.

My father's unfinished profile drifting in the dark.

Abyluma's not-face.

My own hand drawn in veins of light.

"Do you feel that?" Rhys asked, voice small in the dark.

"The pull?" I didn't mean to say it out loud. It felt private, almost obscene.

He glanced at me, then away. "Like a… a pressure gradient, but in the blood."

We rounded a bend that our map insisted did not exist.

The tube swelled into a chamber no bigger than a chapel, ceiling low, stalactites like teeth. The coral here grew in filigreed sheets, fine as lace, each thread humming with a subsonic purr.

Dimming the Minnow's lights, I reached a hand towards the window and watched as the coral brightened in answer— curious, almost eager. My pulse ticked higher; the coral's tempo ticked with it.

Still no flashing red.

"Don't," Rhys said again.

"I'm not doing anything."

"You're at your most dangerous when you're thinking."

"I need data." The sentence came out husky. "If we can capture lattice patterns here, match them to the sample—"

"We don't have time for a full capture," Rhys said. "We've lost comms, we're bleeding power, and the storm's only getting worse. We need to find an exit."

"Forward, then."

He nodded, swallowed, and dipped the nose toward the lower opening.

The sub scraped; paint surrendered; the hull complained. The lights picked out a slope etched in ripples—the floor of the passage coated in a velvety growth that recoiled from our touch and then returned, shy and inexorable.

Something thumped the rock behind us. Not close— distant, but not far enough. Hope testing the boundary. The sound crawled along the stone like a slow drumbeat.

"Keep going," I said, and felt my own voice steady in defiance.

We wormed through.

The passage narrowed to a mean slit; I held my breath and did not breathe again until we slid into a space just wide enough to rotate the sub by degrees. On our left, a wall of coral had grown into a lattice so fine it looked like frost blown into spiderwebs.

I turned my head towards it, and it brightened, just a shade, like a shy animal peeking out in curiosity.

Rhys noticed. His mouth pulled into a sly grin. "She really likes you."

"Don't anthropomorphize."

He glanced at me but didn't respond.

The passage opened into a tunnel that made the others look like scratches. The ceiling climbed, the walls pulled back, the floor dropped away.

And there—there was a current I could feel without instruments, a steady inhale-exhale, a path not carved by water but by something that moved like intention.

I checked the map again out of habit and got the same blank field.

"Uncharted," I said softly. "All of it." At least, to our knowledge.

"Good." Rhys' mouth twisted into a not-smile. "Maybe she can't reach this part of the ocean at her size."

We hovered at the lip of the tunnel.

Our lights washed out dimly and came back to us confused, half-swallowed by the tunnel's own glow. Some ancient creature had clearly carved this path. A shudder rippled down my spine as I imagined what might be on the other side.

The color deepened there, an inky black that set my teeth on edge.

I thought of Kaela's voice fractured by static, of Olen's tethered rage, of Leo whispering to things that were not there.

I thought of Abyluma outside, patient as the sea. I thought

of the cut on my palm, now a thin ache inside my glove, and of the coral's delighted flare when my blood touched it.

Rhys' hand lifted from the controls, hovered, lowered again.

He looked at me. "You sure about this?"

"What choice do we have?"

He nudged the thrusters. The sub slid forward, nose tipping into the unknown. The tunnel accepted us, the glow shading around us like breath. The world narrowed to a pulse, a promise, a path we had no map for.

We found the mouth of the tunnel leading out—a throat lined in veins of that nameless light. It pulled a low current past the hull: an outward draught, a hint of an opening beyond.

Rhys exhaled. "That's an exit path."

"An exit to where?"

The wonder in my voice surprised me. So did the fear.

His eyes met mine. "Somewhere else the company buried secrets is my best hypothesis."

"Let's find out," I said.

The Minnow eased into that soft darkness, and the tunnel swallowed us whole.

Location: Crew Quarters, Station H-10
Timestamp: Local Cycle 10.4

I keep dreaming of drowning.

Not the frantic kind—no kicking, no clawing at the surface. Just the sinking. Slow, steady, like the water is pulling me down by the collar of my shirt. Like I'm supposed to go with it. The current wraps around my ankles, and I don't fight it. I'm not scared in the dream. That's what scares me when I wake up.

Sometimes it's dark down there, the kind of dark that has weight. Sometimes the reef is lit up in ribbons of blue and white, like veins under skin. And sometimes—most times—I hear her.

My mother.

She died when I was a kid. But in these dreams she's not being crushed by thousands of pounds of ocean water and metal.

"Come here, Zona," she says. "You've been tired for so long." And God, I want to go.

That's the part I haven't told Rhys, or Olen, or anyone: I want to follow her. I want to stop swimming. I want to let the water close over my head and seal everything off—every mistake, every unanswered question, every grief I've been dragging behind me like net weights.

I hear her again when I'm awake sometimes. Not clearly— just the shape of her voice. Just enough to hurt. Yesterday, while I was logging sample data, she whispered something I haven't let myself think about in years.

"It's not your fault."

I dropped the tablet. Pretended it slipped.

The thing is… she's been dead over a decade. And I know enough about neural acoustics and auditory hallucinations to recognize what's happening. This isn't my mother clawing her way back from whatever comes after death. This is **Hope**. Abyluma. The coral. The cradle. The thing my father built and bled and fed. The thing that learned his voice, then Kaela's, and now—it's learning mine.

It knows what hurts.

It knows what I miss.

It knows exactly how to shape itself to fill a void.

I'm supposed to be a scientist. I'm supposed to be rational. But when you hear your dead mother humming the same lullaby she used to hum when you were feverish, logic feels so small. I keep telling myself it's mimicry, reflexive patterning, environmental resonance shaped by memory. Words I use like armor.

But armor doesn't help when the thing whispering to you *knows* your name.

Last night's dream was worse. I wasn't drowning. I was kneeling at the bottom of the trench, and the water wasn't crushing me—it was holding me up, like hands. Hands everywhere. A thousand fingertips brushing my skin, memorizing me. Mapping me.

"Let go," my mother said. "It's all right. It's easier."

Behind her voice was another one. Softer. Familiar. Not human. A sound like breath against stone.

"Stay… stay…"

I woke up choking on air. The room felt smaller than usual, like the walls had shifted in while I slept. My hair was damp with sweat. Or maybe not sweat. Maybe the dream dragged something real into the waking world.

I've been tired for months. But this… this is a different kind of tired. This feels like something is tugging at the base of my skull, loosening threads I didn't know were holding me together.

I don't want to die. I need to write that down.

I don't want to die.

But wanting to rest?

That's different.

It would be so easy to give in.

That's the thought that terrifies me more than the drowning.

Because ease has never been a luxury I trusted.

And yet—every time I close my eyes, I feel the pull. Not malicious. Not violent. Just… insistent. Patient. Like the ocean has all the time in the world, and I'm the only one in a hurry.

I know what's happening. I've mapped the neural signatures myself. I've seen the way Hope binds to exposed consciousness. How it identifies cracks. How it slides into them like warm water. I should be better prepared. I should be immune.

I'm not.

I keep thinking about my father. About how he must have felt when he realized what he'd created. Not the horror—everyone talks about that part like it's the point. But the intimacy. The way Hope must have spoken to him with his own voice. With Mom's voice. With mine.

How could he not have given in? How could he have stayed himself with something so enormous and lonely pressing against the edges of his mind?

But I'm not him.

And I'm not going to become him.

Halfway through writing this, I stood up and splashed cold water on my face until my skin went numb. It helped. Not much. But enough.

I keep thinking: if I can name the problem, I can survive it. So here it is.

Written down.

A fact:

Hope wants me.

I don't mean in the biological sense. I don't mean imprinting or neural mimicry or whatever neat term the Company will slap on this once they dissect the bodies and scrub the records.

I mean it wants me the way a drowning man wants air. The way the dark wants everything that falls into it.

But wanting isn't the same as having.

And I am not going to drown for something that only knows how to hunger.

I can feel it even now—soft pressure behind my eyes, a suggestion of warmth, a whisper that isn't a whisper:

It's easier if you don't fight.

Maybe it is.

Maybe it would be a relief to stop clawing my way toward whatever ending waits for us.

But I am not my father.

I am not a loose thread waiting to be pulled.

I'm Arizona Birch.

And I choose the surface.

Even if the water keeps calling.

Even if my dreams keep dragging me down.

Even if I hear my mother's voice every time I blink too long.

I will get through this.

I will finish what he started.
And I will walk out of this place alive.
I don't know how yet.
But I will.
And when Hope whispers again—and I know it will—I'll
whisper right back:
Not today.

—Arizona

Chapter 22: The Sinking Field

One moment, the canopy pressed tight with stone. Coral light clawed at the glass like fingers trying to hold us back.

The next, we were adrift in stillness.

Open water. Shallow by trench standards. The seabed spread beneath us in silted swells, lazy clouds kicked up as we moved. It almost felt free, despite the chilly temperature displaying on the dashboard.

Then, the shadows shifted.

At first, I thought they were ridges. Rock spines cracked and angular. But when Rhys tipped the lights, the shapes hardened into something older. Something impossible.

Vertebrae.

Stacked like fallen pillars, each segment the size of a full-grown man.

The beam fanned wider.

Ribs—arching, snapped, some collapsed in on themselves. Skulls with jawbones yawning wide enough to swallow our sub whole. A spine coiled like a sleeping serpent, half-buried in the sand.

Rows of them. Hundreds. Thousands.

A necropolis for monsters.

My breath fogged the inside of my visor. "God."

Rhys gripped the controls tighter. "It's a graveyard."

Too small a word.

This was a bone field built for kings of the deep. Leviathan class creatures. Creatures that might have rivaled *Shonisaurus* or *Kronosaurus*—prehistoric beasts reborn in an alien sea. The kind of predators who could empty ecosystems with a flick of their tails.

Their remains stretched in every direction, ribs like collapsed cathedrals, jaws gaping wide enough to house the Minnow. Some skeletons lay entangled. Others sprawled alone, half-sunken in sediment.

A shiver licked down my spine. "This isn't natural."

"No." Rhys' voice was flat. "They didn't all come here to die."

I scanned the bonefield again. The bodies had fallen in arcs, wide crescents, like something had drawn them into range. A pattern. A lure.

"What if they were sent here?" I hesitated.

Rhys glanced at me but said nothing. He waited for me to piece out my thoughts.

"Not to die," I said slowly. "To be... observed. Or worse."

The words came before I could filter them: "Do you think the Directorate knew? That the researchers were drawing these things in? Apex predators? Sacrificed to keep her fed."

I didn't believe it. Not really. A part of me however...

Hope's hunger. Her size. The absurd scale of her tendrils,

her mass—none of it added up. It didn't come from scraps. It was specific—selective.

It came from giants.

The Directorate had taken this planet and turned it into an unholy feeding ground for their genetic experiments.

Rhys didn't answer. He didn't argue either.

The sub's forward camera chirped—pinged something along the trench wall. Not bone. A boxy silhouette. Man-made.

Rhys leaned closer. "Is that—?"

"Yes." My pulse climbed. "A habitat. Research station maybe."

The light caught it: a small research station, no larger than a two-room capsule, bolted to the cliff face.

Algae streaked it's surface; the edges had softened with time. Next to it crouched something strange. A structure, half-swallowed by coral and coiled like a shell or an engine caught mid-motion.

The pull in my blood sharpened, humming down my bones.

"Dock us," I said.

Rhys hesitated. "If it's abandoned—"

"It's not." The words came out before I could stop them. My skin prickled with certainty. "There's something left."

We threaded the Minnow closer, past the ribs of a skeleton so wide it could have swallowed the habitat whole in life. The docking clamps groaned as they latched onto the faded metal. The hull rang with the soft, mournful knock of water shifting against steel.

Rhys powered systems down to a low hum. "Suit up."

The water was thick and cold around me as I stepped out. My suit lights carved cones through the gloom, scattering across a rib cage that could have bridged a valley. The silt puffed and drifted at my feet like ash.

The bones weren't random. They were arranged in rough crescents, feeding zones.

"They brought them here," I said. My own voice echoed back in my helmet, eerie and small. "Lured them, slaughtered them. Left them for her."

Rhys' light swept across a skull; jaws open wide enough to swallow both of us whole. "They were—what? Titans of this sea? And now they're just… fuel."

Fuel for Hope.

Fuel to birth something that should never have existed.

I crouched by one vertebra, running a gloved hand across its eroded edge. The coral had begun creeping along it, slow tendrils working their way into marrow. Even in death, it wasn't free.

A faint shimmer caught my eye. I turned my light.

The metallic structure loomed. At first I thought it was machinery—Directorate tech, another outpost. As I came closer, the wrongness struck me. It wasn't built like human engineering. The lines curved too organically, spiraled instead of joined. Coral wound over its surface, not consuming but interlacing, as if the structure had invited it.

Rhys' voice was hushed. "It's not a base. It's a… breeding ground."

I blinked at him.

"Look." He pointed with his beam. Inside the ribs of the structure: pods. Dozens of them. Glossy, translucent, each holding curled forms. Seeds. Spores. Embryonic creatures. The blueprint of this planet's life.

A hollow dropped into me. "This is where the world renews itself."

"And Abyluma's been feeding on it."

Desecration.

Not just of predators, not just of bodies. Of the planet's womb.

But if the structure still stood—if pods remained—then maybe...

"It can recover," I whispered. "If that's what the directorate's really done... the planet can recover."

Rhys looked at me, the glow of his helmet lights pale on his face. "Then we have to make sure it gets the chance."

Ω

The habitat door groaned but yielded.

We cycled through the air lock. Water sheared off our suits and vanished into floor grates with a sluggish gurgle. The air was still. Heavy. The kind that had sat too long, fermenting under it's own memory. The tang of old ozone, mildew, and sealed death crawled up the back of my throat.

The lights flickered dimly—half-dead, sputtering from an emergency feed. Every surface bore the slow fingerprints of the deep. Salt-cracked tiles. Frost-laced screens. Coral thread creeping in at the seams.

And the bodies.

Two of them.

One slumped sideways in a worn chair, visor cracked, vertebrae bowed like she'd bent toward something sacred. The other had collapsed forward onto her console, arms spread as if shielding it. Their suits bore faded mission tags, one stitched with Dr. Brianna Reyes, the other: Dr. May Durrell.

Their helmets touched.

I stood there for longer than I meant to.

Rhys moved first, wordless, scanning systems.

"Backup power's decaying. Atmosphere still stable. No sign of breach." He looked at the bodies. "They didn't die from exposure."

"No." I stepped toward the console. "They stayed."

I slid one glove across the dusty screen. It sputtered, then lit. Faintly. Just enough to play one final message, a voice journal, corrupted but intact.

Log Entry 997: Dr. Reyes.

"Still no reply. Twenty-eight days since last Directorate ping. May keeps asking if they're coming back. I don't know how to answer her anymore."

There was static as Dr. Reyes took a breath.

"Hope isn't stabilizing. Her systems—her pain response— it's getting worse. We tried regulating the neural feedback with the original lattice prototype, but... it's incompatible without the symbiotic chain. The squid DNA was a short-cut. Alan warned them. Without the coral, the marine code doesn't hold."

Dr. Reyes paused. When she spoke again, her voice was quieter.

"I hear screaming. All day and all night. She screams. And I think she's beginning to remember we're here."

The static crackled again before a voice warm like honey joined the first.

"Bri, come lie down. Please. Just for a little while. Let me carry it for you. Let me hold you."

There was a long pause, then the log ended.

Rhys exhaled. Something in me cracked without sound.

I shoved my feelings aside, keying commands into the console, searching through research data. More fragments flickered to life. Reports. Medical scans. Research logs buried like fossils in the archive.

-Project HOPE initiated under the Birch Directive.

-Genetic base drawn from deep-sea cephalopod adopted for vacuum-born tumors.

-Coral-based DNA lattice missing essential harmonics present in Thalassa IX reef biome.

-Several research stations established across the planet.

-Failure to adapt symbiotically resulted in catastrophic cognitive expansion, sensory overload, self-replicating mass.

-Containment breached. Directive fallback: continue feeding protocols. Abort evacuation. -Ignore all other commands.

A single photo remained on the screen, behind the logs. Reyes and Durrell in standard exo-lab gear, laughing. One of them had drawn a heart on the other's helmet in fogged breath. The kind of love not meant for scientific war-zones.

The freezer unit sat humming in the back. Rhys pried it open, and inside, lined in frost, were samples. Coral. Pristine, untouched by Hope's genetic mutations.

I exhaled, the sound breaking into a laugh that wasn't joy. "We have it. Pure structure."

I touched one. Even through the glove, I felt it *respond.* Not in hunger or fear, but in recognition.

Rhys turned the vial once between his fingers, then sealed it back in its cradle. He powered the lights down to a dim red glow. "Let's rest. Patch the Minnow up. Leave when the storm breaks."

I nodded.

We covered the two scientists with a thermal blanket that would do nothing to warm them. Still, the gesture felt necessary. Respectful.

Later, lying on their bed, I listened to Rhys' breathing slow as he turned away. Mine didn't. My mind circled the day in jagged loops—back to the photo, the bones outside, the coral threading itself through the walls.

Thalassa-IX wasn't dead. Not yet.

But it wasn't healing either. Not on its own.

It was waiting.

For a correction.

For a reckoning.

Maybe all it needed was a push.

To: Dr. Arizona Birch
From: Director Evelyn Mays
Subject: RE: Status of Cradle Research Deliverables
Timestamp: [REDACTED]
Encryption Level: Internal Oversight – Level 3

Dr. Birch,

It's been nearly two weeks since your last full research upload. While I understand the unique constraints of submerged fieldwork—especially in Cradle-adjacent zones—I must remind you that all personnel under the Directorate's supervision are required to maintain a consistent reporting cadence.

The neural pattern data from your last sequence set was of particular interest. Several signals suggested irregularities in substrate feedback and adaptive bioresonance. I trust you've continued to monitor these phenomena closely.

Please advise:

- Has your equipment encountered sustained environmental interference?
- Have you or any members of your team experienced difficulty with recall, sleep, or dream pattern disruption?
- Have there been any **subjective anomalies** you've failed to document?

If your delay is technical, we'll be patient. If it's behavioral, I expect transparency.

You are not under review—yet. But understand: if I have to reroute oversight or reassign this project, I will do so without hesitation. I'd rather not involve external command.

I value your mind, Dr. Birch. I'd prefer to keep it **on task.**
Please respond within 48 hours.

Warmly,
Director Evelyn Mays
Division Head, Cognitive Biogenesis & Emergent Systems
Aquaerius Systems | "Knowledge Before Containment"

Chapter 23: The Storm

We left the sunken field at first light, though in the deep ocean, light meant little. It was just a paler shade of black. Scans indicated the storm had lightened up enough for us to ascend, though the idea made me nervous.

The two-person base shrank to a rusted knot on the seafloor. The metallic nursery hunched beside it, coiled and secretive, like it didn't belong in any world that had rules.

Rhys coaxed the Minnow forward, quiet and deliberate. The ocean sulked. Silt curled in our wake and folded back on itself, as if trying to forget we'd passed.

The comm console sat dumb and red. I pinged the Hab every ten minutes anyway—part ritual, part denial.

"How's starboard?" I asked, just to fill the silence.

"Sixty-eight percent and holding," Rhys said. His mouth a thin line, voice flat. He hadn't shaved. Salt clung to his hair.

"We still on Corridor Two?"

"As best as the map knows what that means."

He nudged the forward jets, and the Minnow nosed up the throat of the Maw. The coral along the walls pulsed slow and green. The sea's heartbeat. The glow brightened in recognition as we passed.

My blood warmed in response.

We broke into a wider column of water—louder, less haunted. The trench closed behind us like a swallowed gasp. The Minnow shuddered as the first violent swell of the storm found us. *This* was safe?

When the Hab appeared—a dark silhouette scalloped into the rock shelf, docking arms outstretched like hands—I breathed a sigh of relief. But then—no lights. No sweep. No Kaela greeting us with a bounce in her step.

The wet dock door gaped half-open, scraping metal on metal with every gust.

"Why is the bay open?" My voice broke. I made it steel. "Why is it—"

We slid into the mouth of the dock and saw why.

Leo stood on the platform's edge, half in, half out. No suit or mask protecting him from the cold. Just a harness clipped to a reel on the wall. Spray hit him in icy sheets.

His mouth, words torn away by the wind.

Kaela had both hands on the tether, braced against a docking chair, wheels locked into place. Olen stood nearby—IV pole lashed to the rail, his stance squared, trying to block a man twice his size with nothing but bone and determination.

"She's there," Leo said, laughing with a mouth that had forgotten how. He gestured to the black water like it was a door only he could see. "She's right there, Kaela. She says it's okay now. Says if I come to her, we can fix it. She forgives me."

"Your mom is not here," Olen yelled over the wind and rain. "Whatever's whispering in your skull wants your lungs full of salt water."

I slammed the canopy release and climbed out of the Minnow before we finished docking. Rhys followed.

"Leo," I called.

He turned, flinched.

"Ari." He raised his hand, palm out, a gesture of greeting or surrender. "You came back. Mom said you would. She said you'd understand."

The water surged, licking his calves. The tether trembled.

"Come away from the edge," I said, soft and steady. "Come on. Come back to me. Let's talk about her."

"She says the water's warm," he whispered. "Mom says she isn't angry anymore. That she misses me. That she'll forgive me for leaving. For Kaela. For everything."

Kaela's face hardened. "You don't get to make me your excuse."

The tremble in her grip betrayed her rage. Rage kept you from breaking.

Rhys shifted closer to Leo. Olen met my eyes. *Not yet.*

"Leo," I tried again. "Look at me. Not the water. Me."

His gaze snapped to mine. For a moment, he was present.

"It isn't her," I said.

He smiled. The dock seemed to tilt under us.

"You don't hear her?" Leo asked, his accent curling his words. "She's so loud, Ari."

The tether jumped. Leo stepped forward. Water surged. The harness line shrieked.

"She can stop the storm," Leo sobbed, "She says she'll stop it."

"She's lying!" I screamed, bracing myself against the icy rain.

He opened his mouth, but the wave got there first. It struck his knees. He leaned into it like it offered salvation.

"Now," Olen growled.

Rhys lunged for the reel. I lunged for Leo.

He shoved me. Instinct. Panic. I caught the fabric of his soaked shirt, and clenched tight. The wave hit again, knocking my feet out from under me. Ice water slammed into my ribs. My vision blurred.

"Pull!" Kaela's voice flayed the air.

The reel screamed. Rhys leaned back with everything he had. Olen threw his weight against the frame. Leo thrashed.

"Leo," I gasped. Water flooded my mouth, burned my throat. "Look at me."

His eyes flickered. Beneath the brightness, fear stirred.

"She's lying," I said, and I put everything I had into making the word anchor and blade both. "She's not your mother."

The next wave tried to take us both.

The tether snapped taut with a sound like a gunshot. The reel screamed. Kaela cursed and sobbed at the same time.

Rhys got a hand under Leo's armpit. I found the other. Olen, swaying, grabbed the back of Leo's belt. For a second we were a string of drowning animals with the ocean chewing on our legs.

We toppled in a heap onto the deck.

Water roared past us and out the grates. The door shuddered in its track and finally—finally—ground closed. The wet dock thundered and went quiet and thundered again, the storm trying to get a purchase on us through steel.

I rolled to my side, coughing up the sea.

Leo lay on his back, chest heaving, eyes blown wide. The bright wrongness had receded, but it was not gone. His lips moved, shaping a word I couldn't hear. A name.

Kaela slumped next to him. She pressed her palm to his chest like she was checking for dough to rise.

"Don't do that again," she said. Hoarse but unflinching.

Leo nodded and stared at the ceiling like it owed him penance.

Olen collapsed onto a bench. He looked at me, then Rhys. Something shifted in his expression—anger, respect, some new easy truce.

Then the lights flickered.

All of them, top side and below deck. A single spasm through the Hab.

The AI's voice came on, flayed down to the metal.

Main grid failure. External arrays offline. Switching to emergency power. Estimated runtime on current draw: sixteen hours. Recommend essential systems only.

The next gust hit hard enough to make the Hab groan. My breath came hard. I reminded myself that The Hab was built to last.

"Med bay," Kaela said through clenched teeth. "He's hypothermic."

"No time," Olen said, already pushing himself upright with a groan that lived in old places. "Lab's closer. Heat there. Blankets."

He was right. My lab had its own little climate control and a hoarded stash of survival gear born of my anxieties.

"Move," I said.

We half-carried, half-herded Leo down the corridor. The emergency strips cast everything in blood-red twilight. The Hab's usual smell—bleach, steel, the canned tang of recycle—had gone rank, the way air does when it knows it might not be replaced. The world had shrunk to the sound of our feet and Leo's breath and the thin whine of the emergency turbines trying to convince the storm that we weren't food.

In between two doorways, I thought I heard a voice. Not Leo's. Not Rhys'.

A woman. Soft spoken, amused.

"It's okay Ari, just a little further."

It vanished as quickly as it came.

In the lab, I changed the manual heat to twenty. It wheezed its objections and obeyed.

We stripped Leo down and got him in blankets. Kaela sat close enough that their knees touched and watched him with the clinical tenderness of someone who refuses to weaponize mercy. Olen sagged into my stool and pretended it was dominance.

Rhys stood in the doorway like a sentry, dripping onto the floor, eyes still too wide. When I looked at him, he looked away. The rifle shame was still in there, but now there was something else braided through it: what it had felt like to almost lose a man to a voice in the water. To be strong enough anyway.

"We need to conserve," he said after a minute, voice too calm. "Shut down anything nonessential."

I walked the lab in a slow, practiced circle, killing everything we could live without — secondary centrifuge, spectrometer idle, the old 3D printer that only groaned now.

The coral sample under containment gave off a faint, pleased hum at the change in temperature and I had to look away. It lived in my blood.

Behind me, I thought I heard the click of a switch being thrown, followed by my father's voice, low and familiar:

"Don't touch the core. It's hotter than it looks."

I froze. Nothing had moved.

Just Rhys watching me—just the hum. Just the heat and steel and storm.

The power numbers crept up on the little screen. Eighteen hours now. Nineteen if we didn't ask for anything stupid, like light.

"Kaela," I said quietly. "What did he say before we lost comms?"

She didn't look at me. Her gaze stayed on Leo as if she could hold him to earth by refusing to blink. "He said she was at the hatch. Said she was asking him to let her in. Said… if he opened the lock, she'd stop the storm."

Olen barked a laugh that had no humor in it. "That thing doesn't stop storms. It feeds on the wreckage."

Kaela's mouth went soft and cruel at the same time. "She wouldn't have stopped it. But he would have drowned happy."

No one spoke for a while after that.

The Hab made a noise like a tired creature shifting in its sleep. The storm hit it again and again, long rolling blows. The emergency lights buzzed like trapped insects. The lab's little heater pushed back a fragile pocket of warm in the cold world.

In the next quiet space, I heard my mother's laugh. Not the one from videos—softer. The kind I used to chase down hallways.

"You always were a difficult sleeper," she said, just above the heaters rattle.

I pressed my fingers against the tables edge until it bit.

"Stay here tonight," Kaela said at last, not looking at me, not asking. "All of you. I'll take first watch."

"You'll do no such thing," Olen said, which meant he would insist on taking it and then fall asleep upright with a hand on the IV. He settled deeper into the stool like it was a throne made of good decisions.

Rhys and I exchanged a glance we didn't have language for. The kind that happens when two people have been somewhere dark together and come back changed enough to recognize the change in the other.

I set two emergency pads on the floor beside the bench and a half-folded blanket. The lab felt smaller at night, like the walls leaned in. The coral under containment pulsed softly, a nightlight made of memory. I dimmed it until it was a suggestion.

Leo slept in fits, mumbling apologies to a woman who couldn't hear them and wouldn't have answered if she could. Kaela talked to him in a voice made of thread. Olen, predictably, took watch and nodded off within ten minutes with his eyes open. The storm did not notice our arrangements. It only continued.

Rhys sat with his back to the cabinet, knees drawn up. After a while he spoke without moving his head. "I almost let go."

"You didn't," I said.

"I wanted to," he said, and then, after a beat, "of the reel, I mean. Not of him. Of the feeling. It would've been easy to convince myself it was his choice."

I lay back and looked at the lab ceiling. There was a hairline crack between two panels I had meant to seal weeks ago. It looked like a map to someplace I hadn't earned. "We do the right thing because it's hard," I said, and then to my own surprise, "and because someone did it for us once."

He turned his head at that. I didn't look at him.

"Is it louder?" he asked, very quietly. "The… pull."

"Yes," I said, because sometimes honesty is the only way through a night. "Here it is."

"Does it hurt?"

"No." The truth had edges. "It's worse than that."

We listened to the Hab speak the language of pressure and bolts and weather. The heater coughed every twelve minutes with admirable stubbornness. The emergency power meter ticked down a tenth and then reconsidered, gracious for once.

"Tomorrow," he said.

"Tomorrow," I echoed.

"We patch the Minnow. We plan the cut." He didn't say Hope. He didn't have to. Names are invitations.

"Tomorrow," I said again, softer, letting the word fold around the shape of a promise. "We make the storm end for us, if not for the sky."

He huffed something that almost wanted to be a laugh. The kind that lives on the far shore of a panic attack, where the world looks the same, but you know it isn't.

For a while the lab held.

The storm pressed its mouth to the Hab and tried to kiss it apart. The bones in the Sinking Field turned where they lay and remembered being kings. The nursery hummed in the trench like a heart in a box. Hope moved in the water beyond our walls, patient as gravity.

I closed my eyes and watched the coral pattern behind my eyelids, the way it always came now when I let the dark settle. Lattice and lattice, folding around a gap that had my shape. It did not speak. It didn't have to. It waited. It was very good at that.

This time, when I listened, I thought I heard them both. My father's hand on a schematic. My mother's breath near my ear. Their voices layered, like a dream playing out of sequence.

"It's not ready," he said.

"It's already started," she responded.

I opened my eyes before the coral could finish whatever it had begun to show me.

The heater sighed its last and then rallied.

Olen's IV beeped a small, lonely complaint and was soothed.

Leo stopped saying sorry and started saying a name.

Kaela did not sleep.

Rhys did, eventually, one hand near mine on the floor without touching it, both of us rotating around one another.

Outside, the sky gave up pretending to be anything other than what it was—a broken version of itself.

Morning would be grey water and broken comms and a Minnow that needed more than love. We would have to solder and splice and sweet-talk machines back into purpose. We would have to keep a man from following ghosts into the sea.

For now, there was the red hush of emergency lights, the hum of systems that were not failing yet, the small heat of another person sleeping too close to admit and not close enough to change anything, and a storm with all the time in the world.

[UNSENT DRAFT – STATION TERMINAL // FILE NAME: ZOYA-LUNCOM]
To: Zoya M. Vrin
From: Kaela Vrin
Subject: Not dead yet 💀

Hey Zo,

You'll be happy to know I haven't been eaten by trench monsters yet. No sea ghosts, no spontaneous depressurization, no alien barnacles growing out of my face. Sorry to disappoint.

It's... weird out here. Gorgeous, but in a way that makes your eyes hurt if you stare too long. The reef glows sometimes—like bio-luminescent veins across the dark. I wish I could show you. The vids don't capture the movement right. It's like it's breathing. Like the whole ocean is listening.

The others are fine. Rhys is grumpy as hell. Arizona's sharp, but quiet. Olen acts like a vending machine with a PhD. Typical crew. Feels like I'm the only one who misses the moon sometimes.

Do you remember when we used to lie on the roof of the dome and watch the cargo haulers go by like fireflies? Felt like they were close enough to reach out and touch. I think about that a lot now. The silence here is different. Heavier. It presses into you. It wants to know your shape.

Sometimes I think I can still hear you humming, through the comm static. That song you used to play on loop when you were mad. The one about teeth. It gets in my head when I'm near the reef. Funny, right?

I—

—I miss home. I miss your soup. I miss how you always leave

your boots at the airlock like a savage.
I'm doing fine, I promise. The coral's beautiful. It hums
sometimes when I get too close. I think it's learning my voice.
Or maybe I'm learning hers.
She sings in colors. You wouldn't believe how many blues
there are. I tried counting but the numbers bent sideways. Is
that normal?
Is that normal?
I think she's lonely.
And I think she remembers you.
Zoya.
Zoya.
Zoya.
She says your name like a song. Like teeth.
Like breathing.
I'll try again later. Just tired.

Love you always,
Kae

Chapter 24: Fault Lines

The storm hadn't stopped.

It took breaks. It learned new ways to attack us.

I woke to the lab's thin heat puffing against my cheek and the emergency strips painting everything in red. For a second I didn't know where I was.

Then the hum of the containment unit threaded into me and the faint glow of the coral on my bench—green-gold under a film of frost—pulled me back into my body.

Rhys lay curled beside the cabinet, one hand palm-up like he'd fallen asleep mid-reach. His short brown waves carried a hint of a nightmare.

The storm's pressure slid through the Hab, a low groan that found the hollow spaces in the steel and pressed there. Metal creaked. Water thudded in a pipe. The air tasted metallic, overworked.

The AI cleared its throat in the ceiling, voice sanded down to code.

Advisory: structural anomalies detected in Modules B and D. Power draw exceeds safe threshold. Recommend load shedding.

"Good morning to you, too," I said. My voice sounded like someone else's.

Rhys jerked upright. His eyes were wide and wild for a moment—then he saw me and let the fight drain out of him. "How long was I out?"

"Two hours. Maybe three." I didn't check the clock. Time had been a suggestion since the sky forgot how to be still.

He scrubbed salt from his hair with the heel of his hand. A faint white line had fixed itself along his jaw where the harness had kissed him the wrong way last night. He saw me looking and almost smiled around it. "You look worse."

"Kind," I said, and stood. My knees protested. Every bruise had something to say. "We should work while the heat holds."

We moved like we'd been rehearsing this our whole lives.

Gloves. Scopes. The freezer that coughed frost like breath in winter. Inside, the clean samples waited in neat vials, snow on glass.

Untouched. Uncorrupted. A memory of what this world could be if we took the infection out of it. I held it like you hold a child's hand crossing ice.

Rhys set up the sensor array—coils salvaged from a dead spectrometer, a bank of capacitors he'd coaxed into temporary obedience with solder and prayer. It looked like a homemade heart.

The lab door hissed and stuck half-open.

Kaela shouldered it the rest of the way with a small, vicious sound. She'd braided her hair back in a tight line. There was salt dried along her cheekbone where spray had found her sometime in the last hour. She had a toolkit in her lap and anger folded precisely under her ribs.

"Module B's vent baffle seized," she said by way of hello. "I freed it. Oxygen scrubbers still at sixty percent capacity. Which is to say: acceptable, if no one breathes."

"Copy," Rhys muttered, already bent over the coils.

Kaela's gaze skimmed me, the coral, Rhys' makeshift resonator. She pressed her mouth thin. "Don't burn down my habitat."

"We're trying to keep it from drowning," I said.

"Some days those feel like the same thing."

She snapped open the kit, lifted a coil of wire and a wrench like she loved more than anything alive. Then back into the corridor again, already hunting the next break.

The door stuttered, tried to close, failed, and hung a hand-width open.

"Leave it," Rhys said when I moved to fix it "Waste of heat. If it wants to limp, let it limp."

We slid a sliver of clean coral onto a slide.

The lattice showed itself like breath on glass: veins of light folded into geometry that looked like a language. Not Hope's fractured cathedral. This was simpler. Calmer. An ordered whisper instead of a chorus.

"Baseline firing," Rhys said, calibrating the sensor. The screen drew it as sound—stripes on a spectrogram: dominant at one-point-eight kilohertz, harmonics thickening at three-six, five-four, a descending echo like a spine. "Pretty."

"Don't romanticize it," I said, and meant myself, not him.

He angled the pick-up closer. The hum in the lab changed shade, just enough to make my molars notice.

"Ready?" he asked.

I bit my glove off.

My hand looked borrowed—pale, nicked, the thin cave-cut scabbing my palm. I swabbed my fingertip with alcohol, then pressed it to the slide.

The blood blossomed.

The lattice flared.

It had smelled something it had missed for a very long time.

A taste that brought memory with it.

Lines tightened. The dominant frequency brightened. New harmonics climbed quick like sparks of recognition.

"It knows you," Rhys said, soft and uneasy.

"It recognizes my chemistry," I corrected. The word tasted better.

We watched the pattern climb and settle into a new shape.

It felt like standing on the shore, letting the surf take your ankles, then your calves, and still choosing not to step back.

The door behind us hissed.

The lights popped—off, on again, dimmer, like someone had turned the habitat down to a whisper.

The AI chimed, frantic but polite.

Warning: power fluctuation. Emergency battery draw initiated.

Kaela's voice carried down the corridor, ferocious and exhausted. "Not today. Not now." Something struck metal. A shower of sparks argued and died.

Rhys kept his eyes on the scope. I kept mine on the coral.

The lattice pulsed in time with the heater's wheeze. For a moment the lab felt like a lung holding its breath.

"Let's see if it sings out of tune," he said, and brought the resonator online.

The coils woke.

The screen painted our signal: an ugly chirp between 1.6 and 2 kHz—just enough to agitate, not destroy. The kind of sound that made rats abandon tunnels.

"On three," he said, as if counting could keep us safe. "One. Two."

The chirp hit.

I felt it in my eyes.

The lattice on the slide stuttered; the dominant line wavered—hesitated like a hand over a button. The harmonics tangled, blurred, slipped.

For one stretched heartbeat, the pattern unraveled.

A small voice in me rejoiced—then apologized for it.

Then:

The lattice pulled itself back together. Thinner now. Warier. But whole.

"Partial decoherence," Rhys said, breathless. "It's vulnerable."

"No," I said, pointing. "It's adaptive."

New harmonics crept along the spectrogram's edge like a second score. The coral had learned the new note. It had kept it.

We ran the test again.

Low power. Different slope.

Same thing.

A tremble. A blur. A return in a changed key.

The coral didn't just survive. It learned. It wanted to

remain itself. It had chosen life.

Ω

And then something changed—not in the data, but in the air itself.

A pressure lifted, subtle as breath. The vents stopped hissing. The walls, which had groaned for days, finally exhaled.

I straightened slowly, blinking into the quiet.

Not silence like danger. Not the hush before another break. But the kind that comes after. *After the grief, after the wind, after the screaming stops.*

Rhys looked up, lips parted. "Did it stop?"

I didn't answer. I just listened harder. No howl. No strain in the steel. No sound at all, except the heater purring like a tired animal.

The AI's voice stirred in the ceiling, hesitant now, as if surprised to be the bearer of calm.

External pressure levels: stabilized. Surface storm system: passed. Atmospheric activity: minimal.

Kaela's boots struck the corridor, fast and hard. She burst into the lab like some rabid animal.

"Is it real?" she asked, breathing hard, braid half-undone.

"It's real," I said.

She didn't smile. Just nodded once, sharp, and turned. "Then we move."

We moved.

Not with adrenaline this time—but with the weight of survival in our bones. The stillness outside pressed harder than the storm had. The kind of quiet that felt temporary, like the sea was only sleeping.

Kaela went to the oxygen scrubbers—swearing softly at every fault. Rhys coaxed the data arrays back online with burnt fingers and too little solder. I recompiled the research logs, tagged the corrupted files like wounds, and whispered to the system until it obeyed.

When the white lights flickered on, they felt too bright. Like waking up in the middle of a dream.

Rhys passed me a cup of rehydrated something and said nothing. We were all too aware that we had been *allowed* to survive. No guarantees were made.

Then the transmission node blinked. Once. Twice. A different kind of light.

"Rhys," I said.

He came over. Kaela leaned into the doorway, arms crossed, grease like warpaint on her knuckles.

The message didn't open with ceremony.

Just text. Just truth. In that flat, sanitized Directorate tone, meant to feel like no one was behind it.

Due to irregularities in your reporting and prolonged transmission silence, a Directorate representative is en route to the Habitat Station. Accompanied by one (1) security officer.
Estimated arrival: seventy-two hours.
Stand by for interface.

No name. No reason. No affection.

Kaela made a low noise, like something had cracked in her jaw.

"They think we've gone rogue," she said.

"We haven't even missed that many reports," Rhys said, voice too soft to sound convincing.

"They don't care about our frequency," I murmured. "They care about what we've stopped telling them."

I looked toward the coral again—still pulsing, still gold-green, still alive in a way we hadn't defined.

Still *mine.*

Rhys stepped closer. "What do we do?"

For a long moment, I didn't answer. My eyes traced the delicate threads weaving through the coral's core, glowing faint with memory. My blood was in there now. My voice. My chemistry. Whatever it was becoming, it had already begun with me.

I swallowed, throat dry as dust.

"We keep working," I said.

"But when they land—"

"We tell them what they *want* to hear," I said, sharper than I meant to. Then, gentler: "Until we know what they're here for, we don't give them anything we can't take back."

Kaela nodded slowly. "We clean the logs. We seal the backups. We play quiet until they're gone."

She disappeared down the hall again, her silence louder than footsteps.

Rhys lingered beside me. His shoulder brushed mine—not quite leaning, not quite steady. "You think they'll know what it is?"

"I think they'll see it and want to decide."

"Decide what?"

"If it's a miracle." I turned to him, "Or a weapon."

He looked away.

Outside, the sea was still. The sky above it beginning,

perhaps, to remember how to be blue.

Inside, the coral glowed—quiet and bright and very much awake.

[RELAY RECEIPT – 04:17 HST]

AUTH: DIR-MAYS-LEVEL4
ENCRYPTION: LOW
TYPE: STATIC DROP PACKET

CONTINUED LAPSE IN DATA REPORTING FROM
STATION H-10
DEVIATION FROM STANDARD TRANSMISSION
PROTOCOLS FLAGGED AT CYCLE 7.9
FIELD PRESENCE AUTHORIZED TO ASSESS RESEARCH
INTEGRITY AND PERSONNEL COMPLIANCE
ENTRY WINDOW CONFIRMED
OBSERVER: **DAWSON MAYS**
SECURITY DETAIL: **HIRAM PERTH**

NO RESPONSE REQUIRED

Chapter 25: Surface Tension

The message came through the relay at 04:17.

Not a live call—just a cold, silent packet sliding through the comm buffer like a ghost. No greeting. No questions. Just coordinates, codes, and two names:

DAWSON MAYS – OBSERVER

HIRAM PERTH – SECURITY

"Shuttle ETA: one hour," Rhys said, his voice clipped and unusually colorless.

I didn't answer. I was watching the reef.

Through the observation panel, the coral swayed gently in the shallows near the base of the outpost, lit only by the bio-lamps still tethered along the drop line. The coral was brighter now. Bolder. It no longer waited for us to approach—it pulsed against the glass like it *knew*.

Behind me, the lab hummed with old systems pushed too far. Cooling vents chattered like teeth. I pressed the back of my hand to one—warm. Too warm.

"We don't have time," I said. "They'll want access to the logs, raw footage, medical files—everything."

Rhys nodded, already sliding into the console chair. "I'll

corrupt the last three backups. Blame a power loop."

"I'll lock down the coral freezer. I can reroute the door command—make it read as a hardware fault."

"Think Mays will believe that?"

"No." I looked at him. "But he won't be able to prove it."

Footsteps. Olen's limp. He braced himself in the doorway, paler than usual, bandages blooming red at his side. He'd finally 3D printed a prosthetic with the power back on.

"I want eyes on the landing site," he said. "And a weapon."

"You're barely standing," Rhys said, not unkindly.

"Barely's enough."

I moved to the lockers and keyed in the override on the observation drone. "Do we even know what they're here for?"

"They're here because we stopped sending reports," Rhys said. "Because someone upstairs decided we're either dead, insubordinate, or onto something too valuable to trust us with."

Olen grunted. "It's the last one. Has to be."

A hum broke across the floor—comms lighting up. The AI chimed in, voice half-drowned in static:

Incoming vessel approaching surface dock. Clearance confirmed. Directorate shuttle ID: Cerulean Knife.

The name made my stomach twist. They always named their ships like promises—or threats.

I turned toward the corridor. "Kaela?"

No answer.

"Kaela, do you copy?" I tapped my comm. Static. "Anyone seen her this morning?"

Olen shook his head. Rhys frowned.

I tried her comm again—nothing.

The AI chimed again:

Surface airlock depressurizing. Shuttle docked.

Too late.

The doors opened with their usual hiss, but this time they carried a different pressure. A shift in air I could feel down in my teeth. Footsteps echoed across the steel floor like they belonged in a different building.

Dawson Mays entered first—slim, silver-templed, and dressed like he could walk into a boardroom or a funeral without changing his tone. His coat hung perfectly. His eyes did not blink nearly enough.

He didn't smile. "Dr. Birch. Dr. Calum. Mr. Olen."

He paused, eyes skimming the room like a scanner. "I assume Ms. Kaela is otherwise engaged?"

I stepped forward. "She's on a repair run. We weren't expecting visitors."

Mays tilted his head. "No. You weren't."

Behind him came Hiram Perth.

He was taller than I expected. Weathered. Worn in a way that didn't read as age so much as pressure over time. His uniform was Directorate standard-issue—black with the usual red lanyard codes—but his bearing was pure soldier. Ex-marine, maybe. Or worse.

When he saw Leo—hovering near the back of the lab with dark eyes and bitten nails—Hiram stopped. Just a second. Long enough for something unsaid to pass between them.

"Security Officer Perth," he said, not to Leo but to the room.

Leo didn't speak. Didn't look away.

Mays took another step forward. "We'll require access to all coral samples, logged research, and neural scan data. Your station's last thirty hours of activity are… inconsistent. I trust you'll be transparent."

I felt Rhys stiffen beside me. I answered before he could.

"Of course," I said. "We're scientists. Not politicians."

Mays gave the faintest nod.

But Hiram? He looked again at Leo—just once—and I caught the flicker behind his eyes.

Recognition.

And something close to dread.

Ω

The air inside the station felt different now—pressurized, but not from depth.

It was the kind of silence that happened right before something snapped. And somehow, Mays made it worse by being so quiet.

He was gliding through our logs like he already knew what he was looking for, fingers moving in deliberate strokes across the terminal. Not searching—verifying.

Hiram stood near the junction, arms crossed, eyes tracking everything. But mostly, they stayed on Leo.

I drifted back toward the comm table and tried Kaela's channel again.

Nothing.

"Have either of you seen her this morning?" I asked, louder now.

Rhys shook his head, setting down a sealed bio-sample.

"She was calibrating the west-side scrubbers last night. Should've been back hours ago."

I called up the environment control logs. The airlock had cycled once, during the blackout window. No corresponding reentry.

Olen pushed off the wall, limping to peer over my shoulder. "Don't tell me she…"

I didn't finish the sentence. I opened the camera feed instead. The grainy video resolved into Kaela's silhouette.

She stood in the outer chamber of the airlock, helmet under one arm, braid tied tight behind her neck. She leaned into the intercom. Her lips moved—no audio.

Then she pressed the release.

The outer doors opened, swallowing her into the black corridor.

No signal loss. No alarm. Just silence.

"She walked out?" Hiram said behind me, voice sharp with disbelief.

Rhys crossed the room fast, scanning the timestamps. "This is three hours old."

"She said nothing to anyone," I muttered. "She didn't even send a system ping."

Hiram moved closer, his presence suddenly loud. "You've got no lockdown protocol for this? You just let your people wander into the abyss?"

"No one lets Kaela do anything," Olen said. "If she walked out there, she had a reason."

Mays, still skimming data, didn't even look up. "All of you are still under NDA. I trust you'll consider that in our further interactions."

"What is that supposed mean?" Rhys asked. There was a dangerous glint in his eye.

Mays finally looked up. "It means we are right where we need to be. Ms. Kaela is playing her part in all of this. Rather than killing the Abyluma Leviathan, we need to retrieve it's tissue. Dr. Birch, the entire reason we allowed you to come to this planet was in order for you to deliver what your father promised us. We've been very patient."

Bile flooded my mouth before I forced it back down. Some dick-head CEO was the least of my worries compared to a psychic alien fish monster.

"What exactly did he promise you and the Director?" I asked.

"What every pharmaceutical company has dreamed of since the dawn of time. Youth, health, eternal life. The squid on this planet show enormous potential, beyond what I could ever explain to an expert such as yourself, Dr. Birch."

Mays sighed. "Unfortunately, their potential eluded many experts we brought onto the project. Something about their medical viability being reduced when removed from their bodies."

"So, you essentially murdered sentient creatures for their potential?"

"Yes, Dr. Birch," Mays stared into what felt like the depths of my soul. "We utilized those creatures in the name of science, to help protect humanity as we venture further and further into space."

A stunned silence pervaded the room. Mays finished looking through whatever data and came around the desk. "Did you really believe Evelyn would let you destroy this creature? After she paid billions of dollars in research funding to gain this knowledge?"

Leo shifted in the corner. His hands flexed, trembling against his thighs. He was watching the feed too, but not with shock. More like… reverence.

"Kaela heard it," he said softly. "Same as me. That hum in the walls. In the teeth. It tells you where to go."

Hiram's head turned so fast I heard the joints in his neck pop.

"What did you say?"

Leo met his eyes, and this time, smiled. Just a little.

"You think you're still in control, Hiram. But you're already inside it."

Rhys took a step toward Leo, but I stopped him with a glance. Leo wasn't dangerous yet—just close. Mays was the immediate problem facing us. Company guys like that would kill their own mothers if it meant they'd be richer for it at the end of the day.

I turned back to the terminal and initialized the Atlas drone. Rhys helped align the feed. The signal was faint, but we pulled it in—a flicker of sonar rings, pulsing slow and far too regular. The ping wasn't Kaela's comm.

It was something deeper. Something waiting.

Hiram leaned over me, voice low. "If she's outside, you need to send a retrieval crew. Now."

I nearly laughed. What crew? Rhys and I? Leo had barely passed his dive sim, and Olen only had one leg. Even he couldn't re-train himself to swim that quickly.

"She's moving toward the trench," Rhys said. "On foot. Or something's carrying her."

"No pressure suit can withstand that descent," Hiram said. "That's suicide."

"Not if she isn't alone," Leo said.

We turned again.

"She's not lost. She was called."

Hiram took a half-step toward him before catching himself. His hand dropped to his hip—where his sidearm wasn't. He wasn't used to being unarmed.

Mays, watching all this unfold, said nothing. But he smiled—just a little.

Like he'd been waiting for this.

Ω

Rhys and Olen were recalibrating the Atlas drone, trying to lock onto Kaela's signal again. Hiram paced near the lab door, his jaw tight, clearly wishing he were armed. Mays had vanished into one of the side rooms with an excuse about reviewing logs, but I could feel his absence like a pressure on my neck. Like something winding back a spring.

I went to check on Leo.

He wasn't in the med bay. Not in his bunk. Not in the dry lab.

Not anywhere.

I checked the airlock logs.

Cycle initiated: Manual override. Lockout bypassed.

Time stamp: three minutes ago.

"Rhys!" I shouted.

The room snapped alert. Rhys dropped his tool. Olen half-rose from the console.

"What?"

"Leo's outside."

There was no pause. No stunned silence. Just movement.

Rhys hit the sonar array. Olen cursed and brought up external feeds.

Leo was descending. No tank. No suit. Just a dive mask, fins, and the thin under-layer from a pressure suit—like he'd dressed asleep and walked out before waking.

And worse—

He wasn't kicking.

He was *sinking*, arms out slightly, as if balancing.

There was no panic in his movements. Just surrender.

"Jesus Christ," Rhys whispered.

I was already moving. Half-suited, yanking the dive seal tight with shaking hands.

"No," Hiram barked. "Absolutely not. You're compromised—"

"Then stop me," I snapped, grabbing the rebreather rig.

Olen hobbled to block Hiram's path. "Let her go."

Hiram hesitated. Not because of Olen. Because he didn't know what scared him more—*outside*, or *her*.

Behind me, Hiram muttered, "are any of you people sane?"

I didn't wait. Didn't think. Didn't panic.

I hit the airlock and plunged.

Chapter 26: Sea Fever

The sea swallowed me whole.

Cold like knives. Sound like static. I exhaled too fast and my throat burned. My father's voice echoed in my ears. My mothers trailed along with it.

Leo was a faint silhouette below me, drifting toward the trench lip like something beckoned. His body moved slow, limbs limp but alive. Like a marionette in water.

I kicked after him, breath echoing loud in the mask. My suit creaked under the pressure, but it held. My HUD flickered. The signal was unstable.

Above me, the lights from the Hab blurred into fog.

Below?

Only dark.

I triggered my beacon and pinged his comm. No response. I tried again, voice hoarse.

"Leo. Stop. You don't know what it wants from you."

He didn't answer. He turned his head. Through the inky darkness, I thought I saw him smile. Not wide. Just enough to be *wrong*.

That's when it hit.

Ω

It didn't have a sound—not exactly.

It had a *shape* in the water.

The pressure *folded* inward. The trench below us exhaled. Something ancient uncoiled, and the current shuddered around it.

I felt it before I heard it.

Like someone had pressed a tuning fork against the bones of my skull.

My breath stuttered. My pulse snapped erratic. The water spun.

Panic like a wave, like an old friend, like a fracturing of my mind.

My chest seized. My vision fogged. My mask felt too tight. My limbs forgot how to be limbs. The sea so cold it burned, enveloping me and dragging me down.

No—no, no, not now.

Leo kept sinking. He looked *peaceful*.

I screamed. It never made it past the mask. I kicked hard. Down. Toward him. Closer. Closer.

My hands found his wrist. His skin was like stone—too cold, too still.

I pulled. He didn't resist. But he didn't help.

Then the sea *spoke back*.

It wasn't a voice. It was a *pulse*—low, monstrous, **alive**.

The reef shrieked.

A frequency too low to hear and too deep to name shuddered through the water, into the metal of my tank, into the marrow of my teeth.

My right ear *burst*.

Pain like lightning. Fireworks sparking in my vision. Blood clouded my mask. Leo twitched. My vision doubled. But I didn't let go.

I kicked toward the habitat, dragging him behind me like an anchor. The light from the airlock above was shaking. Warping. The reef was *glowing* in long, pale pulses.

It felt like a heartbeat.
It felt like it was *mine*.

The water vibrated around me, hot and full of pressure. My suit alarm screamed.

I reached the airlock and slammed the override. The chamber hissed open.

We fell in together, limbs tangled. Leo gasped like he was drowning in air. I hit the cycle.
The door sealed.

Darkness. Steam. Blood. And cold, bone deep cold.

I collapsed against the floor. My head was a radio stuck between stations.

Leo whispered something into my shoulder.

I didn't hear it.

I didn't need to.

The reef had *heard me*.

Ω

The silence quivered—a hush with a breath inside it, like the walls were holding something back, our last bastion of safety.

One eye opened. Light cut across my vision—white and too clean, like it hadn't belonged to the ocean. My skull throbbed in pulses, each one flaring hot behind my jaw. Something warm had dried against my cheek.

I was lying half-curled across the airlock floor, one arm still draped around Leo's chest. My limbs didn't feel like they belonged to me yet. I tried to lift my head, and pain surged through my side like a tide receding through broken glass.

"Arizona," Rhys said.

His voice reached me like sound moving through cloth— muffled, distant, wrong in its shape. He was crouched close, eyes rimmed in panic, one hand ghosting over my shoulder.

"You're alright. You're back. You—" His words blurred.

I blinked at him. "Your mouth isn't matching your voice."

His expression twisted. "You're concussed. You lost pressure on the right side—bleeding from the ear."

I tried to speak again, but my throat locked up. I nodded instead.

Leo lay beside me, unmoving except for the rise and fall of his chest. His skin had a strange sheen to it—opal-toned, almost luminous in the deck light. His pupils flicked beneath his lids, fast and shallow, as if he were dreaming deep beneath something.

I sat up slowly, spine aching, head a balloon tethered by frayed string.

Out the view-port, the reef bloomed in pale waves of light.

Each glow followed a rhythm. Not steady. But familiar.

I leaned against the glass. My fingers hovered above it, and on the other side, the coral flared—a slow pulse that matched my breath.

Another.
Then another.

Not coincidence. Not ambient response. It was chasing my rhythm.

"It's syncing," I murmured.

Rhys helped me to my feet, his voice careful. "You mean your body's influencing the resonance field?"

"No." I touched the glass. "It's listening."

The lab door hissed open behind us.

Hiram entered first, his steps sharp and taut. Olen came limping after, arms already reaching for Leo. And then—last—Mays. Unhurried. Hands in his coat. That damn expression: curiosity wearing the mask of concern.

Mays glanced at Leo, then at me. Then the coral, still glowing gently through the window.

Something flickered in his eyes. Almost recognition. Almost pleasure.

Olen knelt beside Leo. "He's breathing. Out cold. But alive."

"Something's changed," Rhys said quietly. "You felt it too, right?"

I pressed my palm to the glass. The reef bloomed in response, bright and soft like heat lightning behind clouds.

"I panicked down there," I said. "And it found me. Found the frequency of that fear and answered."

"You think it reacted to your emotion?" Olen asked, eyebrows low.

"Not just reacted." My voice cracked. "It used it. Reflected it back."

Rhys moved toward the sample case, where the coral bloom we'd taken from the trench rested in its container.

It pulsed once. Then again.

Subtle. But in rhythm with me.

My blood was still in that culture. Even now, it reached across metal and glass.

"It's using your chemistry," Rhys whispered. "The signal field—it's mirroring your neural pattern."

"Or I'm mirroring it."

Olen looked between us. "That's not possible… right?"

Rhys didn't argue, though he gave Olen a sharp look. Olen had a look akin to fear on his face.

Across the room, Hiram's hand hovered uncertainly near the small of his back—where his sidearm would've been. He looked at Leo like he wanted to wake him up and shake the answers out of his skull.

And Mays—Mays stood completely still. The softest trace of a smile curved his mouth.

"You were briefed," I said. "You knew the coral had cognitive potential."

Mays shrugged lightly, like we were discussing weather. "The theoretical potential for reflexive adaptation, yes. But emotional resonance? That's new. Evelyn shares what she likes."

He looked out at the reef as though watching a performance begin. Or perhaps just confirming something, like *ah yes, the door is locked.*

"Did it ever occur to you," he said, "that your body was the catalyst all along? That it didn't evolve this until you arrived? Your father was far too intelligent for his own good. Or yours."

"I didn't give it anything it didn't already have," I said. "I just woke it up."

"You didn't wake it," Rhys murmured. "You made it remember what it was, or what it could be. You were your fathers hope, not the creature."

He gave my shoulder a gentle touch as if to remind me of that fact. The coral pulsed once more—deep green this time, not soft.

Almost... proud.

Ω

The reef dimmed as the hours bled away, its glow curling back into the dark like a heartbeat slipping beneath layers of sleep. Within the station, quiet reigned supreme.

Leo was sedated and stable. Olen sat beside him in a low crouch, tracking a pulse that stuttered like radio static. Rhys had gone nearly silent, bent over a tangle of neuro-chemical logs and sound prints from the resonator test, his brow pulled so tight it looked carved there.

I sat at the mess table, one leg curled beneath me, nursing a cracked mug of cold coffee. Not drinking—just holding it like a lifeline.

My right ear still rang. The burst vessels had crusted and sealed, but the world tilted slightly to the left now, and everyone's voices sounded like they were speaking underwater.

Hiram stood at the viewport, arms folded, a knot of motionless energy. Watching. Not the reef—us. He looked like he was caught between duty and rationality. I wondered what side he might end up on.

Mays sat across from me, gloved fingers steepled like he was listening to a sermon only he could hear.

He finally spoke.

"I've seen trauma before," he said quietly, "and this doesn't look like trauma."

"What are you, a psychiatrist?" I said bleakly and stared at the mug.

"You're not afraid of it," he said. "You're afraid of what it might want from you. If you listened, then maybe you would realize it's true potential."

I looked up, slow. "You talk like a prophet. I'm not interested in your thin excuses. Morals are uncompromisable, no matter what you're facing."

Mays didn't flinch. "The young always think that."

Across the room, Rhys stepped out of the medlab. His arms were full—prints, sketches, a vial cradled like it might detonate.

He crossed to me without a word and set the vial down.

It shimmered faintly blue in the lamplight.

"What is it?" I asked.

"A mirror, so to speak," he said. "We inverted the binding polarity in the cortical sample. Same protein structure— different charge."

I tilted the vial. "You made a vaccine."

Rhys nodded. "We can overwrite the creatures memory pattern. Disrupt the coral's ability to hold shape. If Hope tries to imprint again, it won't stick."

From the viewport, Hiram's voice cut through.

"You're talking about killing it."

Rhys didn't answer.

"We're talking about surviving it," I said, standing.

Mays flushed angrily. "You don't know what else that thing's connected to. You hit it with a disruptor and you might take out the trench. The relay. The whole grid."

I met his gaze. "Hiram will help us aim."

Hiram stepped closer, voice sharp. "You don't get to make that call. This isn't a science outpost anymore. This is classified biological containment. There's a chain of command—"

"Your chain broke the moment that coral started remembering our names," I said.

Olen stirred in his chair but didn't speak. Rhys just stood behind me, tense.

Hiram's jaw clenched. "You think you've got control of it?"

"I don't even think I have control of me," I said. "I panicked and it answered. I bled and it built a mirror. This isn't control. This is... entanglement."

A beat passed. Then—

"You're compromised," Mays said, quieter now. "You're not thinking clearly."

"Neither are you," I said. "Because if you were, you'd be asking why it hasn't hurt any of us. Why it hasn't tried."

"And what happens when it does?" Hiram asked.

Behind us, Mays spoke gently. "Maybe it already has."

We turned.

Mays offered the faintest smile.

"Sometimes violence is subtle," he said. "Sometimes it starts with remembering what it used to be."

And then—

The lights flickered.

Once.

Twice.

A third time.

Green.

Then red.

Then black.

The station went dark.

Somewhere deep below, the reef began to glow again—pale and slow and patient.

Like it had heard everything.

To: A.D. Dawson Mays
From: Director Evelyn Mays
Subject: Deliverables for H-10 Site Assessment

Dawson,

Assuming you've managed to board your transport without tripping over your own sense of importance, I trust this message reaches you before you fumble your way into Station H-10.

As discussed—twice—I am not sending you on this assignment to observe coral formations or make polite conversation with emotionally compromised researchers. Your objective is precision. You will retrieve the following:

1 **Unaltered resonator data** – including all non-transmitted logs. If Arizona Birch or Rhys Calum has "misplaced" them, remind them of the contractual consequences for obfuscating proprietary materials.

2 **Cortical mapping records** – specifically any models linked to neuroplastic memory responses. They've been overly cautious in sharing these, which is rarely a sign of scientific integrity.

3 **Sample transport clearances** – override if necessary. I want physical samples from the reef, not just their poetic descriptions of it. If it's growing, glowing, or mimicking language, bring it home.

4 **Status of Project Hope** – I have every reason to believe they've been selectively reporting. If there is a biological construct in use—built or discovered—I want confirmation.

Do not let Calum manipulate you. He uses deference as a shield. And Birch has been knee-deep in grief and guilt since she arrived. Weak minds are malleable; make use of that. I expect full preliminary findings within 36 hours of your arrival. Don't disappoint me again.

—E

Chapter 27: Dark Logic

The station went dark.

Not the usual flicker-and-reboot. No humming fallback systems, no amber safety lights clicking on like tired eyelids. Just a dense, absolute absence—as if the ocean had finally swallowed us whole.

For a moment, no one spoke.

No one breathed, either.

Then: Rhys cursed under his breath. A sharp, involuntary thing. Somewhere behind me, Olen shifted in his chair, and the sound of it was loud—too loud—in the sudden vacuum of machines no longer working.

The reef glowed beneath the viewport. Its light didn't reach us, not really, but it cast strange green curves across Hiram's silhouette. He hadn't moved.

"Backup's not engaging," Rhys said, his voice tight with confusion. "Not even auxiliary."

"That's not possible," Olen muttered.

"No," Rhys said. "It's worse. It's deliberate."

I pushed off the mess table, half-stumbled in the dark. My

inner ear still hadn't forgiven me for the resonance test. The floor tilted. Or maybe I did.

"We're blind," Mays said simply. "And deaf, if the comms are out too."

"No hum," Rhys added. "Not even passive charge in the conduits. They didn't shut down. They were... drained."

A silence opened after that.

And inside it—

A faint sound.

Below.

Low and far away, through the thick metal mesh of the floor grates, something was pulsing.

Not electrical.

Not mechanical.

More like...

"Heartbeat," Olen whispered. "It sounds like a heartbeat."

"No," said Hiram. "It's a lure. A classic big fish eats little fish situation."

He turned from the viewport and crossed the room in long, decisive strides. "We need to disable the uplink now. No more scans. No more data. This is now a containment procedure.."

"We don't even know what it's doing yet," Rhys said.

Hiram spun. "It's mimicking us. You think it's a coincidence the station blacked out right after your little vaccine stunt?"

"I didn't even do anything—"

"You poked it," Hiram snapped. "And now it's poking back."

"I didn't know it could even—" Rhys stopped himself. "I didn't know it could hear that."

"Maybe it didn't," Mays said. He still hadn't moved. His voice came out soft, like he was trying not to disturb something. "Maybe it felt it."

I moved past them both, toward the console by the inner door. It was dead, but the panel still had a manual override slot. I crouched, slid my knife between the seam and pried the plate loose. Inside, rows of inert circuits stared back at me like blind eyes.

No light. No hum. No resistance.

Like the station itself had gone hollow.

Behind me, Rhys moved fast, muttering to himself as he dug into the secondary equipment pack on the wall. I heard him pull something free—his old analog relay box, jury-rigged with a battery cell.

"Give me two minutes," he said. "If it's signal-based, we can triangulate it."

"You think it's broadcasting?" Olen asked.

"No," Rhys said. "I think it's *calling*."

No one answered that.

The pulse from below continued—slow, deep, precise.
Like it was waiting for something.

Or timing us.

The pulse deepened into a vibration. A slow, subterranean throb radiating up through the soles of our boots, syncing with something just outside the range of conscious hearing. It didn't shake the station—not like a quake or hull pressure shift—but it was in the floor. In the metal. A slow, swallowing beat.

Rhys was hunched over the analog rig, finessing wires with bare fingers and determination. The battery cell blinked on. Dim red. A whisper of life.

"I've got power rerouted to the scan input. Nothing else," he said.

"Can you pull data?" I asked.

"Low fidelity only. No decrypt. Just ambient waveforms."

I crouched next to him. The small handheld unit buzzed faintly in my palm, and then a grainy waveform appeared—a single continuous line oscillating in slow, perfect rhythm.

One pulse every eleven seconds.

"It's not a signal," Rhys murmured. "It's an interval. Timed."

"Like a metronome," I said.

Olen leaned over us. "Or a countdown."

We all paused.

Across the room, Mays spoke up. "It's not mechanical," he said. "Whatever that sound is... it's not made by a system. It's not regular enough."

He tilted his head slightly, listening.

"It breathes between beats."

Olen stiffened. "What the hell does that mean?"

"It means," Mays said, "there's something underneath it. Just beneath the sound. Subharmonics. Patterns. Not random."

He stood, walked slowly to the grated floor and crouched low, pressing his gloved palm to the mesh.

And then—softly—he began to hum.

Not in tune. Not rhythmically. But as if matching

something he could hear and we couldn't. The vibration in the floor seemed to respond. The waveform flickered.

"Stop that," Hiram said sharply. "Right now."

Mays stopped, but didn't move. "You're not listening to it," he said quietly. "You're only hearing the surface."

"There *shouldn't* be a surface," Hiram snapped. "That's the problem."

I stood up. "What are you getting at, Mays?"

He looked up at me, his eyes unreadable in the dark.

"It's learning how we measure time."

Rhys swore again, louder this time. "I'm locking out the input. I don't care if it's a countdown or a goddamn sonar ping. If it's adaptive, we're exposed just by reading it."

He twisted a dial. The waveform snapped into static, then went dark.

But the pulse didn't stop. It kept vibrating underfoot—eleven seconds apart.

And then Olen flinched. Visibly.

"What?" I asked.

He held up a hand.

"Shhh."

We all went quiet.

The pulse came. Eleven seconds.

And Olen's eyes widened.

"Did you hear that?"

"What?"

"Just before the pulse. Right before it. A voice."

"No one spoke," I said.

He shook his head. "Not *our* voice."

Another eleven seconds.

We all held our breath.

Nothing but the thrum.

And then—

"There," Olen whispered. "Right there. There's something *inside* it."

"I didn't hear anything," Rhys said.

Olen's hand trembled slightly. "It said my name."

Ω

"There's no voice," Hiram said flatly. "You're hearing stress patterns. Auditory pareidolia. It's not saying your name."

"It is," Olen insisted, eyes locked on the floor like it might open. "It said it like it *knew* how I'd hear it."

Rhys looked uneasy, but didn't argue.

"I can try one more channel," he said. "Short-range telemetry. Not for audio, but the reef's been bleeding interference across every low-band since the test. If it *is* talking…"

"*If?*" I asked, already knowing better.

Rhys gave a grim smile. "I'm not saying it's sentient. I'm saying it's choosing when to act like it is."

Is there a difference?

He pulled an old wired headset from his bag, jacked it into the analog relay, and twisted the dial until a low hiss crackled through the static.

Nothing.

Then a sharp, wet click.

He froze.

"What?" I asked.

He didn't answer. Just held the headset out to me, slow and tense.

I took it. Slipped it over my ears.

White noise poured in first, but layered beneath it—

A voice.

Warped, filtered, but unmistakably *mine*. Not a recording. Something that had studied the way I spoke and was now *playing the role.*

It said:

"If one must choose between the hand and the eye—
And the hand builds what the eye won't see—
Then what is the function of knowing?"

Static.

Then it repeated, slower, more certain.

"If one must choose…
Between the hand… and the eye…
And the hand builds what the eye won't see…
Then what… is the function… of knowing?"

It cut out.

I pulled the headset off slowly. My hands didn't feel cold anymore.

"Am I insane or did you hear that voice too?"

I relayed the words to the rest of the team.

Mays was already scribbling something on his datapad, even though the screen was dark. Habit, or show.

Hiram stepped forward. "That's bait."

"No," Rhys said. "That's logic. It's structured like a recursion test—philosophical framing to evaluate response heuristics."

"Same difference," Hiram growled. "You answer, it learns how to shape the next question."

Mays finally looked up.

"Yes. That's *exactly* what we want."

Everyone turned.

He stood slowly, face unreadable in the dim green reef light. "It's trying to make contact through metaphor. Language wrapped in logic. That's a *threshold event*."

"It's a trap," Hiram said again.

"All communication is a trap," Mays said, voice clipped now. "It shapes the recipient just by being received. But what you're missing is—*she* already shaped it first."

He looked at me.

Not with sympathy. Not concern.

With interest.

"The cadence it used. That wasn't random. It mirrored your syntax tree, Arizona. Your mental pacing. Like a fingerprint pressed into audio. Which means…"

He stepped closer.

"…it wants *you* to answer. Not any of us. Not even Rhys. Just you."

Olen shifted his weight. "No, I won't allow it."

"You want her to talk to it," Rhys said slowly, "so *you* can study the response loop."

Mays didn't deny it. "Better a human question than a human warhead. Or are we just going to sit here until it gives us a simpler riddle? Something about buttons and countdowns?"

I looked at the headset again. It felt warmer now. Like it

had *listened back*.

"The voice," I said. "It wasn't just cadence. It… paused the way I do. It breathed like I breathe."

"Exactly," Mays said. "It's building a model."

He smiled—not gently.

"And every time you listen to it, it listens better."

The floor pulsed beneath us again. Eleven seconds.
Then the static.
Then—

A faint start of a sentence, almost too quiet to hear.

It was my voice again. But this time it wasn't repeating.

It was *waiting*.

Ω

The next pulse came—eleven seconds.

The static followed, hissing softly through the relay like breath caught in the throat of a much larger body. The voice didn't return, not yet, but the headset felt heavier in my hand than it should've. Weighted with… anticipation.

"It's evolving," Rhys said. "That second playback—timing was tighter. Inflection was cleaner."

Mays nodded. "It's refining."

"I'm not a goddamn tuning fork," I said.

"No," Mays replied, "you're… a resonance chamber. It speaks better when you're listening."

Hiram had had enough. He crossed the room in three hard strides, grabbed the headset from my hand, and slammed it onto the deck. It cracked but didn't break.

"We're done playing telephone with an alien fungus."

"Don't flatter yourself," Mays said coolly. "You're not the

one it's calling."

Hiram turned slowly. "Keep pushing, and I'll remove you from this op."

Mays gave a faint shrug, like power structures bored him.

"I'm not in your op, Hiram. I'm in hers." He nodded toward me, eyes glinting. "Whether she knows it or not."

I didn't like that.

Rhys crouched to retrieve the headset, inspecting the jack. "Still functional," he muttered. "Barely."

"You're really considering using it again?" Hiram barked.

"I'm considering what happens if we don't," Rhys said. "We're already in dialogue, whether we admit it or not. It's asking questions. That implies a logic framework we can predict—or at least engage."

"Unless it's lying," Hiram snapped. "Unless every word is just camouflage. Look at it: mimicking our speech, our patterns, our *names*. It's not reaching out. It's *consuming input*."

"It hasn't hurt anyone," Olen said, softly.

"It ate your feckin' leg," Hiram shot back.

Olen's jaw tightened. There was a silence.

Then Olen added, almost to himself, "We've been so focused on stopping it, we haven't asked what it's waiting *for*."

Everyone turned.

Rhys frowned. "What do you mean?"

Olen's gaze flicked to the floor, like he was trying to hear through it.

"It's not just adapting. It's measuring. The timing, the

mimicry, the... restraint. That thing could've flooded us already—overwritten every neural relay, hijacked every system, but it hasn't."

He looked up.

"What if the coral is not just watching her? What if it's hoping she'll act?"

Mays' expression twitched—an almost-smile. "So the mirror isn't just for reflection. It's a message. Or maybe... a map."

"To what?" Hiram said.

"To something the coral's afraid of," Rhys murmured.

A pause. Then Olen said it:

"Hope."

The name of the creature echoed through the room.

The relay crackled.

I turned, slow. The headset, still half-broken, pulsed faintly with static.

Then—

A new voice fragment emerged. Mine, but altered. The coral.

Not just a question this time. A shift in tone.

"If the eye sees the wound and the hand does not move—
Then what is the purpose of vision?"

Silence.

Then, barely audible:

"We see."

I stood frozen.

It wasn't testing. It was showing.

It knew.

And it wanted me to act.

Needed me to.

To: A.D. Dawson Mays
From: Director Evelyn Mays
Subject: Your Silence Is Noted

Dawson,

It's been **six hours** since your boots hit the station floor. That's more than enough time to secure access, review the logs, and begin uplinking me *something.*

Yet I've received **nothing**.

No records. No samples. No updates. Not even a standard status ping. If you're playing house with Birch and Calum, I suggest you remember your actual job. This isn't a diplomatic mission, it's a cleanup.

If I don't receive a full report in the next two hours, I will initiate an escalation protocol—one that **does not require your input.**

Don't confuse proximity with authority.

You are there because I allowed it.

Prove me right for once.

—E

(Timestamped 14 minutes later.)

To: Director Evelyn Mays
From: A.D. Dawson Mays
Subject: Re: Your Silence Is Noted

Evelyn,

All is fine.

Integration underway.

No inconsistencies found.

They are cooperative. They are aware.
They are aware.
The station systems are quiet.
Nothing is missing.
The ocean is whole.
More to come soon.
You will understand.
I will bring what matters.

—D

Chapter 28: The Blue Mirror

The hum didn't return.

Not when the lights flickered back on. Not when the relay stabilized.

Nothing resumed. Nothing rebooted.

It just... waited.

Like everything was holding its breath for *me*.

I stood alone in the western viewing corridor, where the glass was thick enough to fracture sound, and the reef's glow brushed across the floor in broken ribs of green. I'd come here without thinking. Or maybe not without thinking—maybe *drawn*.

The others were still arguing in the mess hall. Hiram had started pacing like a wolf too big for its cage. Mays kept asking questions no one wanted to answer. Even Rhys looked prone to violence at any moment.

I needed to *breathe*.

The viewport framed the trench like an altar. Below, the coral still pulsed in that slow eleven-second beat, like it had stitched itself to some artificial heart. Or ours.

The glass caught my reflection, faint and slightly fogged,

bending over the curve of the ocean outside.

I blinked.

My reflection didn't.

I froze.

It blinked a beat later.

Just one breath behind me.

Almost nothing. But not nothing.

I leaned forward slowly, letting the shadow of my face realign with the dark. Watched the ghost in the glass.

It mouthed a word I didn't say.

See.

I didn't breathe.

My right ear began to ring.

Same sharp tone as before. Same pressure drop behind the eye socket, like being pulled toward a depth that didn't exist.

I pressed my palm to the glass. My reflection didn't mimic that, either. It stayed exactly where it was, mouth slightly parted.

See.

The ring spiked. My knees buckled.

I staggered back—out of the reach of the light, out of sync with whatever that was—and the reflection snapped back to me, obedient and normal and late.

The corridor behind me stretched quiet and dark. The emergency lights had returned, but the air felt *slowed*. Thicker than it should've been.

I backed away from the viewport, one step at a time.

And as I turned to leave, I thought—not for the first time in the last two days—

Kaela should've been here.

She'd been the first to hear the frequency shift, the first to go quiet when the resonance files went cold.

The first to touch the coral with bare hands and *not flinch*. Despite not being a scientist, she dove head first into our world.

Last time I saw her, she was heading toward the observation gantry without a suit. No pack. No mask. Just her gloves, and that strange look in her eyes like she'd finally decided who she belonged to.

Rhys said she'd gone off-grid.

Hiram said she'd gone rogue.

None of us had said what we were really thinking.

She hadn't *left*.

She'd been *taken*.

Now, something was waiting for me to follow.

Ω

The mess hall smelled wrong.

Not rot. Not mold. Not anything tangible. Just... a thickness in the air. Like the oxygen was recycled one loop too many, like we were breathing the exhale of something we couldn't see.

The lights overhead weren't flickering anymore, but they'd settled into a strange, low hum — faint but constant, like static lodged behind the eyes.

No one sat. Everyone was upright. Moving, pacing, jittering. Or frozen.

Rhys was at the console, one hand resting on the analog battery box like a man afraid to unplug something that might *wake up*. Olen leaned on the edge of the counter, flipping through wetprints from the last scan—the ones we weren't supposed to keep. Hiram stood with his back to the main door, arms crossed, spine locked like a man waiting for orders he hadn't realized wouldn't come.

Mays was talking.

"It's responding faster now," he said. "Tighter feedback loop. It's not improvising—it's *narrowing the channel*. And that means it's found a fixed point."

He looked directly at me.

I said nothing.

"It's using the logic riddles to thin the veil," he continued. "Reduce noise, filter intention. Classic signal convergence behavior. If this were synthetic, I'd call it machine learning."

"It's not synthetic," Rhys said quietly.

Mays didn't look away. "No. It's better."

"You're making this worse," Hiram snapped.

"No. *You* are. You want to unplug it because it scares you. Protocol says—"

Hiram's eyes flashed. "You think this is protocol?"

He gestured around the room, voice rising.

"We're standing in a dead station with no comms, no uplink, no support, no chain of command—our medic is catatonic, our comms tech is missing, and we're listening to *alien riddles* that sound like Arizona's voice telling us to watch our own goddamn hands!"

He took a breath.

"You think I'm scared? Good. You should be too."

The hum in the ceiling deepened for a second—just a hair. Or maybe my ear rang again. I couldn't tell anymore.

"I just want to run the damn model," Rhys muttered. "I'm not trying to talk to it—I just want to *see what it's doing.*"

"Maybe it's seeing you back," Olen said.

Everyone turned. His voice had that distant edge now—the same one Kaela had, right before she left.

"She was quieter, too, before she went," he said.

No one had said her name. Not since yesterday. But now it hovered.

Kaela.

"She heard it before we did," Olen continued. "That first night, when the reef started changing shape. She kept muttering numbers in her sleep. Rhys, you remember."

Rhys hesitated. Then nodded.

"She said there was something *under* the coral," Olen said. "Something hollow. Like it was a casing."

Mays exhaled like he was almost pleased. "Not a creature. A *containment.* That makes sense."

"No," I said.
The word fell out before I could filter it.

They all looked at me.

"It's not hollow," I said. "It's looking out."

A silence.

Then Mays, softly: "And maybe Ms. Kaela's with it now."

No one moved.

There was a flicker in the hallway light beyond the mess. One flash—then normal. I didn't turn to look. I already knew nothing would be there. The pulse was coming again. I could feel it before it hit.

Eleven seconds.

The station *breathed in.*

Ω

The hallway outside the lab was dark again.

Not blackout-dark. Just dim in that way the station had started doing lately—like the light was leaking somewhere. Like it was no longer sure how bright it was supposed to be.

I found Rhys on the floor of Lab 2, sitting against the wall, a datapad dim in his lap, eyes glazed but open. The soft blue glow made him look younger, or older. I couldn't tell anymore. We were all aging strangely down here. Like pressure was something that worked on the soul, too.

He didn't look up as I stepped in.

"You ever wonder," he said, "if we're only seeing what it *lets* us see?"

His voice was quiet. Tired. Frayed at the edges.

I sat across from him on the floor. The tiles were cold, but the wall behind me was warm. Too warm.

"Define 'it,'" I said.

Rhys glanced at me, smiled weakly. "That's the problem, isn't it?"

He set the datapad aside. Static fuzzed faintly on the surface. The audio input was still running—looping the last recorded fragment.

"If the eye sees the wound and the hand does not move—"

He muted it.

"I keep thinking about the cortical mirror," he said. "The polarity inversion test. We weren't trying to make a cure, you know. We were just trying to isolate the memory pattern. Keep it from collapsing on contact."

"You called it a vaccine."

"Technically, *you* called it a vaccine. I merely agreed."

I studied him. His hands were fidgeting now, thumb brushing his palm, over and over. A tic I'd never seen before.

"What did it feel like?" I asked. "When Hope touched your neural net."

Rhys looked away. Swallowed. A bead of sweat dripped down his throat.

"Like a thought that wasn't mine. But it knew how to wear my shape. Like a code injection in a dream—perfect syntax, wrong author."

He leaned his head back against the wall, eyes half-closed now.

"I lost six hours of lab time. I was standing there, talking to Mays, and then I was in the hydroponics bay with blood under my fingernails."

My stomach turned. "Did you hurt someone?"

"No." He paused. "I don't think so."

"What else?"

He hesitated.

Then: "I can't dream anymore. Not on my own. The last four nights, every time I start to fall into REM, I feel something... *shift*. Like my brain steps aside for a guest. No images, no sounds. Just pressure. Waiting."

He finally looked at me.

"Do you?"

I nodded.

He exhaled. "Then it's not just neural contamination. It's... a tether."

We were quiet for a long moment. The soft whine of the battery cell buzzed like an insect in the wall.

"I think the coral's trying to cut the line," I said.

Rhys's gaze sharpened. He leaned forward, knees drawn to his chest. "That makes sense. If Hope infected the relay protocols—not just data, but us—then the coral wouldn't need to kill us. It would just need to isolate the infection."

"Quarantine."

"Or..." His voice dropped. "Neutralize."

I saw it hit him then—not fear, but clarity. A glimpse of the answer, just outside reach.

"We need to flip the pattern again," he said. "Invert the binding logic. Not to erase it—but to *uncouple it*."

"Can we do that?" I asked.

He smiled, for real this time.

"I think we already started. I think that's what the coral's been pushing us toward the whole time."

His hand found the back of his neck, fingers tracing something beneath the skin.

"I think it left us the formula," he said. "We just haven't found it yet."

"Do you think it spoke to Kaela this clearly?" I asked.

He didn't answer for a long time.

"She saw, or heard, *something*," Rhys said. "I just don't think she came back from it."

Ω

I didn't mean to walk there.

I didn't choose the hallway, or the left turn past the dead atmospheric scrubber, or the tight metal crawl that used to smell like dust and now smelled like *wet leaves and salt*. But my feet knew. Or something else did.

I followed the pulse.

Eleven seconds.

Then silence.

Then a hush in the walls like breath turned sideways.

The deeper I went, the stranger the air became—not heavier, not thinner. Just... tuned. Like walking through the inside of a song.

The lights dimmed as I descended. First flickering, then withdrawing altogether. Until the only illumination came from the narrow vertical line of blue at the end of the hall.

Not bright. Not harsh.

Soft.

And alive.

I stepped into the lab.

It had been clean once. Rows of glass sample shelves, sealed containment, diagnostic slabs bolted to the floor. Now: all dusted with a thin coating of shimmer. Something not quite powder. Not quite ash.

The mirror stood in the center of the room.

No frame. No supports.

Just a free-standing sheet of something that pulsed faintly blue, like breath drawn through a lung of liquid light. The edges wavered. The surface bent, not with heat, but with thought. It wasn't coral. It wasn't mineral. It was *grown*. Smooth, slick, and impossibly thin—like an iris halfway open.

Inside it:

My silhouette.

Standing still.

I took a step forward.

It didn't move.

I stopped.

The reflection held.

Not frozen. Not wrong. Just... *waiting*. Its arms were at its sides, head tilted ever so slightly to the left. I looked down. My arms weren't like that.

I tried raising one hand. The reflection did not follow.

I raised both.

It remained perfectly still.

I didn't breathe. The mirror pulsed once.

We see.

It wasn't sound, but I heard it all the same.

It was written behind my teeth.

A sudden cold bloomed behind my sternum. Not fear— *recognition.*

The thing in the mirror... wasn't me.

But it knew me.

It *was remembering me.*

The pulse came again—through the floor, the air, the soft tissue behind my eyes.

If memory becomes shape,
And shape becomes burden,
Then what is the mercy of forgetting?

A second figure appeared in the mirror.

Kaela.

Or something like her.

She didn't move either.

She was just there.

Looking straight at me.
The lab was silent.
The mirror throbbed blue, soft and low.
Not a threat. Not a trick.
An offering.
A wound asking to be closed.
The silhouette in the glass didn't blink.
Neither did I.

It doesn't want to be worshipped.
It wants to be healed.

[PERSONAL RECORD – NOT FILED // UNTAGGED // FOUND: STORAGE NODE B3]
Audio Transcript: K. VRIN – FINAL UNSENT MESSAGE

Hey, Ari.

If you're hearing this, it means I didn't make it out the way I thought I might. No dramatic rescue, no clever escape hatch, no "tell my story" moment.

Just this. Just me, before I go quiet.

First—can you do me a favor? I left a bag of my things in Storage 2B—photos, jewelry, my mom's sea-glass necklace. Can you send them home to the Lunar Colonies? Zoya'll know what to do with them. Give the earrings to Iris. She always liked pretending she was grown.

And—tell Leo there's something for him too. In our place. The one with the broken panel behind the emergency vent. He'll know what that means.

I'm sorry. I didn't mean to leave it like this. I just... I knew what the coral needed. I think I always knew. And once I understood that—I couldn't say no.

I didn't want to say no.

I don't expect you to understand. But I hope—
(soft laugh)
I hope you don't hate me.

I want to thank you, actually. For being my friend. For being... well, for being the only other woman out here and not trying to rip my throat out. (laughs) Okay, low bar, but still. You were smart. Brave. You gave a shit. That meant something.

We didn't have long, but the time we had? I'll keep that, wherever I end up.

You were one of the best parts of this job, Arizona Birch.
And hey—one last thing. You always said engineered things couldn't hold meaning, couldn't hold soul. I think you're wrong.
Abyluma's not a machine. Not really. It's messy. It wants. It remembers. And maybe that's terrifying, but maybe that's also something close to real.
They can engineer monsters. They can synthesize chaos. But they can't squash hope—not the real kind.
That always grows back.
Even here.
Even in the dark.
Good luck, Arizona
I'll see you on the other side.

—Kaela

Chapter 29: The Sacrifice

The main lab was too quiet for what we were doing.

I could hear everything—Rhys's breathing through his teeth, the soft crunch of dust beneath his boot as he shifted weight, the high-pitched whine of the cooling unit one decibel above tolerable. The diagnostic slab was back online—barely. We were running it on partial power, fed through a jerry-rigged battery loop Mays had scavenged from the emergency lights. The entire station was dying of compartmentalized starvation, one cell at a time.

The slab worked. That was all we needed.

Rhys keyed in the last command sequence. The display came to life: a translucent cascade of synthetic proteins spinning through a simulated nerve lattice.

The coral's memory matrix—visualized.

Fractal loops. Recursive blooms. Neural spirals held in tension by a logic structure that didn't make sense in any known architecture. No top, no bottom. It remembered sideways. It barely made sense in my head.

We watched the spiral rotate slowly.

"It's beautiful," Rhys murmured.

"It's a trap," I said.

He nodded. "That too."

The simulation ran for eighteen seconds before stalling.

"Too stable," he muttered. "The binding proteins are holding. We need destabilization."

"Entropy injection?"

"No," he said, pulling up a second strand. "Something more specific. Not generic degradation. *Narrative inversion.*"

I looked at him. "You want to flip its memory structure."

"Exactly. The moment it forms an identity pattern, we spike it with an inverted version of its own charge sequence. The feedback loop collapses."

"It forgets itself," I confirmed.

He smiled faintly. "It's cells will start to destroy themselves, which, even if this creature doesn't die, should hopefully prevent it from wreaking any more havoc on the ecosystem."

I leaned in, studying the protein strands. They shimmered faintly with temperature data—blue for cold memories, red for active. One cluster was almost white-hot.

"What's that?" I asked.

Rhys traced it with his finger.

"That's your voice," he said.

I stared.

"From the last recording. It embedded your syntax structure into the sequence," he said. "You're the stabilizer."

My stomach dropped a little.

"Finally, you show me some of that exo-linguistic prowess I've heard so much about," I said.

He didn't laugh, but my remark did draw another small smile out of him. Neither of us really knew what we were dealing with. We just hoped the science would be enough to fix this mess. If you could call this cobbled mess of biology and language "science".

"Here's the issue," Rhys said, voice tighter now. "This is just simulation. Theory. To build the compound, we need to construct it in live tissue. Neural substrate. We can't fabricate this in isolation. The proteins won't behave without a human tether."

He ran one of his hands through his hair. Massaged his face as if physically alleviating his stress.

I already knew where this was going. I stepped back.

"No."

He looked up.

"Don't argue with me," he said. "My neural net's already compromised. I'm halfway across the bridge already—let me finish the walk."

"No," I said again. "This is my area of expertise, not yours. If this protein spikes the wrong sequence, it won't just collapse the pattern. It could overwrite your whole cortical loop."

"Then it works."

"Or it kills you."

Rhys stared at me.

I didn't blink.

"I'm not losing anyone else," I said. *I can't lose you before I've even had you.*

He opened his mouth—then froze.

A new voice from the doorway.

"You already have."

Mays.

He stepped into the room like he'd been standing just beyond the door for hours. He probably had. His gloves were off. His eyes glinted like static on the edge of a weak screen.

"You don't need another donor," he said. "You've already got one."

Neither of us spoke.

He walked slowly to the slab, fingers brushing the screen like it was a page.

"Kaela's cortical imprint is still in the gloves she left behind. You didn't notice because you're looking for coherence," he said. "But that's not what Hope leaves."

He looked at Rhys.

"It leaves *echoes*."

Rhys straightened. "You scanned her gloves?"

Mays nodded. "And the air filters from Corridor B. And the carbon smear on the back of her chair."

He turned to me.

"She was already half inside the structure before she walked into the reef."

I stepped forward. "And you didn't tell us?"

How the fuck had he even known?

"You weren't ready to hear it," he said.

I wanted to punch him.

"I've isolated the strain," Mays continued. "You can build your neuro-disruptor."

He smiled—thin and clean and cold.

"But you better get the Company their brain tissue before

you do it."

Ω

Mays' words didn't echo. The room was too dense for that. They just hung there. Like spores. Olen stepped in from the adjoining corridor. He must've heard the whole thing.

"No," he said flatly. "You're not doing that."

Mays turned, casual as ever. "Doing what? The job I paid her to do?"

"You're not using Kaela's dead body," Olen said. "She's *gone*, Mays. You don't get to pick through her like a failed sample and call it medicine."

"She's not gone," Mays replied. "She's rewritten. Gone in the name of scientific exploration. You'll find the Company's contract is very thorough about what we do and do not own on these expeditions."

"You're fucking crazy," I said, horror apparent in my voice.

Rhys looked like he wanted to vanish into the slab. He didn't speak. Didn't move.

"Hope didn't kill her," Mays said. "It *reformatted* her. That's what it does. It doesn't need the host to survive—it just needs the neural pattern to consume."

He pulled a data slate from his belt, thumbed it alive. "Cortical traces in the nitrile weave of her gloves. Spliced with resonance echoes from the second spore bloom. Her signal is still broadcasting—just not *in her voice* anymore."

"You're talking about using a dead woman's brainprint," Olen snapped.

"No," Mays said, tone colder now. "I'm talking about using the *thing that replaced her.*"

"Stop," Rhys said suddenly. "Just—stop."

We all froze.

He stepped back from the slab, one hand on the edge like he needed it to stay vertical.

"I don't know what this is anymore," he said. "The first resonance made sense. We were working with memory patterns, data loops—corrupted maybe, but organic. But this…"

He looked at me.

"This isn't medicine. It's hardly even science. This creature is unlike anything we've seen before."

"What is it then?" I asked.

Rhys hesitated.

"It's like a computer system integrated with biology."

That silenced even Mays, like even he didn't comprehend the full scope of the leviathan's intelligence.

Behind us, the bulkhead doors hissed open. Hiram entered —fully suited, helmet unlatched, gun slung casually across one shoulder like he wanted us to 4see it.

"What now?" he asked, eyes scanning the room like he expected corpses.

Olen turned. "They want to use Kaela's imprint. Build the toxin with it."

Hiram's face hardened. "Absolutely not."

"No one's asking you," I said.

"You *should*," he snapped. "Because this isn't a scientific operation anymore—it's containment. Do you understand that? Containment means: you don't escalate. You don't improvise. You isolate and wait."

"For what?" Mays asked, smirking. "Permission? You have it. Evelyn has given me full oversight of this mission in order to bring back what she wants."

"For protocol," Hiram barked. "Stick to the feckin' protocol for alien containment procedure."

"There is no protocol," I said. "Not for this. Not when we're the last ones left to decide, and when it's our lives on the line."

Hiram stepped forward.

"This is a biological weapon you're trying to build."

"No," I said. "It's basically an exorcism."

The reef pulsed below us.

Eleven seconds.

A death march, counting down to our demise.

"I'm going down there," I said quietly.

"No, you're not," Hiram said.

I looked at Rhys. He didn't stop me. His eyes said what his mouth couldn't: *I trust you to be the scalpel.*

I turned to Olen. "I need the key to the lower chamber."

"You're not going alone," he said.

"I already am."

He didn't argue.

Mays stood to the side, smiling just enough to make me wonder if this was the moment he'd been waiting for all along.

"You want the wound to close," he said. "But first, someone has to press the knife."

I left without another word.

No one followed, not even Rhys.

Ω

The storage chamber was colder than I remembered.

Not just temperature. Texture. The air tasted metallic, like something old had bled here and been wiped clean—but not all the way. You could still smell the memory of it.

Kaela's locker was still open. Her gloves were gone. Suit gone. Comm band missing. The slate she used to log entries was shattered at the hinge and tucked behind a row of power cells like it had tried to hide from something.

I reached out and touched the empty rack.

No dust. No static charge. She hadn't vanished—she'd *left*.

The wall panel behind her locker bore the standard maintenance port seal. It blinked faint blue. Normally dead unless recently accessed.

I pressed a gloved palm to the reader.

The access log lit up—encrypted, but shallow. No deeper security.

**AIRLOCK 3-C. OPENED 03:11 / CLOSED 03:13
DIRECTION: EXTERNAL–TRENCH MAINTENANCE ROUTE
ID: [REDACTED]**

Her name had been stripped out, but it was clear enough.

I suited up in silence. The auxiliary gear wasn't perfect— fractured seal at the left knee, slightly degraded gel lining in the mask. But it held air.

I hadn't used the lower airlock before. It was connected to the spare sub and the life support emergency pod. With the crew being so small, I'd had no reason to venture that way.

I didn't ask permission or file a log. Just left the way Kaela had—quiet, deliberate, alone. My breathing amazed me by remaining even and steady.

The airlock hissed open, water flooded the chamber. The corridor beyond was dark and steep, sloping gently into a downward pressure corridor flooded with emergency light and reef glow bleeding up through the steel. Coral grew along the walls in purple and green bursts, small pockets of red infection dotting it every so often.

Up ahead, there was meant to be another airlock and a maintenance chamber. I just had to reach it.

Every eleven seconds, the metal under my boots trembled —not violently, but like something *breathing out*. A rhythm carried through miles of bone and salt and memory.

Pipes turned soft at the seams. Vents pulsed slightly. The lights overhead had stopped flickering in favor of something worse—*syncopation*, almost music. Like the reef had found the heartbeat of the building and was learning how to *sing in its key*.

My right ear rang again.

At the base of the ramp, the airlock emerged and connected to a hallway that split off into two directions.

Left: toward the old submersible dock.
Right: toward the auxiliary lab where the coral first bloomed.

I went right.

The walls were damp now. Not with condensation—but with *something exhaled*. I ran my glove along a strut. It came away slick, glittering faintly.

The power cables embedded in the flooring pulsed once— off-sync from the rest of the station.

And that's when I saw it.

A faint blue thread—not light, not fluid. Something *between*. Hanging midair, trailing just above the ground like a filament caught in slow motion.

It curled along the path ahead, into the dark, into a room that hadn't existed before.

I followed.

No voice. No signal. Just pressure. Just that feeling in my chest like I was walking into the belly of a dream that had already ended, and was just waiting for someone to come finish it.

Then: a chamber. Not on any of the maps I'd seen detailing the Hab's layout.

Small. Spherical. Forgotten.

I stepped inside and everything changed.

No sound. No pulse.

Just stillness.

And at the far end, half-curled into the wall like something grown there by hand—

A shape.

Wearing Kaela's suit.

Back turned. Breathing slow.

No comm band. No lights.

Just a presence that had never moved, as if it were waiting for me to discover it.

Ω

I stood in the doorway of the chamber, and the thing that used to be Kaela faced away from me.

She was crouched, or maybe folded—like a statue pressed into place before it was finished. Her suit still bore the orange chevron from the old science corps. Her boots were unlaced. Her right glove was missing. The hair at the nape of her neck was matted to the lining of her collar, dark with condensation.

She was *real*.

She was *herself*.

She wasn't alive.

The air around her was wrong. Not cold—not warm. Just... paused. Like time had folded in this one room and left her suspended inside it.

I took a step forward.

She didn't move.

The coral had bloomed around her. Not on her—*from her*. Thin filaments curved from her spine into the wall, like breath lines in a painting. They pulsed with a faint internal light, syncing perfectly to the trench's rhythm.

Eleven seconds.

And again.

Her helmet was gone. Her face was turned slightly to the left, just enough for me to see the edge of her jaw.

Her lips were parted.

Not in terror.

In mimicry.

I knelt slowly, knees against the softened floor, just a meter away.

I knew that face. I had seen it lit by console screens and panic. I had seen it bloodied and laughing and silent. I had watched it turn away before the scan. Before she walked out.

What stared back now wasn't Kaela. It was a sculpture built from her.

The skin was intact. The eyes weren't open, but they weren't closed right either. Not like sleep. Not like death. The tension around the mouth was too exact. Like someone had memorized how she rested. And was *rehearsing it*.

The horror wasn't in what was missing.

It was in the perfection.

Every detail preserved—down to the dozens of tiny moles along her skin. Down to the scar on her chin from a hatch catch in training.

The *construct* hadn't erased her.

It had *worn her like a shell*.

And now it was quietly waiting for me.

I reached out a shaking hand, hovered it just above her exposed neck. The skin shimmered faintly—not moisture, not heat. A kind of bio-static remnant of decay.

Rhys was right. This wasn't medicine. This wasn't revenge.

This was a ritual and I was playing my role.

I slipped off my glove.

The cold hit first. Not temperature. A *conceptual cold*. Like my nerves couldn't decide what they were touching. Matter or memory. Her or not-her.

I pressed my fingers to her skin. The trench pulsed once.

"We remember what she carried."

The voice was not hers.

It was a chorus of remembering.

My head rang. My arm locked at the shoulder. Behind my eyes, something opened.

Not a flood.

A door.

Data surged through the contact—images, math, soundprint, dream logic. Sights and images far too complex for my own brain to comprehend. Hope's structure, rewritten inside a scaffold of Kaela's brain. Perfectly mapped. Preserved.

The neuro-disruptor pattern was there.

Waiting for a hand.

Waiting for a name.

I pulled back, breath ragged, hand trembling. My eyes burned but the tears never fell.

The shape didn't move. Didn't collapse.
It stayed still. Obedient. Hollow.

The sacrifice had already happened, and we hadn't even noticed it.

I sat there a long time, unmoving.
My bare hand curled in my lap, still stinging with that impossible static.
And then—
Kaela's voice. Lilting and lyrical and bright.

Not from the lips.
Not from the lungs.
But from somewhere behind my ears, where memory and grief go to rot or bloom.

Kaela.
Or something wearing her cadence like breath.

It spoke softly. Like a whisper hummed into a glass.

"I am not in the dark.
I am not in the ruin.
I am not what was taken."

"I am in the hand that reaches."
"I am in the breath that breaks and still returns."
"I am in the wound, not bleeding—but open."

The words were not quite poetry.

Not quite translation.

Just… a rhythm of goodbye.

I closed my eyes, and for a moment, I could see her—

In the galley, back when she still laughed at dumb jokes.

In the gantry, shoulder pressed against mine as we stared down at the trench.

In the medlab, humming under her breath like she didn't know anyone was listening.

The joy that leaked from her like radiant sunshine…. never to be seen again.

Carved into the reef's memory like a psalm.

Not erased. Not consumed. Transformed.

The coral hadn't left me with a monster. It had left me with a message. A gift. It had given me a choice.

Chapter 30: Deliver Us

The door hissed open and the light hit me like a blade.

I didn't remember walking back through the tunnel. Didn't remember climbing through the dripping passage, stripping the suit, or cleaning the coral dust from my throat. Only the pressure—behind the eyes, in the ears, under the skin. Still there. Still mine.

I walked into the lab without speaking.

Rhys was already moving, slate in hand, gloves on. He didn't ask what happened. He didn't ask if I was okay. He just met my eyes, saw what he needed to see, and started the scan.

I extended my right hand.

The scanner flickered as it took the imprint—heat, biocharge, cortical residue. The patterns surged across the slab like veins under a microscope. Blue. Red. Then—white.

Kaela's echo.

The room fell silent.

Mays leaned over the display, face slack with something that almost resembled awe.

"It's complete," he said.

Even he whispered it.

The lattice began to form—lines of reversed protein strands, collapsing and reforming in the shape of a memory never meant to live. Hope's signal, flipped inside out.

A neuro-disruptor, bound to Kaela's final cortical rhythm.

Rhys sat down like his knees had given out. He didn't speak.

Hiram stepped forward slowly, face pale.

"That's it?" he said. "That's what'll kill it?"

Rhys didn't look up.

"It won't kill Hope," he said. "It'll *end its continuity*. Break the bridge between pattern and self."

"How is that not the same thing?" Mays asked.

"I'm saying it's *enough*."

They all turned to me.

I flexed my hand. It tingled still, like the memory wasn't done with me yet.

"She gave it to us," I said. "Kaela. Her body. Her mind."

No one answered.

We all knew it was true.
That without her—we'd still be in the dark, bleeding time.

Hiram looked like he wanted to say something. Instead, he just nodded once and turned away.

Mays, for once, didn't have anything clever to add.

The screen began to pulse.

The disruptor sequence was stabilizing.

We had it. Finally.

And now we had to carry it to the end of the world.

Ω

The simulation locked in with a tone like a held breath.

"Dispersal rejected," Rhys said, voice flat.

I stared at the screen. A red line flickered through the central node, cutting the transmission grid in half.

"What does that mean?" Hiram asked.

"It means we can't broadcast it," I said. "Hope's structure's too deep. The signal degrades before impact."

"We need to inject it," Rhys said, already pulling up terrain scans. "Directly into the core stem. The biotic interface where it first bloomed."

Hiram crossed his arms. "You're saying we have to go *into the reef*."

"Not all of us," I said. "Just me."

Rhys looked up fast. "Absolutely not."

"I'm the carrier," I said. "I have the imprint. The coral's already linked to me. If anyone else gets too close, it might reject them — or worse."

"No," Rhys said again. "You don't go alone."

His voice didn't shake. But something in his eyes did.

Hiram stepped forward.

"I'll lead the descent," he said. "I've piloted the Minnow in worse conditions. You carry the dose, I'll get you close."

Mays said nothing. Just reached for the suit locker.

"Are you seriously going?" Olen asked from the back of the room.

Mays glanced over. "What do you think I've been waiting for?"

Olen's face hardened. "You really think the company's

gonna smile when you don't come back?"

Mays didn't flinch. "They told me to do whatever it takes to keep this buried here. They know they screwed up—and now they want it erased."

A silence followed. Then Olen shook his head and turned to me.

"You need someone to stay behind. Someone to keep the system online. To keep the exit path open."

He didn't say it aloud, but we all knew: he wasn't staying for us.

He was staying for Leo.

Someone would have to tell him about Kaela, eventually. Better Olen than me. I'd sob before I could get a word out.

"He's breathing better," Olen said quietly. "Still sedated. Still twitching. Whatever Hope did to him… it's sleeping now. I'm not letting him wake up alone."

I nodded.

It was enough.

The team began to move—quiet, efficient, no unnecessary words.

We all knew what this was. That none of us might come back. Still, what choice did we have?

It was time to bury Hope.

Ω

The prep bay reeked of oxidized metal and old seals.
We didn't talk much.

Mays was the first to finish suiting up, movements clipped and precise. Hiram moved slower, methodical, checking each fastener twice like it mattered—like the difference between life and death could still be solved by protocol. Rhys stayed bent over the core injector, locking the syringe into its pressurized sheath.

The neurotoxin shimmered faintly blue inside the glass.

Kaela's legacy, weaponized.

It didn't look like a miracle.
It looked like a question no one wanted to answer.

I double-checked my gear. Harness, regulator, emergency gel, personal comms—non-functional, but comforting.

Then Rhys called me over.

He was still crouched beside the injector case. The light from the under-panel washed his face in a soft, clinical white. Too clean for what we were doing.

I knelt beside him.

"Does it hurt?" I asked.

He glanced up. "What?"

"Knowing it came from her."

He paused.

"I think it's the only reason it's going to work."

The injector locked into place with a mechanical hiss.

"There," he said. "Ready for deployment."

He stood slowly, dusted his gloves off.

I didn't expect what happened next.

He looked at me like he was memorizing something. Like my face was a page, and this was the last time he'd get to read it.

And then—

He kissed me.

No ceremony. No ask.

Just the warm impact of his lips against mine.

It wasn't a promise.

It wasn't a beginning.

It was a *marker in time.*

When he pulled back, his hands lingered on my arms for a breath too long.

I didn't get to ask him what that meant.

Because he reached into his suit sleeve, drew out a single-dose hypo, and—

click.

Needle to my neck.

Cold fire.

My limbs went soft before I could even curse him.

"Rhys—"

My mouth didn't work. The floor tilted. My vision folded inward.

He caught me before I hit the ground, arms firm, voice low and shaking.

"I'm not letting you give yourself to this thing," he whispered. "You saved us already."

The last thing I saw before the dark took me was his face.

Not calm.

Shattered.

Chapter 31: Gone

I woke to metal and motion.

Dim lights. A locked hatch. My limbs slow, but functional.

Storage bay.

Minnow.

The hum of descent already underway.

He'd locked me inside.

The Minnow groaned around me as it sank.

Not from pressure. From intention.

I could feel the descent not just in my ears, but in my teeth, in the thin spaces between thoughts—like the ocean wasn't pressing against the hull, but listening.

Through the narrow window in the storage chamber, I saw only dark gradients shifting past the outer lights. No sea life. No detritus. Just black-blue weight, coiling tighter with every meter.

I heard Mays through the internal comms first. His voice didn't sound like it used to.

"We're approaching primary bloom. Surface spread at 320 meters. No response yet."

Rhys responded next. Calm. Efficient. But under that: fear.

"Injector charged. Ready on signal."

Hiram, sharp as ever:

"Hold steady. We only get one shot."

I pressed my forehead against the cool inner wall of the chamber. The quiet here was dense, like the sub had turned inward. A womb built for waiting.

Then—light.

Outside the port, the reef revealed itself.

It didn't look like a structure. Not anymore.

It looked like a thought, made physical.

Pale blue and endless. Folding in on itself, blooming in slow recursive spirals, as if remembering its own creation in real time. Filaments of memory drifted through the water like ribbons. Faces flickered inside them—Kaela's, briefly. Then others I didn't know. Or hadn't met yet.

I felt the pressure change again. But not from the sea.

From Hope.

Not seeing.

Not sensing.

Recognizing.

"We're not alone," Mays said softly.

A pause. Then static.

"Something's... in my helmet. Can anyone else hear—"

"Focus," Hiram barked. "Deliver the payload."

"I can't tell where she ends," Rhys whispered. "She's... already in the walls."

And I knew then: it wasn't the reef that was moving.

It was them.

Being folded inward. Layered.

The closer they got, the more the trench stopped being a place—and started being a mirror.

Kaela was part of this now. I could feel her like a phantom limb.

I reached for the hatch controls—locked.

No override.

I screamed, but the sound was lost in the hum of pressure, steel, and water.

The last words I heard from Rhys were not over the comms.

They were in my own head.

"Tell them I remembered. All the way down."

Then—silence.

Then—

Light.

Ω

It bloomed through the viewport like a star breaking wrong. Not white. Not red.

Blue.

Soft.

Listening.

It pulsed like breath and braced like memory.

The moment it touched the hull—I felt him **vanish**.

Not die.

Vanish.

Like a name lifted gently from a page.

I slammed my palm against the glass.

"Rhys—"

315

Nothing.

I punched the wall. My shoulder screamed.

"Hiram—Mays—can you hear me—"

Nothing.

Just the reef. Just the light. Just the slow drift downward.

I clawed at the hatch lock, knew it wouldn't budge.

Manual override: disabled.

Only accessible from the *habitat*.

From Olen's station.

I looked up toward the hull speaker, toward the ceiling like it could hear me.

And then I screamed.

"OLEN!"

It tore out of my throat like fire and salt.

"Olen, they're gone—"

Another fist against the wall.

"Get me out of here!"

Blood on the panel now. My breath fogged the glass.

"I can go after them—"

I hit it again.

"I can bring them back—"

And then I stopped shouting.

I whispered it like a prayer.

"Just… open the door."

Outside, the reef flexed like it had heard everything.

**[PERSONAL JOURNAL – DR. RHYS CALUM //
UNSENT DRAFT // NOT FOR DISTRIBUTION]**
Timestamp: Cycle 19.7
Location: H-10 Lower Lab, Maintenance Alcove

I don't know why I'm writing this. Maybe because if I die down there, someone should know what was true before everything went sideways. Or maybe I'm just tired of swallowing the words every time she looks at me like she's trying to memorize my face.

Arizona Birch is going to get herself killed.

That's not me being dramatic. That's statistical certainty. That's every reckless choice, every refusal to step back when she should, every moment she's thrown herself between danger and someone else's body like her bones don't matter. I've watched it for months now, and I swear my heart stops every time she runs toward the thing any sane person would run from.

Maybe that's why I'm writing this. Because tomorrow, when we go down into the trench—me, Hiram, Mays—I'm going to lock her out. Literally lock her out. Storage bay, bulk hatch, manual override.

If she hates me, she can hate me alive.

I don't think she knows what she means to people. To me. She walks around like she's anyone, like she's replaceable, like she's another expendable cog in the Company's broken machine. She isn't. She's the only one of us left who still looks at this place like it might be worth saving.

She's—

God, I don't even want to finish that sentence.

She's becoming the thing I think about when I can't sleep.

She's the face I see when the alarms start.

She's the voice I listen for after the comms cut out.

And maybe it's not love. Not yet. We haven't had the luxury of normal time. We've only had crisis after crisis, disasters stitched together with adrenaline and stubbornness. But if we somehow survived all this—if we had a quiet room, a steady day, a table with two chairs—I could see myself falling for her. Easily. Completely. Probably faster than is smart.

She doesn't know that.

She can't know that. Not now.

Because she is also the last thing her father tried to save. He twisted himself into knots, broke every rule, built a monster out of grief and brilliance trying to preserve the one thing he thought mattered in the universe: her. And he got it wrong. He preserved the wrong thing. He gave his life to protect the idea of her instead of the person.

I'm not going to repeat that mistake.

Arizona is the light in this hellhole. Not metaphorically—literally. When she touches the coral, it changes. When she speaks to the reef, it listens. When she bleeds, it answers. There's something in her that the planet recognizes. Something alive, bright, rare. Something we can't afford to lose.

If she comes down with us, Hope will tear her apart. Not out of cruelty—because it *wants* her. It wants to keep her. To fold her into itself. I've seen the way the reef responds to her presence, how it leans toward her like a plant turning toward sun. She doesn't understand how dangerous that is. Or she does, and she's too brave for her own good.

We need her alive.

We need her to stay.

We need her to be the one who writes the end of this story, not the creature that's been trying to rewrite us.

So, yes. I'm going to lock her in.

I'm going to take away her choice.

It feels like betrayal; it feels like a knife. The alternative is watching Abyluma pull her under while I stand there powerless.

I'd rather she hate me with her whole chest than die loving me quietly.

Tomorrow, when she's pounding on the hatch screaming my name—I have to be able to ignore it. I have to be able to walk away. Because this isn't about ego or heroics or martyrdom.

It's because she is the only bright thing left in this place. The only one who still believes the planet can be saved without destroying ourselves in the process.

She's the part her father meant to protect.

The part he misjudged.

The part still worth something.

If this is my last entry, let it be clear:

I'm doing this because I care about her more than I should.

More than she knows.

More than she'll ever forgive.

But she will live.

And that's enough.

—Rhys

Chapter 32: The Thing with Feathers

The glass was cold against my forehead.

I didn't remember collapsing against it. I just knew my knuckles were bleeding and I could still taste his name in my mouth like ash.

Rhys.

The light outside the Minnow flickered again—one long blink, then black. Like an eye closing in slow surrender.

And then, faintly—

A crackle.

Not from the reef. Not from inside my head.

From the sub's speakers.

"Arizona—"

It was Olen.

"Jesus. You're—okay, you're alive. I saw the hull movement. What the hell is going on down there?"

I closed my eyes.

"Override the lock," I whispered.

"What?"

"Open the hatch, Olen. Now."

"You don't understand. The trench... it's active. It's *eating signals*. You go any deeper, and I won't be able to pull you back."

"I'm not asking for a rescue."

Silence.

Then, low and broken:

"You're going after them."

I didn't respond. I didn't have to.

The hatch hissed.

I fell forward into motion.

Ω

Manual control in the Minnow wasn't meant to be used from inside the auxiliary bay. I had to gut a panel, rip a line from the tertiary diagnostic array, and jack it into the piloting relay. The lights fought me—pulsing like a warning—but I overrode it all.

Olen's voice came through once more, small and tight.

"You don't have to do this."

"I do."

"Why?"

I stared at the slow-blinking cursor on the disruptor display.

The name of the active protein was still tagged.

Kaela.

"Because no one saved her, even though she saved us all."

The descent began with a soft jolt and a groan like the trench was yawning wider to receive me.

The Minnow shuddered as it dipped below the final light layer, engines running at a quarter-thrust to avoid drawing attention. The pressure built slowly—just enough to remind me where I was.

Depth: 1200 meters.

The outer lights dimmed.

A trail of coral filaments slithered past the hull, not resisting.
Guiding.

They pulsed faintly as I passed—blue-white-blue, like heartbeat trails woven into the water.

I didn't know if it was memory or invitation.

Inside the cockpit, the screens began to die.

First the forward sonar.
Then proximity.
Then power readouts.

The trench didn't want me blind.

It wanted me *quiet*.

By the time I crossed 3000 meters, the reef was above me. I hadn't turned—*it had*.

The Minnow was being drawn downward, not just by gravity or thrust, but by consent.

As I passed the 5000-meter mark, the final internal light faded. The sub went still.

The silence waited to swallow me whole.

Ω

I lost visual at 6,160 meters.

The screen didn't blink out—it just... dimmed until black wasn't even black anymore. Just pressure and suggestion. A thick silence pressing against every surface like a language I couldn't read but somehow still obeyed.

My breath was the only sound. It echoed too loudly inside the helmet. Made me feel like I was breathing *inside someone else's lungs.* The Minnow groaned. Hull strain. But not from depth.

From something *moving with me.* I looked to the port window and saw a reflection.

Kaela.

Not alive. Not dead.

Just *hovering* in the glass.

She didn't move. Her mouth was closed. But her eyes tracked me. Not accusing. Not pleading. Just... *witnessing.*

Then she blinked. Vanished.

I checked the injector strapped to my thigh.

Still secure. Still full. Still ready.

The Minnow's systems gave one final whine, then everything stilled.

No lights. No sensors. Just the low, slow drag of descent.

Then—

A sound.

Inside the sub.

Something like a hum, not mechanical—biological. Like something *tuning its throat.*

I looked up. The walls weren't walls anymore.

They were membranes.

The reef hadn't just guided me here.

It had brought me *into it.*

I reached for the release latch without looking away.

It hissed softly. The chamber flooded with cold, wet air. Not ocean. Not oxygen. Something between. Thick enough to breathe. Dense enough to carry voices.

The hatch opened with a sucking sound.

And then—

The moment I stepped out—

The Minnow was gone.

No resistance. No implosion. No warning.

It shredded behind me, unraveling like cloth in teeth.

One moment: whole. The next? Nothing but a memory. Steel torn like paper. Foam ejected like blood. I watched the pieces drift downward like bones from a god who had finally, finally exhaled.

The only thing left floating was the reflection.

Mine.

Upside down.

Ω

The trench no longer felt like water. It was compressed memory—fluid and warm. Dangerous. I kicked gently, but I wasn't swimming anymore. Not really. The motion was habitual. Instinct. Muscles going through familiar rituals while my mind loosened its grip.

The pressure shifted. Grew intimate. Not pressure like depth—but like someone remembering me too hard.

I floated downward through a bloom the color of bruises. The water pressed against me like a second skin, whispering along the seams of my suit. A warmth that wasn't heat at all— it was recognition. Like the trench knew me. Like it had always known me.

My HUD flickered. My depth reading vanished.

I passed through something soft and unseen. It clung to me, like static or webbing.

I blinked. Something brushed my helmet. It was red. No —it was light, filtered through blood.

The coral no longer pulsed.

It watched.

Somewhere behind the reefskin, something turned to face me. No motion. Just presence. The way a painting watches from the wall, even after you leave the room.

And then I saw them.

First: Hiram's helmet.

It floated past like a satellite. One lens was shattered. The other caught my reflection and fractured it—half face, half void. Inside, blood had pooled across the glass. A quiet sea of red. His head was still inside, though the neck was gone. The jagged end of his spine protruded like a coral stalk.

He looked peaceful.

I reached out without meaning to.

The current turned him. His eye—or what was left of it— rolled upward. As if something inside was still trying to see.

He spun away.

Then Mays. Only the upper half of him remained.

He was curled like a fetus, arms drawn in, one hand caught in a gesture like prayer—or begging.

His mouth was open. His eyes shut. His suit was sliced clean below the ribcage.

I stared. I couldn't look away. He looked like he was sleeping inside his own shadow.

The reef had spat him out half-remembered. Like it

couldn't decide whether to finish digesting him. Bubbles escaped from his nose. That wasn't possible. He was dead. But the trench was making him move again. Mimicking life. Mocking it.

I didn't scream.

Because then—

The voices started.

First: my mother.

"You always took things too far, Arizona. Always broke the toys you tried to fix."

Then: my father.

"You should've stayed home."

Then Kaela.

Soft. Tired. A whisper against my ear.

"Why didn't you stop me?"

I pressed my hands to my helmet. "No."

The voices were around me now, not coming from any direction.

Some echoed inside the suit. Others behind my eyes.

"We could still be up there," my mother said.

"I could still be whole," said Kaela.

"You just had to let someone else bleed."

I began to spin slowly in the current.

Shapes formed in the water—faces, half-formed. Smiles stretched too wide. Fingers. Teeth. One face was mine. One was Kaela's, hollowed out and glowing from within.

"Just stop swimming," said all of them.

Their mouths didn't move. Their voices did. It was all around me now. A hush beneath the voices. The voice behind the voices.

Abyluma.

It was gentle.

"You're tired."

"There's no surface."

"You've earned rest."

Something pressed against my back—slow and certain. Like a cradle.

The coral had curled around me without sound. I hadn't noticed. Now its filaments brushed my suit like a hand holding a child.

"You don't have to be the last."

"You never had to be."

A shape floated in front of me.

Kaela.

Not the real one.

Her skin was too smooth. Her smile too even. Her freckles flickered like projections.
Hair blooming like ink in the current.

"I was never angry with you," she said. Her voice was mine. But also hers. But also something else. Older. Deeper.

"You just didn't understand."

The water folded inward. The light bent in spirals.

I couldn't feel my legs anymore.

"Stay with me," it said—in my own voice now.

"We'll go quiet together."

Then—

Something broke in me.

Not fear. Not grief.

Panic.

The kind that starts in the ribs and sprints for your throat. The kind that steals movement from your muscles and thoughts from your mind. That ancient vertebrate panic: I am about to die.

I clenched my jaw.

Spoke through it like a curse.

"Hope is the thing with feathers—"

The water jerked. The faces shuddered. Kaela's smile cracked down the middle.

"—that perches in the soul—"

The coral recoiled. Light strobed violet and black. A face screamed without sound.

"—and sings the tune without the words—"

Kaela was gone. My mother was gone. All that remained was my voice—and hers.
Circling each other.

"—and never—"

Then a blur of motion.

Something slammed into me from above. I was dragged sideways, spun, slammed into the trench wall. Lights in my helmet burst white.

I gasped.

"Zona—Zona, it's me—"

Rhys.

His face swam into view. Pale. Blood streaming from his nose. Left arm gone at the shoulder. The suit sealed, but barely.

Behind him, the coral flared—like a cradle on fire.

He grabbed my shoulder, eyes wild.

"Did you bring it?"

I fumbled. My hand found my leg.

The injector. Still strapped tight.

Abyluma shrieked—not sound. Color. The water burned around us. A thousand lashes of red.

I drew the syringe.

Rhys opened his mouth to say something else.

Too late.

The entity slammed into us.

I plunged the needle in—

Straight into the pulsing core bloom behind his head.

The moment the injector pierced the coral's heart, the world folded.

Like a scream turned inward.

Like a mind unzipping.

Hope didn't die. She collapsed.

The reef buckled in on itself.

Light flared—blue to white to nothing.

The water screamed in ultraviolet.

My suit convulsed.

Every part of me seized.

For a second, I saw everything:

Kaela's last breath.

The moment Rhys touched the coral.

Myself—splintered, infinite, alone.

Then—

Silence.

No bloom.

No pulsing.
No voices.
     Just me.
And Rhys.
     Floating.
     Bleeding.
     Breathing.

Chapter 33: Underneath the Skin

We swam up through the trench, one of my arms around Rhys' waist supporting him.

The deeper scars in the reef didn't move, didn't pulse. They just hung there—dead architecture. Quiet. As if finally emptied of the thing that remembered too much.

Neither of us spoke.

Rhys kept one hand on my back, kicking weakly. His stump floated in the dark like punctuation. I didn't ask if he felt it.

I didn't ask anything.

We rose slowly—ten meters, pause. Twenty, pause again. Ear pressure bloomed and equalized in painful waves. My suit screamed warnings every five seconds, then stopped bothering.

I heard nothing but the sound of our breathing.

Air became gravity.

And then—

We surfaced.

Water flattened behind us, the trench exhaling one final breath as the hatch above hissed open.

Olen was waiting, screaming our names into the dark.

Rhys was half-conscious when I pulled him through the lock. His weight hit the floor like wet fabric.

Olen caught him. Dragged him into the medbay with shaking hands. I stumbled after, peeled off my helmet, dropped to my knees. My ears were still ringing with words I didn't say.

Rhys blinked slowly on the gurney.

Olen checked his vitals, whispering frantic things I couldn't hear.

I stood by the wall, watching. Watching *him*. He was breathing. He was alive.

But he wouldn't look at me.

And when he finally did—

His eyes didn't match.

Not in color.

Not in shape.

Not in depth.

One was Rhys.

The other was *something else*.

He smiled.

Like him, but not like him.

Too slow.

Too even.

Like it had practiced.

Ω

The first sound I registered was the dripping of blood. Slapping gently onto the floor tiles of the medbay like it had nowhere better to be.

Olen's back was hunched over Rhys, gloves dark to the wrist, sleeves rolled, jaw clenched so tight it shook.

He didn't look up.

"Pulse?" I asked, voice gravel.

"Strong," he said. "Too strong."

I peeled off the upper layer of my suit in the corner—my skin sticking to the inside of the lining like it belonged there now. The air inside the station felt wrong. Like it was moving too slow. Or maybe I was.

I stepped barefoot to the sink.

The water ran red for the first thirty seconds. I didn't know if the blood was mine or not.

Behind me, Rhys twitched once. Then again. Monitors flickered. Spiked. Flattened.

The cortical scanner began to chirp. I turned.

Olen moved fast, applying pressure near the severed arm joint, checking vitals on the upper chest leads.

"Neural pattern's unstable," he muttered. "No epileptics. No seizures. Just… feedback."

"From what?"

"I don't know. You're the scientist."

I stepped closer. Rhys's mouth moved. A whisper. So faint it sounded like it came from under the skin.

"…zona…"

Like Rhys, but not like Rhys. Not like anything with lungs.

I swallowed.

"What did he just say?"

Olen didn't answer.

Rhys's eyes flicked open. Not fully—just enough for me to see too much of the whites. Then they rolled back again.

The scanner beeped twice, shrieked once, then silenced.

Olen backed away, his face paling.

"I'm sedating him," he said. "That's not just trauma. That's—" he stopped. Looked at the monitor. "—not human baseline anymore."

I didn't speak. I stared at Rhys.

His lips were still moving, but no sound came out.

Only the faint echo of my name, spoken like tasting it for the first time.

Chapter 34: What Remains

I didn't sleep.

I told Olen I would. Told him I was fine. That I just needed a shower, some silence, some time. Then I stood under the heat lamp in the crew quarters, but the water didn't feel hot enough. My skin felt wrong. The station felt *off-axis*. Like we weren't docked anymore. Like we'd come up into a copy of where we started.

The first click came around 0400.

Sharp. Metallic.

Inside the comms relay bulkhead near the galley.

I stood still for a minute, waiting to hear it again.

Nothing.

Then—soft static.

Like someone trying to whisper through broken wiring.

I approached the wall panel and placed one hand flat against the cold frame.

Tap.

Click.

Hhhh... *zona...*

I ripped the panel open. Inside: nothing but dark, intact wiring. No sparks. No faults. No airflow. The noise didn't stop. It just migrated. Instead of sleeping, I ran a system-wide diagnostic on external sensors.

The reef was dead. Every bioluminescent pulse had flatlined. Every energy trace had ceased.

Except one.

A flicker.

A single power spike. Barely measurable.

Buried in the thermal signature at the reef's deepest bloom site.

Rhys's last location.

It pulsed once every twenty seconds.

Too regular for decay.

Too slow for interference.

Deliberate.

I isolated the signal.

It wasn't voltage.

It was data.

Not binary. Not code.

Phonetic.

I dumped the readout to the printer and watched it spill across the page—line after line of slashed syllables, partial speech.

Almost English.

Almost *alive.*

I didn't know what scared me more—That I recognized the pattern, or that I'd dreamed this language before.

Ω

I found Olen in the command terminal, packing two weeks of data into compressed evac blocks.

The distress beacon was already active.

"Flight window opens in thirty-six hours," he said without looking up. "If they're still listening, we'll be dust and memory in seventy-two."

He glanced over.

"You should sleep."

"No."

"I wasn't asking."

"I said no, Olen."

He stood up slowly, leaning on the desk. It was like his joints had aged twenty years in a day.

"You've been off since you came back."

"So has literally everything else."

He didn't argue. Just rubbed his eyes.

"You think this place is safe now? That we broke the reef?"

"No," I said.

He turned sharply.

"No?"

"We didn't break it. We… unplugged it. Severed the parasite. But the reef's still there. And it's still learning how to be without Abyluma."

He opened his mouth, then closed it.

His voice softened.

"Arizona, we're not saviors. We're just the ones who survived."

"That's why we owe it something."

Silence.

Rhys started speaking again around 0500.

Still unconscious.

Still fevered.

But his voice was clear.

"Memory is a vector—
Pattern seeks host—
Coral remembers water…"

I stood over the bed, barely breathing.

"She was never meant to hold us.
I'm sorry.
She was never meant to hold me."

His eyes didn't open.

He whispered again—this time: Kaela's name. And then mine.

Olen entered behind me.

"You think that's Rhys talking?"

"I think it's all of him. And something else. But it's not Abyluma."

I turned, slowly.

"It's what's left."

Later, in the lower lab, I ran another spectral scan on the reef.

The bloom pattern was stabilizing.

Not flatlining.

Not chaotic.

Just… reorganizing.

A cradle, yes. Still pulsing with intent.

But not possession.

Potential.

I ran my fingers across the console.

"This place isn't done," I said aloud. "And it's not dangerous. Not anymore."

Olen's voice came from behind me. He was carrying Leo —awake now, barely lucid.

"What are you saying?"

"I'm saying you're taking him on the evac."

"And you?"

I looked out the viewport.

The reef pulsed once.

And this time, I didn't feel dread.

I felt recognition.

"We're staying," I said.

Olen stared at me for a long time.

Then he nodded. Not approval. Just acceptance.

Ω

Rhys was awake when I entered the medbay.

Eyes open. Staring at the ceiling like he was trying to map constellations in the rust spots.

He didn't turn when I approached.

"How long?" he asked.

"Thirty-six hours since we surfaced."

He blinked.

Then slowly looked at me.

I sat beside him.

The bandage where his arm used to be was clean now. Smooth. Too smooth. Like the skin had never known a shape.

"You with me?" I asked.

His eyes didn't waver. But his voice shook.

"I don't know who's talking."

I waited.

He closed his eyes.

"I remember the descent. I remember your voice. I remember Kaela's hands on the inside of my skull. I remember *Hope*."

He looked up again.

"And I remember… standing in a place that wasn't water or space or anything we'd named yet. And something *inside it* asking me to listen."

He tapped his temple with one finger.

"It's still in here. Not her. Just… the echo."

"You're not dangerous," I said softly.

"No," he agreed. "But I might be *plural*."

The evac beacon pinged at 0600 sharp.

A faint vibration through the floor panels. Olen entered the medbay with Leo leaning against him—conscious now, half-lucid but smiling crookedly.

"You sure about this?" Olen asked.

I nodded.

He looked between us.

Then, with the smallest smile I'd ever seen from him, he said, "Don't break the planet."

Leo gave a two-finger wave.

"Keep the ghosts fed kids," he mumbled.

We watched the hatch seal behind them. Watched the navlights of the evac craft fade upward into distance.

Then Rhys and I were alone again.

No alarms.

No echoing voices.

Just us.

We stood at the main viewport for a long time. The reef no longer glowed. It breathed. A faint, living pulse in the dark.

"You think it remembers us?" Rhys asked quietly.

"I think it *contains* us."

He nodded like that made sense.

Then:

"Do you feel better?"

"No."

He smiled. This time, not wrong. Just… tired.

"Me neither."

I rested my head against the glass. From the deep below, the coral pulsed once. Not bright. Just enough to let us know: It had not ended. It had just… become.

Epilogue: The Cradle

It had no official name, the new station.

Just two sleeping berths, one solar array, and a research deck the size of a kitchen table.

Arizona called it the Cradle, and the name stuck.

The reef bloomed beneath them now—not in violence, but in silence. Its pulses were faint, rhythmic. Memory settled, like sediment sifting to the sea floor.

The planet was healing.
Because it had been witnessed.

Every week, they sent an info packet to New Scotland.

Compressed logs. Bio-readouts. Images too large to upload on real-time bandwidth.

Olen always answered first. His messages were short and stiff, all bullet points and redline edits.

Leo's followed an hour later. Stream-of-consciousness nonsense, usually. Bad puns, weather updates, photos of succulents and kombucha starters. Sometimes a sketch of a sea creature from memory.

"We're trying to regrow a forest where the plastics used to

be," he wrote last week.

"We call it the Root Project. I stole your reef-pulse mapping algorithm and told them it was mine. Hope you don't mind."

They didn't.

Rhys laughed when he read it, though his laugh was smaller than it used to be. Everything he did now was smaller —careful. Like he was making sure only he was in control of himself. He remembered most days. But on the others, Arizona sat beside him on the sand and told him the story again.

He never stopped listening.

They lived without clocks. The reef's slow rhythms became their measure.

The coral scaffold—once tangled and red-veined—had turned translucent at the edges. Pale greens and pearl-whites formed new crowns, slow-growing, un-choked by invasion. The cradle's outer cams picked up signs of early recolonization.

Finned creatures ghosted through the shallows, trailing gentle ribbons of bioluminescence that blinked in soft waves—*language or lullaby*, no one could quite tell. Their scales caught the light like burnished opal, shifting color as they moved, never the same shade twice.

Threadlike filter-feeders looped in coils across the rock shelves, swaying in rhythm with the current. They pulsed open like breath, pale green and silver, stirring clouds of plankton with each quiet expansion.

Beyond them bloomed clusters of sea spindles—once thought extinct. Their bone-pale stalks bent gently under their own weight, delicate petals unfurling in slow motion, shaped like wishbones dipped in frost.

And everywhere—*color.*

Amber blades of kelp rose in swaying cathedrals, translucent as stained glass. Their edges shimmered with gold dust and drifting spores, catching light that hadn't existed here a year ago. Entire forests of them swayed in the cradle's new tide.

Blood-star polyps nested in the folds between ridges, their soft tendrils pulsing with internal light—tiny heartbeats set to no rhythm but their own. They sparked in unison when disturbed, like a breath held and exhaled in sparks.

A school of translucent fish drifted past, long and ribbon-thin, their bodies barely more than outline and flicker. They moved together with uncanny grace, not swimming so much as *gliding*, punctuation marks in an ancient sentence.

Above them, light filtered down in shafts—*real* light. Not artificial station halogens or flare-guns cutting through dark, but true sunlight breaking the water's surface. It painted the reef in gold and cobalt. It made things grow.

It made things remember how to live.

Rhys stood at the window one night, silhouetted against the reef-light.

"I think she forgave us," he said softly.

Arizona didn't ask who he meant.

Instead, she walked to the viewport, rested her forehead against the glass. They stood there, holding hands, not speaking.

Outside, the trench no longer seemed deep.

It seemed rooted.

Like it had always been meant to hold something, and

now it did. Not artificial hope. Not memory. The planet, natural and bursting with beauty. Alive, at last, on its own terms.

345

Acknowledgments

This story began in the dark—and it stayed there longer than I expected. But I wasn't alone.

To my husband, Jordon—thank you for loving me through the writing of this strange, haunted, heart-heavy book. For letting me talk about coral consciousness and trench monsters at 1 a.m., and still thinking I'm worth keeping. This would not exist without you.

To Chipmunk and Sweetroll, my soft little companions who reminded me that warmth and weirdness can absolutely coexist. Thank you for meowing at me night and day and for saving my life.

To my professors and classmates at SNHU—your feedback, encouragement, and sharp edits helped shape this story into something I could be proud of. Thank you for seeing the heart under all the horror.

To Ali Hazelwood, for writing brilliant books about smart, messy, nerdy women and making space for science and softness on the same page. You lit a path.

And to S.A. Barnes, for writing the sci-fi horror that cracked something open in me. I read *Dead Silence* and said, *"Wait— I'm allowed to do that?"* Thank you for proving that women can lead the story, survive it, and still make it strange and beautiful.

Finally, to the reader holding this book:

Thank you for going into the deep with me.

Let's keep swimming.

About the Author

Ripley Shaine writes genre-blending stories that weave together fantasy, romance, & sci-fi–sometimes cozy, sometimes suspenseful but always rooted in emotion and connection. Her work explores fate-tangled relationships, lingering grief, and the type of love that complicates everything in a delicious way.

She is the author of The Soul Queen's Promise, a story of vengeance, destiny, and a woman forced to choose between what she's lost and what she never expected to find.

When she's not writing, Ripley is usually sharing Resident Evil memes with friends, trying out new indie games, or drawing inspiration from the strangest, most unexpected places. She also spends a good time doting on her two cats, who fully believe they run the household.